Murphy Murphy
and the Case of the
Commission on Cliches

By Keith Hirshland

For information, or to order additional copies, please
contact:

Beacon Publishing Group
P.O. Box 41573 Charleston, S.C. 29423
800.817.8480| beaconpublishinggroup.com

Publisher's catalog available by request.

ISBN-13: 978-1-961504-03-5

ISBN-10: 1-961504-03-5

Published in 2023. New York, NY 10001.

First Edition. Printed in the USA.

Murphy Murphy
and the Case of the
Commission on Cliches

"Every story needs a simple place to start"

Pat Green

Murphy Murphy and the Case of the Commission on Cliches

THE CALM BEFORE THE STORM

"You a silly willy Uncle Murphy," the toddler said. From his little mouth it came out "Unko Moophy". "And you wacky too!" He added for good measure.

Murphy Murphy found himself buried in sand with just his neck, head, and the toes of his size 10 feet visible. With a high-pitched giggle, the little boy dumped another bucket of Malibu beach sand on his uncle's body.

"That's redundant Louie."

"What's dundit?" the kid asked.

"It's something characterized by verbosity or unnecessary repetition in expressing ideas," detective Murphy Murphy responded.

"For goodness sake Murphy, he's *THREE!*" The detective's girlfriend, and the boy's aunt, Charlie Carlucci said. She was sitting on a blanket a few feet away.

"And a half," retorted Murphy, "and as far as I'm concerned that's high time for him to learn these things. I mean seriously, what *are* his parents teaching him?"

"They're teaching him to share his toys with others at preschool. Oh, and they're teaching him not to spit out his mashed bananas," she answered. Murphy shook his head. "In other words," Charlie continued, "they're teaching him to be a kid."

Murphy turned from Charlie to Louis who now stood inches from his head holding firmly to another bucket full of beach. But instead of dumping it on his uncle the lad set the bucket down, squatted, and pooped in his diaper.

Detective Murphy Murphy had returned to Southern California. A movie was currently in production, the subject of which was the story of his most notable Department of Redundancy Department investigations. A case involving the popular rock and roll band, Serious Crisis. It had garnered headlines in all the music trades and at one point Murphy found himself with members of the band posing at a photo shoot for the cover of Rolling Stone magazine. The band's star was on the rise as streams of their music went through the roof. The story of the case caught the attention of a struggling Hollywood screenwriter named David Kamens who called in every one of his last favors to get in front of decision makers at several studios. The folks at Universal bit.

While working the case the detective had befriended some of the band members including its lone female, Lyndsay Howlund. He also met her uncle who just happened to be an actor named Matthew Laurance. He had enjoyed a modicum of fame thanks to roles in the Eddie and the Cruiser movies, St. Elmo's Fire, and television series including Duets, Saturday Night Live, and Beverly Hills, 90210. He had been cast, naturally, in the Serious Crisis movie as himself but was also responsible for bringing Murphy Murphy on board as the film's technical adviser.

"I told the director it was a *basic necessity* that we had someone on set who had a grasp on the *actual facts*," Laurance told the detective needling him with the redundancies known to drive Murphy Murphy crazy. "We *mutually agreed* it was *absolutely essential,*" he concluded, unable to suppress a giggle.

"I hate you," was all Murphy had said in response.

"No. You hate that you love me," the actor answered, "and you'll love me even more when you hear how much the studio just paid someone else for the *same identical* role." The giggle became an all-out laugh as Laurance ended the call.

"Let's call it a love/hate relationship then," Murphy said to the dial tone.

The money and the opportunity brought Murphy Murphy to Hollywood and he invited his girlfriend, Charlie Carlucci, to join him. Charlie, in turn, asked her brother Gaston and his son, her nephew, Louie to come along.

After the day at the beach Murphy and Charlie were back at the hotel relaxing on a couch. Little Louie lay between them. His head on his aunt's lap, his feet on Murphy's. The boy, exhausted from the sun and the exertion needed to bury Murphy Murphy on the beach, snored lightly. The movie studio had put the detective up at the tony Malibu Beach Inn. He hadn't bothered to look up how much a room like this would cost the hoi polloi but Charlie had. Murphy let loose a long whistle when she told him.

"Why Louie?" he asked his girlfriend.

"Why Louie what?"

"Why did Gaston and Belle name this slightly annoying, yet incredibly adorable, child Louie?"

"Oh that," she nodded and looked at her nephew. "Simple answer?"

"Sure."

"Louie is a Carlucci family name. My daddy's brother"

"Your uncle," Murphy interrupted.

"Yes. Mine and Gaston's uncle was a Louie. A grandfather on my mother's side was a Louie *and* my great, great grandmother was a Louie."

"Your great, great grandmother was named Louie?"

"She was."

Murphy Murphy and the Case of
the Commission on Cliches

"Short for Louise I presume."

"You'd presume incorrectly," she said as she leaned over and kissed him on the cheek. "Just Louie. Short for Louie. Families, you know, sometimes do funny things." Little Louie snored on.

Murphy knew all right. In fact he was certain some folks would say his own family's naming tradition sped right through *funnyville* into *crazytown*. He was, as of now, the last in a long line of Murphy Murphy's. As far back as he could remember, and even further back than that, each male offspring in his Murphy family tree was named Murphy. Every. Single. One. Not the first-born male, every born male. That's because the first-born male was the *only* born male in that particular Murphy family. Once a boy was born the baby making stopped. Oh sure, the family could have as many girls as they could produce as long as all the baby girls came before a baby boy. Even more bizarre than elective population control and then naming the boy Murphy Murphy was the fact that for generation after generation, mother after mother, father after father, no one bucked the system. At least not to the extent that any Murphy would acknowledge or admit.

And now the existence of his familial lineage rested squarely on the shoulders of one intrepid detective, sitting in a two thousand dollar a night hotel room, gazing out over the Pacific Ocean. This particular Murphy Murphy. He knew it and for the longest time he was completely at peace being the last of the line.

Then he met and fell in love with Charlie Carlucci. He now sat alongside her and smiled at the prospect of being at her side forever.

"What are you smiling about?" she asked catching a glimpse of his goofy grin.

"Just thinking about you," he answered somewhat honestly.

"You're full of it, detective," she said punching his arm. "Sweet, but full of it." She was right about the full of it part, and the sweet part he hoped. He realized he wasn't quite ready to spill the beans about his Murphy Murphy conundrum. At least not yet.

THE DIE IS CAST

Murphy and Charlie met Matthew Laurance for dinner at his home in the Hollywood Hills. On the menu was take out from Vic's Food to Go. The restaurant website insisted the Pa Nang Chicken was "to die for" and Murphy had to admit it was delicious but the Teriyaki Beef over Fried Rice was the best he had ever tasted. Charlie was less adventurous and stuck to the Egg Rolls. Much to Laurance's delight, and Murphy's chagrin, she stated emphatically that if they were to eat at this restaurant at another time hers was an order she would "repeat again".

"How did you find this place?" Murphy asked between bites. "It might be the best Thai food I've ever had." Laurance scooped more of the chicken dish on his plate.

"Oh gosh," he looked at Murphy and then Charlie. "I've been eating Vic's Food to Go since the early '80's." He took another bite, chewed, and thought some more. "We were shooting St. Elmo's Fire," he resumed after a swallow, "and Emilio Esteves's old man came by the set one day."

"Martin Sheen!" Charlie blurted.

"What about him?" Murphy asked.

"He's Emilio Estevez's old man," she answered.

"He is indeed," Matthew nodded. "Always has been." He nodded approvingly at Charlie then smiled at Murphy Murphy. "Anyway," he continued, "Sheen pulls into the lot driving a baby blue, Ford LTD woody wagon. Charlie was riding shotgun."

"Charlie Sheen?!" Charlie exclaimed.

"One and the same," Laurance nodded again.

"He's my namesake," Charlie admitted.

"Excuse me?" Murphy asked.

"At least that's what my parents claim. One night they were a little tipsy after a dinner party and I was supposed to be asleep."

"But you weren't," it was Laurance.

"Nope. My parents' dinner parties were a hoot. There was always something to learn if you listened closely enough."

"Go on," Murphy pushed.

"So, I heard them tell some friends that I was conceived the night they saw Grizzly II: The Revenge."

"George Clooney was masterful in that!" Laurance deadpanned.

"Wait!" Murphy looked at Charlie, "a movie called **Grizzly II: The Revenge** was the impetus for a night of love making for your mom and dad?" Charlie shrugged. Murphy turned to his friend, "and you've heard of this movie?" Laurance also shrugged and after a glance at Charlie they both broke out laughing.

"You two are hilarious," Murphy said and he stuffed a piece of beef in his mouth.

"Go on with your story Matthew," Charlie encouraged the actor.

"As you wish my lady," the actor bowed. "So, Charlie Sheen was in the front seat."

"Wait again!" it was Murphy Murphy.

"What now?" Laurance asked.

"If Martin was a Sheen and Charlie was a Sheen why wasn't Emilio a Sheen?"

"Have to ask him," was all Laurance offered.

"No more interruptions Murphy," Charlie scolded her boyfriend.

"Me?"

"Yeah you," Laurance said, "now, don't you want to hear the *end result*?" He smiled. Murphy did not. "Where was I?" Laurance wondered aloud.

"Martin had just pulled in with Charlie riding shotgun," Charlie reminded him.

"Right. So, Charlie leans most of his body out of the front passenger window and calls out to Emilio, 'we're going to Vic's Food to Go!' he yells." Charlie walked over and stood next to Murphy.

"You have to admit it's a good story," she whispered. He had to admit it wasn't bad.

"So, Emilio turns to all of us and says, 'come on gang we're going to Vic's!'"

"Wow!" Charlie said.

"Did you go?" Murphy asked.

"Of course!" Laurance laughed, "and so did Ally, Rob, Andrew, Demi, Judd, and Mare." He ticked off each name with the fingers on both hands. "Andie didn't go," Laurance shook his head, "she was kinda stuck up." Charlie clapped her hands. "Then we all piled into Martin Sheen's wagon, all eight of us with me, Rob Lowe, and Mare Winningham all the way in the back and we went to Vic's Food to Go. First time in my life that I ate Thai food, nowhere near the last."

"What about additional joyrides with Martin Sheen and the Hollywood Brat Pack?" Charlie asked.

"I'll take the opportunity to go with my *natural instinct* and plead the fifth." Murphy tossed a chopstick at his friend.

Murphy Murphy and the Case of
the Commission on Cliches

While Laurance related the tale, Murphy felt his phone vibrate in his pocket. Wishing not to be rude and realizing the only people in the world he wanted to talk to were currently in the room, he let the call go to voicemail.

"I'll do the dishes," their host said as he gathered up the paper plates and cartons and dumped them in the trash. Murphy excused himself, went out on the balcony and listened to the message.

"Detective Murphy Murphy, I'll lay my cards on the table. My name is Adalindis Orval Katterwomp and I currently head the world-renowned Commission on Cliches. You can bet your boots I need your help."

"I'm sure you are and I bet you do," Murphy said under his breath. The message continued.

"The commission has an issue that we need to get to the bottom of and a little bird told me you were the right man for the job."

"Good grief," Murphy said.

"I can sit tight but not for long. I'm hopeful you'll allow me to bend your ear so please RSVP." Katterwomp left his number.

"Cliches and redundancies," Murphy whispered entering the digits in his phone, "the only thing left for the trifecta is a pun. How could I possibly resist?" Murphy headed back inside.

"Who was that?" asked Charlie. Murphy smiled and held up the index finger of his right hand.

"Hey Matthew, ever heard of the Commission on Cliches?" His friend considered the question.

"Can't say that I have," was his answer. Murphy turned back to Charlie.

"Have you?" he asked. She shook her head. "Apparently they're *world-renowned*."

"Of course they are," Laurance said with a smile.

"I think I may have a new case," Murphy added.

"Well, that calls for a celebration!" Laurance said as he reached into a cabinet and pulled out a bottle of Remy Martin XO and three glasses.

A HOBSON'S CHOICE

Murphy Murphy and Charlie sat in the gate area waiting to board their flight back home. The movie didn't need him because they were shooting scenes involving the band, Serious Crisis, for the next several weeks. He did swing by the set before they headed to the airport just to say hello to Big Joe Lionns, DeMaio Turrell, and Lyndsay Howlund. Three bandmates who had become friends with both Murphy and Charlie. Howlund, the niece of Matthew Laurance and the main figure at the heart of the case of Serious Crisis, gave Murphy a big hug and presented him with a thumb drive containing the band's newest single, *Annual Anniversary*. She told him writing it was a "creative process" as she "blended together" some of the events that united them ending up with a "brief summary". She added, with a wink, that he might have made a "cameo appearance" in the song. The detective fought the urge to smack her upside the head and thanked her instead.

At the gate Charlie sat next to Murphy, earbuds in, listening to the song. Murphy decided to use the time to call Mr. Adalindis Orval Katterwomp back.

"Hello," a hesitant voice answered.

"Is this Adalindis Orval Katterwomp?" Murphy asked.

"You've hit the nail on the head," he said. Murphy considered hanging up right there and then but he didn't.

"Mr. Katterwomp this is Detective Murphy Murphy returning your call."

"Oh joy!" the man actually shouted, "I was hoping against hope you would call. You see I'm afraid we're in a pickle."

"Mr. Katterwomp," Murphy started but was interrupted.

"Please call me A-OK. I'm guessing you'd prefer not to beat around the bush and get right to the heart of the matter."

"That would be nice but first could you tell me how you found me?"

"Of course. You see, as fate would have it, I know someone who knows someone who knows someone who knows your Chief of Police."

"Dud Hill," Murphy said softly.

"Right as rain," Katterwomp confirmed, "and he said you'd leave no stone unturned while helping solve my, uh I mean, the commission's dilemma." Murphy made a mental note to have a word with the newly appointed Chief.

"So," the detective started, "how can I help?"

"Here's the long and short of it. The commission, which I may have mentioned I head, has discovered its sacred text has gone missing. I fear foul play and intend to move heaven and earth to retrieve it."

"Sacred text?"

"Exactly. Between you, me and the fence post it's our Seven Valleys, our Talmud, our Dead Sea Scrolls."

"And it's disappeared?"

"Gone with the wind," Katterwomp said sadly, "and I fear getting it back may be fraught with danger."

"Why don't you let me be the judge of that," Murphy said holding back a chuckle.

"Then you'll put your best foot forward and help?"

"I'll help," Murphy said.

"Oh, thank you detective, from the bottom of my heart. Your chief told me you'd be our ace in the hole. So, onward and upward!"

"There may be one small problem."

"Now detective, I do hope you're not thinking of putting me behind the eight ball by mentioning the almighty dollar. After all, I fought tooth and nail to bring you on board."

"Nothing like that Mr. Katterwomp."

"Remember it's A-OK," the man jumped in.

"Right. Sorry. It's nothing like that A-OK. It's just that I'm working on another project that has me in Los Angeles quite a bit."

"Then we've come up smelling like roses!" Katterwomp cried.

"Why is that?"

"It seems there will be no reason for me to get my nose out of joint. Our headquarters are near Hollywood so your other project can absorb the lion's share of your expenses. Penny wise, pound foolish I always say."

"I'm sure you do," Murphy replied. "You're headquartered near Hollywood?"

"We are, have been for years. What better place than this neck of the woods for a commission on cliches. The politicians in Washington were more than happy to give us a wide berth so we got the lead out and headed west."

"Then I guess you can count me in."

"The devil is in the details and we'll work them out but I'm going to go out on a limb and declare this is the best of both worlds!"

Murphy Murphy and the Case of
the Commission on Cliches

"A-OK?"

"Yes detective?"

"May I ask you a question?"

"Of course, and I promise to answer without fear or favor."

"Do you always speak in cliches?"

"That, my good man, goes without saying." Murphy ended the call and looked at Charlie who just happened to be looking at him.

"That sounded interesting," she said.

"I guess it's back to the salt mines," he said. "It would appear I do, indeed, have a new case." Just then the gate agent called for their row to board.

A SIGHT FOR SORE EYES

It was Friday and that meant Charlie would spend most of the day, and night, at The Gas Pump Lounge. It was the establishment she owned with her brother, Gaston. Alone, Murphy Murphy finished unpacking, put a load of laundry in the wash, then checked the pantry and the fridge. He made a list of necessary provisions and headed down the street to visit his friend Judith Colman at her place of business, Bar Flight.

Until recently the bar was owned by the prize fighter Richie "The Pizzer" Pizzoni. Succumbing to prostate cancer 'The Pizzer" had moved on to the big ring in the sky but before passing he had rewritten his last will and testament leaving Bar Flight to Judith. He also left a healthy chunk of change to his best friend, former sparring partner, and Bar Flight bouncer, Buck. Despite the windfall Buck, at Judith's request, had stayed on standing guard over the club's front door.

"Thanks for asking Ma'am," Buck had said when Judith made the offer of continued employment.

"There's no place I'd rather be and no amount of money will change my mind about that."

"Glad to hear it Buck," Judith replied, "and by the way it's Judith, or boss, but never Ma'am."

"Yes Ma'am," Buck answered.

As Murphy approached the entrance to the bar, he immediately noticed a few changes to the outside of the building. Most notably the new owner had decided to fix the "L" in the neon sign. Pizzoni had purposely disabled the one neon letter because he liked the sound of "Bar Fight" for the name of a place owned by a world champion prize fighter. Judith relit the "L" but the thing that brought a tiny tear to Murphy's eye was the addition, in neon, of "Richie Pizzoni's" name above the original sign.

"Nice touch Jude," he whispered as he approached the door.

"Hey Buck," Murphy said as he entered, "how's it hangin?"

"No complaints deeeeetective," was Buck's reply extending the first syllable. "Welcome back," the big bouncer added.

"Thanks. Is the boss lady around?"

"Does today start with a "t"?" Buck answered the question with a question.

"As a matter of fact, it does," Murphy said, "that's not how the saying goes but I get your point."

He walked to the bar, noticing along the way other changes Judith had made to the place since taking over the reins of Bar Flight. He saw several framed pieces of memorabilia commemorating "The Pizzer's" career. Posters, magazine covers, pictures and a Championship belt were now on display in an area now named "Pizzoni's Corner". It was chalk full of mementoes Richie would never put on display when he was alive. There were other changes that Murphy could only describe as an homage to his friend, and Judith's favorite actor, Matthew Laurance. One was an Eddie and the Cruisers movie poster, signed by Laurance, that hung in a prominent place behind the bar. Judith had also added a few more flat screen televisions, dispersed around the joint, to show not only Eddie and the Cruisers in a continuous loop but episodes of two television series, Duet (in which Laurance played Ben Coleman), and Beverly Hills 90210. That cast included Tori Spelling, Luke Perry, Jenny Garth, Brian Austin Green, and Matthew Laurance as Dr. Mel Silver.

Judith noticed Murphy looking around the room and took the opportunity to pour him a couple of fingers of Jameson Irish whiskey in a glass. Murphy made it to the bar, grabbed a stool, and plopped down. Judith slid the glass his way.

"I love what you've done to the place," Murphy said before taking a sip.

"You like the positive improvements?" she asked with a smile. Murphy just shook his head.

"You people are going to drive me to drink." He took another sip.

"Too late," she said then added, "How was So Cal?"

"Good. The movie industry is interesting. Oh, and Matthew sends his love."

"That's swell. Can't wait to meet him." As she said it, she leaned in close until her face was just inches from his. "Of course, that would necessitate me traveling to Hollywood with you."

"Maybe next time," Murphy nodded. "Did I tell you they cast Rebecca Hall to play you in the movie?"

"You did not but that's cool!" She clapped her hands, "I loved her in **The Town**."

"I liked her in **Iron Man 3**," Murphy countered.

"Of course you did."

Murphy finished off the rest of his drink as Judith slid a glass of water his way.

"Thanks," he said taking a long pull of the cold liquid, "and there's more."

"Pray tell," she prompted.

"I think I have a new case."

"Really?" Judith perked up, "tell me all about it and start at the beginning."

"Knock that off," Murphy scolded his friend and then told her about the Commission on Cliches.

An hour and another Irish whiskey later Murphy was headed home. Along the way he stopped into the Triangle Market to pick up, among other things, a case of his favorite beverage The Mountain Valley Spring Water. Pratik Patel owned the Triangle but most nights left it to his son, Pravit, to manage.

"Welcome back Mr. double M squared," Pravit exclaimed with delight when Murphy Murphy entered the store.

"Hello Pravit," Murphy returned the welcome, "you do understand that's too many "M's".

"Have you stopped in to procure some basic necessities?" Pravit asked ignoring Murphy's admonishment.

"Oh god," Murphy said under his breath. "Just the water," he said out loud.

"Of course, of course," Pravit replied. "Allow me to rise up and get a case of 12 for you. Thanks to prior planning we have plenty on hand. Pardon me while I disappear from view for just a brief second."

"You're incredible," Murphy said wishing he had brought his gun.

Murphy Murphy and the Case of
the Commission on Cliches

"Why thank you Mr. Double M squared. Both my father and I mutually agreed that good customer service is absolutely essential."

"Please just go get the water, Pravit."

Murphy carried the case of water home. A home, like Bar Flight, that had been recently remodeled. For years the detective had slept on a Murphy bed but his paramour Charlie Carlucci was having none of that. She told the story about a friend, or a neighbor, or a distant relative (Murphy couldn't remember which) had suffered both physical and psychological trauma after the murphy bed on which he, or she, (Murphy couldn't remember which) slept had unexpectedly slammed shut. Murphy had tried, complete with demonstrations, to convince Charlie that that could never happen with his state-of-the-art Multimo Royal bed but nothing could put her mind at ease. Nothing save a complete remodel of Murphy Murphy's apartment. One thing that remained intact was his stereo system which currently played Mozart whilst Murphy, fully clothed, dozed on the couch.

STRAIGHT FROM THE HORSE'S MOUTH

The ringing phone woke Murphy. He opened his eyes and reached for his phone. A photo of a smiling Charlie Carlucci greeted him.

"Hey," he said sleepily.

"Up and at 'em handsome," his girlfriend said.

"What time is it?"

"Time for you to be up."

"Isn't it Saturday?"

"All day. Now get up, get dressed, and meet me at Planet of the Crepes so you can buy me breakfast."

"I'm up," Murphy said rolling off the couch.

After a hello kiss, a delicious meal, and a goodbye kiss, Charlie went back to The Gas Pump Lounge. She had to prepare for a big night. Three bands and hundreds of live music starved fans. Thirsty, cash paying, fans. Murphy also had plans for the day as well. Laundry, the grocery store, the record store, and a call to Adalindis Orval Katterwomp was all on the "to do" list and not necessarily in that order. Noon came quickly, "as good a time as any to call my new friend," Murphy said picking up his phone.

"Katterwomp here. Well not actually here," the voice started. "I hate to put you on ice but I'm currently busy as a beaver. Please leave a message. If I consider it a dilly, I'll return your call and we'll get to the bottom of your reason for getting in touch." Murphy waited and heard the beep.

"It's detective Murphy Murphy, please call me back." He figured he had some time so he decided to listen to his newest vinyl purchase. He unwrapped a rare recording of Mozart's *Serenade KV 361 pour 13 Instruments a vent*. He powered up his stereo system and grabbed his headphones. Just then the phone rang. Murphy noticed a 213 area code and decided it must be Katterwomp calling back so he shut down the stereo and answered.

"Murphy."

"Detective, it's A-OK," Katterwomp said.

"That was quick," Murphy responded.

"Quick as a wink!" A-OK agreed. "Actually, believe it or not, I wasn't busy. It's just, all things being equal, I like to have all my ducks in a row before getting down to brass tacks."

"Uh huh," Murphy said questioning once again his decision with regard to this case.

"You called and I'm guessing it wasn't just to shoot the bull."

"It wasn't," Murphy agreed, "but before we dive in can I ask a favor?"

"Of course," Katterwomp answered, "I'm an open book."

"Right," Murphy said as he considered the best way to make his request, "if it isn't too much trouble could you try not to use so many cliches?"

"Well, son of a gun detective," Katterwomp blew out a slight whistle, "I thought I was trying."

"Okay then," Murphy mentally shrugged, "let's get down to business."

"A man after my own heart," Katterwomp replied. "Oh, sorry."

"No worries, A-OK," Murphy smiled. "Tell me all about the Commission on Cliches and your sacred text. And start at square one please."

"Well done, detective. Well done."

Katterwomp started with the commission and its formation. Murphy learned it had been the product of Congress during the Gerald R. Ford administration. He was the 38th President of the United States and the only person to serve as both Vice-President and President without being elected to either office. Ford became VP when Spiro Agnew was shown the door and assumed the top spot when Richard M. Nixon resigned. Ford knew all about commissions because Lyndon Johnson appointed the then Michigan Congressman to the Warren Commission. That was the special task force convened to investigate the assassination of President John F. Kennedy.

"Are you still with me detective?"

"Right here," Murphy answered, "I'm taking notes and recording this conversation."

"By the book I see," said Katterwomp, "by the book."

"Please continue," Murphy prodded and A-OK did.

He told Murphy that apparently Ford enjoyed his time on a commission so much he wanted others to have the same experience. During his presidency Ford, according to Katterwomp, had to deal with a Democrat House of Representatives that enjoyed a veto proof majority, rising inflation, the swine flu pandemic, an ongoing Vietnam war, a weekly comedic bludgeoning on television thanks to Chevy Chase, and 2 assassination attempts.

"The Commission on Cliches was Ford's way of taking a load off," Katterwomp told Murphy Murphy. "He would often sit in on the meetings when he felt like he was in a rut or burning the candle at both ends."

"Good grief," Murphy whispered.

"And when the meetings would come to an end all the commissioners said the President promised that his lips were sealed."

"How did this happen in the first place?" Murphy asked. "How did your commission get created?"

"It was easy as pie detective. Ford simply asked a high-ranking Michigan congressman for a courtesy. Said congressman was more than happy to appease the head of his party and fellow Michigander. An aide slyly introduced a line of text into the 1976 Government in the Sunshine Act. He did as he was asked and that was when our little commission first saw the light of day."

"Just like that?"

"Just like that."

"No one noticed? Nobody raised a red flag?"

"Nobody flipped their lid, that's for sure," A-OK chuckled. "The bill was more than 5,000 words long. One short sentence made the commission on cliches a foregone conclusion. I suspect nobody bothered to read the bill."

"I find that hard to believe."

"I'd prefer not to beat a dead horse but allow me to shed some light on how the government operates."

"Please do."

Murphy Murphy and the Case of
the Commission on Cliches

"During each congressional session more than 10,000 pieces of legislation are considered. Frequently those bills run more than a thousand pages long, that's *millions* of words. I hate to burst your bubble but you can bet your bottom dollar nobody goes through all of them and that suits me to a t."

"That's just so disappointing," Murphy lamented.

"On the contrary detective it's just business as usual. Anyway, those first commissioners are either long in the tooth or dead as a doornail but we, the commission, soldier on."

"How long have you served?" Murphy asked.

"I've been around since god's dog was a puppy," Katterwomp laughed at his own joke. "Seriously, Roberto Francis Picozzi, my third cousin twice removed, was appointed to the original commission. He was a man among boys, as honest as the day is long, give you the shirt off his back actually, and I wanted to be just like him. I told him I wanted to be a commissioner, put my best foot forward, and threw my hat into the ring. When he called to advise me of my appointment it was a red letter day!"

"You're exhausting," was all Murphy thought to say.

"Runs in the blood I'm afraid."

"Who pays you?" Murphy thought to ask.

"Why *you* do!" the man said with a chuckle.

"What do you mean *I* do?"

"You as in the American taxpayer. That was another legislative sleight of hand slipped into The National Defense Authorization Act."

"Another 5,000 word bill?" Murphy said with contempt.

"To the contrary my good detective. The Sunshine in the Government Act can't hold a candle to the NDAA. That one is more than 3,200 pages and includes hundreds of thousands, if not millions, of words. I believe we can be found on page 2,455 or is it 2,456. Oh wait, maybe it's 1,472."

"It doesn't matter," interrupted Murphy.

"That's my point exactly. I realize all of this sounds as dull as dishwater but you did ask."

"I know," Murphy admitted. "Who appoints new commissioners?"

"We do," Katterwomp answered, "well to be on the up and up, I do. But, of course, any new appointee must be up to snuff."

"Of course."

"Anyway, thanks to the powers that be in Congress, the long and short of it is the commission on cliches is renewed and funded every time the government passes the NDAA. In essence we've been on the gravy train since the 1970's."

"Terrific," Murphy said shaking his head. "Now, tell me about the sacred text." The detective waited for a response as several seconds passed. "Mr. Katterwomp? Are you still there?"

"I'm here detective. It's just that when I think of the missing pages I sink into a blue funk."

"Give it the old college try," Murphy poked.

"I'll bite the bullet," Katterwomp conceded. "What has gone missing is actually a book that was first authored years ago by a commissioner named Roger James. He felt it wise to put pen to paper and document the history of every sacrosanct word or phrase that, over time, rose to the level of cliché worthy," Katterwomp paused. "It MUST be found detective! The words need to be preserved so future generations going forward know the origins and backstories of our most cherished sayings!!" A-OK was yelling now.

Most impressive, thought Murphy Murphy, *cliches mixed with redundancies. This guy is really talented.* "Calm down sir," Murphy advised, "Take a deep breath."

"My apologies detective," A-OK said after composing himself, "this conversation has gotten my dander up. I mean if there's no history there can be no future. Hey wait," Katterwomp stopped, "I need a pen and paper so

I can write that down, put it on ice so I can insert it in the book once you find it. It's good as gold!"

"You do that," said Murphy. He waited until A-OK returned. "So, what does Mr. James think happened to the book?" Murphy asked.

"Alas and alack I have no idea."

"Why not?"

"It seems Roger James has cut and run."

"He's disappeared?"

"In the wind."

WATER OVER THE DAM

Brian Katrek a.k.a. Johnny "Mags" Maginnes stood outside the closed door and admired the gold leaf letters stenciled onto the center of the glass. His name, one of them anyway, gleamed directly above the title, "Captain". He had gotten the job when the police department's former Captain, Dave "Dud" Hill was promoted to Chief of Police a few months prior.

The appointment by the City Council was the next logical step in the career progression of the local law enforcement legend nicknamed "Dud" after performing what would have been the ultimate heroic act. Hill appeared to sacrifice his own life attempting to shield others from an explosive device he discovered in the city's largest indoor mall. As it turned out it only "would have been" the ultimate act of valor because the bomb was poorly constructed and turned out to be, you guessed it, a dud.

Hill's ascension to the cop shop's top spot left a hole in the chain of command. When the Captain became the Chief, the Chief needed to hire a new Captain. After briefly considering promoting from within Hill decided to go outside the department and hire a decorated veteran and former private investigator. Thus, with the stroke of a pen, Detective Murphy Murphy had a new boss. A boss, as it so happened, he knew quite well. Katrek, or Maginnes, depending on which suited the man best at any given time, was the ex-Army Special Operator and private investigator hand-picked by Hill. He had teamed with the new Chief to help Murphy Murphy in the case of Serious Crisis. Although if you asked the detective who actually solved the mystery neither the former nor the current Captain was much help during the investigation. In fact, Katrek/Maginnes was considered a viable suspect at one time. But nobody asked Murphy Murphy.

Katrek turned the doorknob and entered the reception area. It was still too early for his special assistant, Courtney Cagley, to be at her desk. Katrek liked getting to work before everyone else. There was another door, plain wood, no glass, which led to the Captain's inner office and through that door he went. Once inside Katrek looked around and he liked what he saw. A large oak desk, a big comfortable chair, and a nice sized picture window through which he could see Posey Park. In one corner of the room, he noticed a small round table with three less comfortable chairs. In another corner stood a seven foot, potted, fiddle leaf fig. He wandered over to the plant and rubbed a leaf between his forefinger and thumb.

"Fake," he said and smiled.

Murphy Murphy and the Case of
the Commission on Cliches

The former Captain's pictures, commendations, and tchotchkes had been replaced with his own. He was most proud of the framed Silver Star, awarded for military operations involving conflict, and a Butterscotch Blonde Fender Maple Fingerboard guitar signed by Serious Crisis cofounder DeMaio Turrell. He noticed the time, took a seat behind his desk, and punched the intercom button on the phone.

"Yes, Chief?" came a female voice in return.

"Miss Cagley, could you please locate Detective Murphy Murphy and let him know his presence is requested."

"Yes sir."

"And tell him, in these exact words, that I'd like a reply back as soon as possible."

"Must I?" Courtney Cagley asked.

"Thank you, Courtney," was the reply.

Murphy had always liked Courtney Cagley. They met years ago at the police academy and became friends. They both cruised through the academy and became beat cops at the same time but their careers soon took divergent paths. Murphy moved up through the ranks to become a detective while Courtney, who also showed a tremendous amount of promise, was injured in the line of duty. She single-handedly stopped three gun wielding teenagers from robbing a liquor store. In the process one of the thug's guns discharged and officer Cagley was hit. Post recovery and rehabilitation she moved into the administrative division and was now the Special Assistant to the police captain.

Murphy followed his friend's career and had mixed emotions when her extension appeared on his phone's caller ID. He was happy to hear from her but more often than not her calling meant he was going to have to talk to her boss. Courtney, as instructed, delivered the message verbatim. Murphy thanked her and said he'd be right up.

"You are nowhere near as good as the last guy," Murphy said as he pocketed his shield and headed for the elevator.

"Hey Courtney," Murphy said as he entered the office area.

"Hi Murphy," she replied. "It's good to see you."

"You too. How are the boys?" Murphy knew she had three.

"Amazing as always. Thanks for asking. Brandon was named the ace of his high school pitching staff. His first game is next week."

"Wow that's impressive. Isn't he only a sophomore?"

"He is!" Courtney said with pride.

"And how are Lucas and Trevor?"

"They're great too. Thanks for remembering. Now, are you finished stalling?"

"I guess," Murphy said with a shrug.

"Go on in. He's expecting you."

"If I must," he said and opened the door to the inner sanctum.

Katrek sat behind his desk, hands behind his head, a big smile on his face.

"Detective Murphy my friend and amigo. Come in. Have a seat." He pointed to the chair opposite him.

"Those two words mean the same thing," Murphy said taking a seat.

"Which two?" Katrek asked, still smiling.

"Friend and amigo," Murphy answered. "But you knew that."

"Did I?"

"I noticed the gold leaf on the door outside," Murphy changed the subject. "Why did you pick Katrek over Maginnes?" When Murphy worked the Serious Crisis Johnny "Mags" Maginnes had been a suspect before the detective learned he was working for Lyndsay Howlund's mother as a private detective. While running a background check Murphy found the PI went back and forth between names depending on the situation.

37

"Dunno," the Captain answered. "I guess I like the alliteration of Captain Katrek and Maginnes can be hard for folks to spell. You know is it one "n"? Two "s's"? Katrek is easier. Don't you think?"

"Don't care," was all Murphy said. "You called. What can I do for you?"

"Why so icy detective? I was hoping we were past the point of competing with each other. It's unnecessary."

"So is being redundant."

"Touche," Katrek said, getting up from his chair. He wandered over to the window and peered outside. "I know you think I got this job under false pretenses but my hope is you'll disavow that notion. Personally, I think, because of our past experience, we can do good work together."

"If you'll stop doing *that,* I think you might be right."

"Copy that, detective. Now, tell me about this Adalindis Katterwomp and his Commission on Cliches."

IT'S NOT THE HEAT IT'S THE HUMIDITY

Roger James wasn't alone in the darkening room but he was the only human. A sliver of light from a crescent moon made its way through one of the windows. The book of cliches, the manuscript he had authored, the volume that had consumed a big part of his adult life, sat on his lap. As he stared at it, he laughed out loud. His dog, a big, beautiful, Landseer Newfoundland, lifted his large, hairy head toward the sound. A dollop of drool escaped through the left side of the mouth of the only other living thing in the cabin.

"It's okay Cooper," James told the black and white behemoth. "Don't mind me."

He had gotten the beast as a puppy two years before on November 9th. James knew that date was the anniversary of the infamous D. B. Cooper incident, a still unsolved mystery concerning America's first airplane hijacking. James had been fascinated by the Cooper caper from the beginning so, since he picked up the pooch on the anniversary date, he named his furry friend after the mastermind. The earlier burst of laughter had come about because James knew the truth.

He hated cliches. He hated them with a passion. He hated them with every fiber of his being. That's the reason he memorialized so many of them in the 305 page, red and blue book that now lay on his lap.

He wrote all the grandiose, outdated, overused phrases down as a first step toward the goal of eliminating their usage altogether. He figured if he put them all out there for the world to see he could convince the public writ large to rid them from everyday language. But he hadn't counted on a couple of things. Things like an explosion of uncritical, over-emotional thinkers graduating from sports broadcasting schools and littering a 500 channel, every game on television, universe. Watching football, golf, and basketball with his nephews drove this point home. He loved sports, was a huge fan, but the experience of being a viewer was becoming less and less enjoyable. Maybe eliminating a resource that documents the offending phrases would facilitate a cleansing that James felt was necessary.

He also couldn't have foreseen a zealot like Adalindis Orval Katterwomp who imagined his simple, little, book of cliches to be an English language element version of the Rohonc Codex. He had lobbied to be a member of the Commission on Cliches so that he could destroy it, and all the hackneyed expressions that came with it, from within. But Katterwomp's hold over the other commissioners was too strong. He couldn't find an ally so his plan never gained traction. Katterwomp convinced a majority of his colleagues that the preservation of English cliches, and more importantly self-preservation in the form of his commission, was the top priority.

James had fallen out of favor and now it had come to this. He now had a different plan. The first part involved the purchase of a Royal brand, fireproof/waterproof, document box from Hammacher Schlemmer. Next, he needed to devise a plan that would keep the book away from Katterwomp at all costs. He could hide it in plain sight, he thought, as long as A-OK was never able to lay eyes on it. The third pillar of his plan was the elimination of Adalindis Orval Katterwomp and the dissolution of the Commission on Cliches. He had letters to congressmen and senators prepared which included a decades long litany of abuse and deceit carried out by Katterwomp and his minions. The silly, needless, commission was created with a clandestine stroke of a pen and it would disappear the exact same way. He was extremely confident about the odds of success for the execution of the first two elements. James continued to ruminate on how to accomplish the third.

FOLLOW YOUR NOSE

Murphy was back on an airplane headed West. In a United Airlines middle seat. Because this time his ticket was purchased by the Commission on Cliches and not the movie studio, Murphy had to take what he was given. At least Katterwomp had splurged for an upgrade to economy plus. Murphy had been a little lucky because the window seat was occupied by a nice, quiet, little old lady who couldn't have weighed more than 80 pounds. Murphy figured the woman freely gave up her claim to the armrest for the entire flight when, immediately after takeoff, she leaned all the way against the side of the plane and fell asleep. But the detective's luck ran out on the aisle side. That seat was now occupied by a 300 plus pound mountain of a man who, Murphy discovered, was on his way to L.A. to interview for a marketing job with the NFL's Rams.

"I played a little bit in college," the man offered while buckling the seat extender.

"I'm not surprised," Murphy replied. Moments later than man introduced himself as Randy Snow.

"Big R to my friends," he added, "and I'd be proud to consider you a friend for the next several hours."

He turned out to be a perfectly delightful, albeit huge, traveling companion. Big R was quiet and respectful, a decent conversationalist when, and only when, conversation was warranted. Murphy figured Mr. Randy Snow would be a welcomed addition to the Los Angeles Rams front office staff and he told the man so.

After about a half an hour of chit chat Murphy and Randy settled into their seats. The detective, left arm on the armrest, immersed himself in the latest crime procedural he was reading. It was a mystery titled, *Song Girl*, and it was recommended by his pal Courtney. He found it to be a fairly interesting cop vs killer story but it had, Murphy thought, a unique and intriguing twist. One of the characters had suffered a serious brain injury and after coming out of a coma found she was only able to speak in song titles. Hence the name of the book. Murphy wondered what that would be like if it happened to him, or Charlie, or Judith. He asked Randy too and the big guy just shrugged his shoulders. But several minutes later he saw his seat mate write the title on a napkin. Murphy also found himself singing a line or two of the songs, Song Girl mentioned in his head. The ones to which he knew the words anyway whenever they popped up on the page. He enjoyed the read.

When the flight attendant arrived, Murphy purchased the "Takeoff snack box" while his rather beefy buddy chose the "Tapas box". They both would have liked to enjoy an Irish whiskey but apparently United no longer served anything alcoholic except beer, wine, and hard seltzer in coach. Big R opted for a White Claw while Murphy stuck with water. With just more than an hour left in the flight the detective set aside his novel and began to solidify a plan for once he hit the ground. He'd rent a car, drive to the Commission on Cliches headquarters and have a look around before meeting with A-OK. He also bandied about the idea of calling Matthew Laurance. He enjoyed the actor's company a great deal and knew the man would be furious if he learned Murphy had been in town and not reached out. But he also didn't want to commit to a social engagement when he had no idea how much time and attention Katterwomp would demand. After a brief internal debate, he made a mental note to call his friend once he was safely on the ground if only to make no promises. A bell dinged and the cockpit announced the plane's final descent into the Los Angeles area. Big R opened his eyes while the old lady snored on.

Murphy Murphy and the Case of
the Commission on Cliches

BEWARE OF GREEKS BEARING GIFTS

Katterwomp knew detective Murphy was arriving that day but he had forgotten when. Earlier he wandered around the commission campus making sure everything was in order for the visit. He wanted to put on a good face. When he returned to his office, he found both a box and a note on his desk. Intrigued, he opened the box to find a dozen donuts from Earl's Donuts, his absolute favorite, staring back at him. He selected a devil's food old fashioned from the confections and took a big bite.

"I am in hog heaven," he practically moaned.

After another healthy bite he turned his attention to the note and tore it open. It's message nearly made him choke. It was written in an even, steady hand.

Katterwomp, the note began, *my time with the commission has come to an end but before I leave I'm ready to bury the hatchet if you are. I know you know I have what you want. Meet me at the zoo, near the entrance to the elephant exhibit. One week from today, 11 PM sharp. Alone. If you're not there or I see you brought company I'm gone for good and so is your precious prize. We'll lay all our cards on the table and see what happens.*

The note was unsigned but Katterwomp knew from whom it came. He'd make the trip to Griffith Park, alone, at the appointed time, and put an end to this madness once and for all. Murphy Murphy couldn't know, nobody could. He'd take care of the matter, like he had always done, by himself. In the meantime he'd enjoy another cake and wait for the detective.

FULL STEAM AHEAD

Murphy Murphy decided to rent a Mercedes sedan. Partly as retaliation for the middle airline seat but mostly because he now knew Katterwomp's commission was flush with taxpayer money. Before getting in the car, he called the commissioner.

"Hello?" A-OK answered. Murphy thought it sounded like the man's mouth was full of food.

"Mr. Katterwomp, it's detective Murphy. Is this a bad time?"

"No time like the present my good detective. No time like the present. Have you arrived in the City of Angels?"

"Indeed, I have."

"Well make hay while the sun shines and get over here."

"That's precisely why I'm calling A-OK. Where, pray tell, is *here*?"

"Ahhh. Here would be 5931 west 18th street. The zip code is 90035. Enter it into your GPS. Even if you don't know the ropes, it should take about 20 minutes, a half an hour tops."

"See you soon," Murphy hung up before another cliché could assault his senses.

"I'll be here with bell's on," A-OK said seconds too late.

It took Murphy exactly twenty-three minutes. A sign outside the entrance on 18th Street read, **The Los Angeles Center for Enriched Studies.** He rechecked the address wondering if Katterwomp had made a mistake. As he pondered that question, he realized he had yet to call his friend Matthew Laurance.

"Speak now or forever hold your peace!" the actor said with authority.

"Too much caffeine?" Murphy asked.

"Murphy Murphy! My friend," Laurance sounded excited, "no caffeine I assure you. I was just practicing for a role as a priest," he clarified. "To what do I owe the pleasure of your call?"

"I'm in town but I'm not sure for how long. I just wanted to give you a heads up."

"I'm touched," Laurance said, "since you're here you absolutely must join us for dinner."

"Who's us?" Murphy asked. "Is Lyndsay here too?"

"Sadly not. I'm having dinner with Ronny, Brie Larson, and Domhnall Gleeson at Providence on Melrose."

"Ronny?"

"Ron Howard silly. He's directing our little film. Brie has been cast as the lovely Charlie Carlucci and Dom is playing you. This is serendipitous and, of course, dinner is on the studio."

"Sounds great," Murphy said because it did. "What time?"

"7:00. We'll save you a seat."

Murphy hung up. *Domhnall Gleeson* he thought. He had to admit part of him was hoping for Ben Affleck, Chris Pratt, or Bradley Cooper. But he knew of Gleeson's work and remembered liking him in a movie called, *About Time.*

"I'm a fan," he said as he steered the Mercedes toward a guarded entrance. He rolled down his window and pulled to a stop.

"Detective Murphy," he said showing his shield, "I believe I'm expected." A man in a private security company uniform looked at the shield, then down at a piece of paper on a clipboard, and finally back at Murphy.

"Straight through," he said pointing toward a group of buildings. "Second one on the right."

"Thanks," Murphy said saluting. He rolled up his window and drove into the complex. He found a space across from the building, parked the Mercedes, and got out. By all appearances Murphy found himself smack dab in the middle of a school campus. A sign outside one building said "Administration". Across the street from where he'd parked sat another building with another sign. This one read, "Classrooms". That's where Murphy headed.

The door was unlocked so in he went. The hallway further cemented the feeling that Murphy was in a school. Fluorescent lights overhead illuminated a long hallway of white tiles speckled with black dots. Lockers lined the halls. Walking through the building he made note of doors with windows of frosted glass. Doors, which Murphy instinctively knew opened to classrooms. His intuition was rewarded when one of the doors he passed was open a few inches and from inside it he heard what he believed to be instructions.

The detective stopped and slid a little closer, careful not to be noticed for fear of interrupting. Peeking through the opening he could see the backs of the heads of young men and women seated in chairs. Pens and pencils in some hands, pads of paper on the desk. Others, Murphy saw utilized lap top computers or tablets. Their attention was focused on the front of the room and a tall, lanky, man with close cropped blonde hair. He stood at a blackboard and Murphy took the measure of the man. He was wearing khaki shorts and white sneakers with black ankle length socks. He also wore a navy polo shirt covered by what looked like some sort of long bib with pockets in the front. There was a name on the back. Murphy noticed it was "Thomas" but he wondered if that was a first name or a last.

From one of the pockets the man, who Murphy assumed was teaching this particular class, pulled a four-inch piece of white chalk. He turned to the blackboard and wrote the words, "firing darts." That phrase took its place directly beneath others. Murphy took note. They included, but weren't limited to, "In the Zone", "A Bounce in His/Her Step", "Flying Under the Radar", "Firing on All Cylinders," and He/She won't Beat Herself/Himself". The spindly teacher turned back to his students.

"Learn these," he said tapping the chalk on the board. "Live these. Because these most fundamental descriptors are your friend. They will help you successfully navigate through any broadcast situation. They form the bedrock for every good announcer, believe me I know. I used them all, for crying out loud, every chance I got."

Murphy saw heads bob up and down as the students wrote furiously on their pads or pounded relentlessly on their keyboards. For the first time Murphy felt like he

51

was, indeed, in the domain of the Commission on Cliches. Having heard enough, he moved on.

Several steps later the detective noticed another door to a different classroom. This door was wide open. As he made his way closer, he saw another teacher at the front of an identical classroom but oddly, Murphy couldn't help but notice, there were no students. He stepped inside. The teacher looked to be in his 50's, early 60's at the oldest. He had salt and pepper hair slicked straight back ala NBA Hall of Fame member Pat Riley. The man sat in a wooden chair with his feet up on his desk. Unlike the previous instructor this one had on black, pressed, cuffed slacks which partially concealed wildly decorative over the calf socks inside black dress shoes. Murphy looked from teacher to blackboard and back. The blackboard may have been a mirror image of the one in the previous classroom but the words written on its surface could not have been more different. On it, printed in neat letters, were two columns. At the top of one "Never Say" was written and underlined. The other column was headed by the words, "Instead Say". Beneath the first column was a row of words. Murphy read, "Perfect", "Unbelievable", and "Very Unique". He understood completely the third admonition but wondered about the other two. It made more sense when he followed the arrow that pointed to words in the other column. "Perfect" was linked to the alternatives "Perfectly Placed", "In Perfect Position", and "Ideal". Across from "Unbelievable" he noticed "Hard to Believe", "Amazing", "Incredible", and "Fantastic".

Murphy Murphy and the Case of
the Commission on Cliches

There were no alternatives for "Very Unique" and Murphy Murphy agreed there shouldn't be. The detective stared at the board while the teacher stared at him.

"Help you?" he broke the silence. Murphy met the man's gaze. He saw blue eyes that, to the detective, looked a little sad.

"Class over?" he asked and the teacher checked a gold watch on his wrist.

"Not for another thirty-five minutes."

"But there aren't any students." When Murphy said it the teacher's mouth formed a small, cheerless, smile.

"Very perceptive. You should be a detective," he said and Murphy offered a smile of his own.

"Where is everybody?" the detective asked.

"In other classrooms I suppose," he said and waved his hand in the direction of the hallway, "learning to be sports announcers," he emphasized the final two words with air quotes, "from *NITWITS!* " he practically spat.

"But not from you."

"Clearly not," he shrugged. "It would appear today's youth are more interested in butchering the English language as opposed to respecting it." Murphy considered the man's words. He liked this guy. Truth be told he felt sorry for him because his students had deserted him but he liked him nonetheless.

"Do you know an Adalindis Orval Katterwomp?" Murphy asked. The teacher looked up.

"Of course. He's the big cheese. Just ask him."

"Do you have any idea where I might find him?

"You might find him in his office. End of the hall," he pointed, "to the elevator. Go down three floors," he stopped.

"Then what?"

"Then nothing. The elevator opens up into Katterwomp's office."

WHEN IN ROME DO AS THE ROMANS DO

As suggested the elevator doors opened into a room but Murphy would be hard pressed to describe it as an office. It was expansive. There were no windows, fitting for a space three floors underground, but the space was uncharacteristically bright. It was a semi-circle with alcoves every several feet featuring trees and shrubberies standing as high as eight feet. The floor was covered with a silvery gray carpet. As Murphy stepped inside, he felt his feet sink at least half an inch in the plush pile. There was a huge official looking seal in the center of the room. Interlocking capital "C's" were the main feature. A beautiful bald eagle, complete with an olive branch in its beak, was perched on the C at the top of the crest. The words, *Ye Who Enter Here, Abandon All Hope* ringed the bottom. Murphy Murphy giggled.

The room smelled of fresh paint but he thought he detected a faint whiff of smoke in the air. *Not from a cigarette, cigar or pipe,* thought the detective, *more like the scent of paper recently set alight.* There was no reception area. In fact, Murphy saw no furniture at all. He did see three doors, spaced equally between the alcoves. They made Murphy think of a riddle his dear, departed, Grandfather Murphy Murphy told him when he was a child. He ran the riddle of the three doors through his brain.

A man is trapped inside a room with three doors but only one of the three exits allows him to escape the room alive so he must choose wisely. He's told behind one door he'll find hundreds of assassins ready to shoot whomever comes through. The second door conceals a pride of lions that hasn't eaten in three months and on the other side of the third door is deadly flames that burn for a length of two miles. Which door does the man choose to make his escape?

Murphy remembered sitting on his grandpa's lap and thinking about the riddle. It didn't take him long to come up with an answer.

"I think I know pop pop."

"So soon grandson?"

"Yes sir!" he recalled saying with confidence.

"Then what is your answer?"

"The second door," he remembered saying with pride.

"Are you sure?"

"I am sure."

"Then why the second door Murphy Murphy?"

Murphy Murphy and the Case of
the Commission on Cliches

"Simple," young Murphy said, "Because if the pride of lions hadn't eaten in three months, they would be long dead. That is why the man must choose door number two."

"Very good grandson," he remembered his pop pop saying with a pat on the knee. "You are a wise lad indeed." The memory made Murphy Murphy smile but only for a moment.

"Hello! Anybody here?" he called. In a matter of seconds, a man, who Murphy assumed was Adalindis Orval Katterwomp, emerged from door number two.

"Detective Murphy I presume. I welcome you with open arms."

The man was smaller and thinner than Murphy expected but his voice, in person, was deeper and more sonorous than it sounded on the telephone. But it emanated from a body that appeared wholly ill equipped to contain it. He had plenty of hair, mostly dark with odd streaks and patches of white and grey. Murphy pictured a drunken skunk or a mischievous toddler with a brush and a bucket of paint. Katterwomp's eyes were of average size and brown and even though he had plenty of hair on his head his eyebrows appeared non-existent. The mouth was small and round. Above it sat A-OK's most prominent feature, his nose. Murphy thought it resembled the beak of the bald eagle on the floor. It was slender and sharp and pointed down so the tip seemed to kiss the man's upper lip. The nose brought to Murphy's mind something else his loving grandfather used to say. It happened to be the man's favorite joke.

"What did the elephant say to the naked man?" he would ask Murphy or anyone else who would listen.

"I don't know pop pop what?" he responded despite the fact that he had heard the joke dozens of times.

"How do you breathe through that thing!?" The answer always made both of them giggle. Every time. Murphy successfully suppressed a giggle in front of Katterwomp.

"I'm happy to finally make your acquaintance," he said instead. Then he allowed his eyes to take in the entirety of the ante chamber one more time. "Quite a place you have here," he added feeling less and less guilty about renting the Benz.

"I've led a charmed life, detective, and I know this place cost a pretty penny. I'd be crazy as a coot to take any of it for granted." Murphy stood speechless as Katterwomp turned toward the door from which he emerged and held out his hand. "After you," he implored. Murphy walked past A-OK, through the door, and into what Murphy decided must be the man's private office. Katterwomp followed.

"Take a load off," he said and Murphy sat. The commissioner circled his desk and took his seat directly across from Murphy Murphy. The desk was spotless

and devoid of clutter save for a single box. "Donut?"
Katterwomp asked tilting the box so Murphy could see
the confections inside. The detective counted seven
delicious looking circular cakes.

"They look fantastic," Murphy confessed, "but I'm
afraid I have to pass."

"Your loss is my gain," A-OK smiled and grabbed a
glazed donut, with what looked to Murphy like pieces
of the kid's cereal Fruit Loops on top and took a bite.

"Tell me more about the guy who wrote the book?"
Murphy asked then waited as Katterwomp chewed and
swallowed.

"The book?" he asked.

"The book of cliches, your sacred text, the thing I've
been tasked to find. You told me it was a book."

"I did indeed and it is. I'm impressed that you're not
letting any grass grow under your feet. I like that."

"The guy you mentioned before? Was he the only
author?" Murphy asked.

"Well, actually a few of us, yours truly included,
contributed through the years but if I was being an
honest Injun I'd have to reiterate the author most
responsible for our most precious piece of writing is a
commissioner named Roger." Murphy pulled a pen and
his notebook from a jacket pocket, found the page on
which James was mentioned and underlined it.

"I'd like to speak with him."

"So would I," A-OK responded a little too quickly thought the detective. Murphy looked up from his pad.

"Let's talk to him together then," he suggested.

"There's the rub, my good man. You see, I've tried everything, called everyone, looked everywhere," Katterwomp lied with a straight face. "I have no idea where Roger James is."

A GOOD TIME WAS HAD BY ALL

Murphy spent a few more minutes with Katterwomp before leaving his office. In that time the man had inhaled another donut. It made the detective curious as to how the commissioner stayed so skinny. He took the elevator back to the ground floor and walked the empty hallway past deserted classrooms. School had clearly ended for the day. Outside he looked around the campus again now knowing some of what was both above and below ground. Oddly, he felt, there wasn't a soul in sight. He had some time before dinner so he grabbed his phone and called Charlie.

"Hi there handsome," she said after picking up on the first ring. Murphy's heart skipped a beat when he heard her voice.

"I'm crazy about you," he blurted. It wasn't how he had planned to start the conversation but it felt right.

"Why thank you," she answered, "I'm pretty fond of you too. How's it going out there?"

"Strange to say the least," he was honest, "this Katterwomp fella is a character and a half."

"An odd duck huh?"

"Might be the oddest duck I've ever encountered."

"So, how goes the case?"

"Honestly, I have no idea. The guy wants me to find this book but I'm at a loss as to how to go about doing that."

"No clues? No leads?"

"Well, there *is* one guy. The missing book's supposed author."

"There you go."

"Maybe," he agreed, "except for one problem," Murphy then countered.

"Which is?"

"He appears to have disappeared."

"A minor hiccup for the world's best detective," she encouraged her man. "Start there. Find him."

"Did I mention I love you."

"Nope." They both laughed.

"Oh, guess what?"

"What?"

"I'm having dinner tonight with Matthew and a few of his friends."

Murphy Murphy and the Case of
the Commission on Cliches

"The Sheen family?" she wondered.

"Hah," he laughed remembering the conversation they had in Laurance's home. "No."

"Anybody I've heard of?"

"I'm thinking probably."

"Ooooh," she said excitedly, "spill the beans already buddy!"

"Okay. Okay. Calm down. Ron Howard for one."

"Oh my god!" he heard her scream. "Is he directing the movie?"

"He is. That's good, right?'

"Better than good you ninny. It's fantastic! Who else, who else?"

"An actor named Domhnall Gleeson," he answered.

"General Hux!"

"Who?"

"General Hux. The Empire General in the final three Star Wars movies. In *The Rise of Skywalker* he helped Finn, Poe, and Rey escape because he hated Kylo Ren, remember?"

"How could I forget?" he said even though he had forgotten. "Anyway, he's playing me."

"I like that choice although he has red hair and you don't. I'm sure they can dye it but even if they don't, he'll be perfect! Okay, who else?"

"Just one more. The actress playing Charlie Carlucci."

"Me?! Oh gosh, I'm nervous. Who?"

"Brie Larson." The only thing heard from the other end of the phone was another, even louder scream. "Are you okay Charlie?"

"No! I think I'm going to faint. Captain Marvel is playing little 'ol me. I can't believe it."

"I'll be sure to pass along your approval."

"Please do."

"Better yet let's get you back out here and you can tell her yourself."

"I'm ready when you are."

"I'll get the shooting schedule and we'll make that happen."

"This is so surreal," Charlie said in a faraway voice, "Your life, *OUR* life, being made into a movie."

"Tell me about it," was the only reply Murphy could come up with.

"By the way," Charlie said in a calmer tone, "where's dinner?"

"Some place called Providence," Murphy started to answer.

"On Melrose? That Providence?" Charlie interrupted.

"You've heard of it?"

"Of course, silly. It's legendary. It's also pretty pricey."

"Really? How pricey?"

"As much as $350 a person pricey if you indulge in the tasting menu which, if I'm reading the guest list correctly, you will be."

"Holey Moley!" Murphy exclaimed. "I'm glad I didn't have lunch."

He told Charlie he loved her one more time and hung up. Before getting back in the car he spied his reflection in the Mercedes's driver side window. He realized he hadn't packed much and the cable knit sweater he currently had on his back was as fancy as it got. He knew it wasn't going to cut it at a $300 a person dinner with some of Hollywood's heavy hitters. Checking his watch he decided he had plenty of time to go shopping. He knew there were plenty of places nearby on Rodeo Drive including Tom Ford, Bijan, and the Ralph Lauren Flagship store where he could pick up a $4,000 sport coat to wear over a $600 shirt. Luckily for him, when he was in town during the Serious Crisis case, Matthew had introduced him to Ron Thomson. It was a men's store where Murphy knew he could get what he needed for less than a tenth of the price he'd spend in Beverly Hills. Murphy and Matthew had encouraged Serious Crisis band members DeMaio Turrell, Big Joe Lionns, and Chuckie Gruber to get outfitted there too. Drummer Herbie Albanese preferred The Gap.

The only potential complication was the store was downtown and he was in a part of town known as Mid City. If he was lucky, he could get there in thirty minutes, unlucky it could take more than an hour. He decided the trip was worth it so he rolled the dice and was rewarded with a smooth, relatively traffic free ride. Once there he spent forty minutes inside before deciding on an RT Symmetric Button Down Closure jacket in grey and a blue Tie Bar Hidden Placket shirt. Conrad, the salesperson, promised he looked "smashing" and the ensemble went perfectly with his black jeans.

A stop over at his hotel for a quick shower meant Murphy was right on time as he pulled up in front of Providence. The restaurant was on Melrose Avenue just a couple of blocks from the Paramount Studios. Murphy put the car in park, got out, and handed the key to a valet. The young lady seemed offended taking the key and holding it between her thumb and forefinger like a bag of dog poop. Murphy wondered what the problem was until he looked over his shoulder at an Aston Martin Victor and a Bentley Bacalar that had stopped on the street behind him. He felt slightly embarrassed but supremely relieved realizing he could have rented a Chevrolet Spark. Another valet ran out to grab the keys to the Aston Martin, laughing at Murphy's girl as he passed.

"Murphy! Buddy!" the detective heard Matthew Laurance and turned toward his voice. He saw the actor emerge from the passenger side of the sleek black sports car. "Meet my friend Ron," Laurance added as Ron Howard climbed out of the driver's side.

"I'm with them," Murphy said to the valet who ignored him and drove away. He made every effort to not look, or act, overly starstruck as pleasantries were exchanged. The three men went inside.

"Is that a Ron Thomson?" Laurance asked running his right hand down the lapel of Murphy's new jacket. Calls of "Hello!" and "Hey there Ron!" greeted the group as they made their way to the bar. "Big shot," Laurance whispered as they followed Howard in relative obscurity.

"Dom!" the director shouted, "and Brie! My goodness you look fantastic!"

"Why thank you," the man who Murphy assumed was Domhnall Gleeson, said with a smile. Brie Larson punched him on the upper arm.

"Do you guys know Matt Laurance?" Howard asked the movie stars.

"Matt?" Murphy said to his friend. Laurance rolled his eyes.

"That's Sal Amato!" Brie Larson said pointing at Laurance. "Eddie and the Cruisers was my absolute *favorite* movie when I was a kid. I must have seen it a hundred times. Of course, I know Sal Amato."

"I'm flattered," Laurance said shaking her hand, "I think."

"I don't believe I've had the pleasure," Gleeson said extending his own hand. "I'm Domhnall but please call me Dom."

"The pleasure is all mine," Laurance took and shook his hand. "And this," he said turning to Murphy, "Is my dear friend Detective Murphy Murphy. He's the reason we're all here tonight."

More greetings and pats on the back ensued and drinks were ordered. Matthew offered a toast and Murphy took what he felt was an obscenely large gulp of his whisky.

"Jameson, huh?" Gleeson addressed Murphy pointing to his glass. Murphy nodded. He knew by the brogue, and from what Charlie had said, the actor was from Ireland. "I'm a Red Breast 21 year man myself," Domhnall offered.

"Nice. But a bit steep for a guy on a copper's salary," Murphy said smiling.

"Was there honestly a department of redundancy department?" Gleeson asked.

"Still is as a matter of fact," Murphy answered taking another gulp.

"Iontach," Domhnall shook his head. Murphy knew the word meant fantastic or wonderful in Irish.

"I'm actually not Irish but because everyone thinks I must be, I know a few words," Murphy admitted. "So, gan dabht," he replied which he also knew meant "without a doubt".

"Irish or not I believe we are going to be fast friends," the actor said in English.

"Mister Howard," a tall, beautiful, redhead, made her presence known, "your table is ready when you are."

"Thanks Allie," the director acknowledged her. "Ready folks?" They were. Murphy excused himself and went to the men's room. On the way he recognized at least a dozen famous faces. They paid him no mind in return. In the restroom Murphy did his business then washed his hands and splashed cold water on his face.

"Can be a bit overwhelming, can't it?" Murphy hadn't noticed the man three sinks down.

"That's an understatement."

"Hang in there. Try to enjoy it," the gentleman said. "The food here is exquisite." He dried his hands and patted Murphy on the shoulder on the way out. Murphy stood staring at Morgan Freeman's back.

The seating arrangement at the table had the detective sitting between Larson and Gleeson. Laurance and Howard faced them from the other side of the table. Domhnall rose to let Murphy slide in. He had to admit he felt a little lightheaded and a lot out of his league. His friend Matthew was an accomplished actor but Gleeson, Larson and especially Ron Howard were horses of a different color. He conjured up an image of Katterwomp as he thought it.

"Can I ask you a personal question?" He said to Brie Larson after getting settled.

"Uh," she started to answer, "I guess so."

"Do you really drive a Nissan?" he asked referring to her work in commercials. He felt a not so gentle kick from under the table and snuck a glance at Laurance who was shaking his head.

"That's not personal," Larson said sounding relieved, "but it is funny." Murphy took that as a no.

"I finally got Bacon," Howard was saying to Matthew Laurance. "The guy still owes me for Apollo 13 so he'll be playing the roadie Martin Kaufmann."

"What about the band," Murphy turned his attention away from the actress and toward the director at the same time revealing that he'd been eavesdropping. Howard didn't seem to mind.

"Honestly Mr. Murphy."

"Just Murphy please," the detective offered.

"Fair enough. Honestly Murphy, that is still a work in progress. We do know we have Trace Adkins as Big Joe Lionns and a really talented young actor named Joe Keery has been cast as DeMaio Turrell."

"Can he sing?" Murphy asked.

"Like a bird," Howard responded. "He used to be in a band called Post Animal. You should check them out." The name sounded somewhat familiar to Murphy but he couldn't remember why.

"I realize it's probably none of my business but what about Lyndsay?" It was Laurance this time. "I know it's been a *difficult dilemma* but, after all, she is my niece." This time it was Murphy's turn to deliver an under the table kick.

"Ahh Lyndsay," Howard nodded, "that has been problematic."

"How so?" Murphy wondered.

"Well, let's see," the director touched the forefinger of his right hand to the same finger on his left. "First, and I'll try and put this as delicately as possible." He looked at Brie Larson. "it's not easy to find female leads these

71

days," Murphy saw Larson shrug her shoulders. "Especially ones who can convincingly carry a tune. Believe me we have had actresses volunteer for the role," his gaze remained on the actress. "Anyway," he looked at Murphy again, "we want to get it right so, for example, we approach Gaga but she was busy." He moved the finger on the right to the middle finger on his left hand. "McKenna Grace is too young," the finger moved again, "Faith Hill is too old."

"And she's not an actress," Larson interjected. Howard's finger moved again.

"And Billie Eilish can't act a lick," he spread his hands wide, palms up. "We're currently in communication with Emma Stone's people and we've reached out to representatives for Hallie Steinfeld and Anna Kendrick." Murphy could have sworn he heard Brie Larson whisper "whatever".

Ron apparently hadn't heard and he continued, "You'll be happy to know we are going to have a diverse cast. I think we convinced Idris Elba to play Captain David "Dud" Hill, and Dev Patel, Keenan Thompson, Danny Dae Kim and Tessa Thompson are all on board."

"That's great," Murphy said trying to sound enthusiastic at the same time wondering why perceived diversity was such an issue. He briefly wondered which people would be played by the aforementioned actors. He decided he couldn't care less, he just liked the fact that so many movie stars were going to be in the film.

"Bravo for you," Brie said without much conviction. It was clear to the detective that there was tension between the actress and this particular director. It made him wonder if she would make it through dinner let alone the entire movie production.

"Oh!" Howard interjected suddenly remembering something, "how could I forget to tell you that Ving Rhames will be playing Morris 'Mo Mo' Morrissey."

"That's so cool," Murphy said remembering his restroom encounter and thinking it would have been even cooler if Morgan Freeman was Mo Mo.

"Doesn't sound like there will be much to *protest against*," it was Laurance again. The redundancy made Murphy shake his head.

"You're hilarious," Gleeson said to Matthew. Murphy felt Brie Larson's hand on his forearm. He turned and looked at her.

"I guess you better tell me all about Charlie," she said with what sounded like resignation in her voice. Murphy happily acquiesced.

The remainder of the evening was a bit of a blur to Murphy Murphy. Food and wine begat more wine and food. Nobody ordered a thing but it all kept coming. Two and a half hours later he was back in his hotel room and even though he was still wired from the heady company, a bit tipsy from all the alcohol, and it was late, he called his girlfriend. Charlie had once told him it was never too late for him to call.

"How was dinner?" asked a sleepy voice.

"Absurdly bizarre," were the first words that came to Murphy's mind.

"Isn't that redundant?" Charlie asked through a yawn.

"Undoubtedly," he admitted, "but man it was wild. I almost ran into Morgan Freeman in the men's room. I wish so much that you could have been there."

"In the *men's room*?" she asked. "That would have been weird."

"Very funny. I just mean I'm not doing that again without you."

"I'll hold you to that," she said stifling a yawn. "Did you like Ms. Larson? Will she make a good Charlie Carlucci?"

"I did," he said after a beat, "and I think she will."

"Do I sense a 'but'?"

"Maybe," he hesitated again, "it's just that I got the impression she and Ron Howard didn't see eye to eye on certain things. It was almost as if she wanted the role of Lyndsay and not you."

"I've read she can be difficult on set sometimes," she said trying not to sound disappointed.

"And off it too I noticed."

"Oh well," Charlie said, "maybe I'll get Charlize
instead."

"That would be cool," Murphy admitted.

EVERY CLOUD HAS A SILVER LINING

Murphy woke up the next morning still feeling a little tired and more than slightly hungover. He had a few hours until his flight so he decided to revisit the Commission on Cliches headquarters. His goal was to get more information on Roger James. Ron Howard had given him the shooting schedule for the Case of Serious Crisis movie after dinner and had highlighted several days during which he thought the detective's attendance would be helpful. He knew he'd be back in less than a month but there was still work to be done on this day. So, he forced himself to get out of bed. He showered, packed, checked out, and drove toward mid-city.

The guard at the gate recognized the detective and waved him through. But he was one of the only things that was identical to the day before. Murphy parked in the same spot but this time it was behind a relatively new, silver Cadillac Escalade. Another difference was the eerie silence in the building's hallway. There were no professors speaking from in front of blackboards. The building was devoid of students frantically pounding on keyboards. Murphy made it to the end of the hall and entered the elevator. He started to push the button for the third floor but his curiosity made him press number one instead.

When the doors opened Murphy saw a parking garage. A simple concrete floor with numbered spaces. There were no names to identify spots save one. The one right next to the elevator. The block letters on the sign in front of the area read **ADALINDIS ORVAL KATTERWOMP**. The space was empty. Every space in the garage was empty. Murphy stepped back into the elevator and pressed the button for the second floor. Nothing happened. The number failed to light up and the elevator didn't move. Murphy saw what appeared to be a sensor on the panel and figured a special key card was required to access that particular floor. He reached for his pen and pad and made a note to ask Katterwomp about that. Then he hit the button for three.

The antechamber was also unchanged from the day before. All three doors were closed. Murphy knew A-OK's office was behind door number two so he went, instead, to the first door. It was unlocked so in he went. There were no assassins firing at will. What there was instead was a large oval oak table surrounded by 12 office chairs. The chair at the far end of the table was larger and looked more comfortable than the other eleven. *Katterwomp's chair* thought Murphy. This was clearly a board room or a meeting room. The place where the Commission on Cliches held court with Adalindis Katterwomp presiding. On the wall behind the big chair Murphy saw a smaller version of the seal that adorned the antechamber's carpet. Fanning out from either side of the crest were twelve, 11" by 14", framed photographs of people. Twelve professional headshots to match the number of chairs.

There was an additional photograph, this one slightly larger and more ornately framed, on the wall directly opposite the seal. It was a color picture of President Gerald R. Ford. Murphy strolled all the way into the room and looked at the pictures on the wall. There were nine men and three women. All three of the women appeared to be African American. By contrast eight of the nine men were white. The lone male person of color was identified as Roger James. Murphy wondered how, why, or even if, the man's ethnicity was important and he wrote as much in his notebook. He also wrote down the names of the other eleven commissioners with the hope of finding and interviewing as many as possible. It took him a few minutes before had had them all. He looked at the list hoping against hope a connection might become obvious.

MATTHEW ADAMS

BRANDI SEYMOUR

DANIEL V. "DANNY" BRIGGS

GAYDEN CARR

REBECCA "BECKY" GASTON

PERRY G. FURMAN

DR. CAMMIE DIERKING

SIR GAVIN COLES, MBE

PAUL "YOKKY" JOKLIK

DARRYL JAMES MARSHALL, ESQ.

MICHAEL BLOOM

ROGER JAMES

ADALINDIS ORVAL KATTERWOMP

As Murphy perused the list, he thought he heard the elevator doors open but when he rushed out of the conference room they were already closed. Murphy did notice the "UP" arrow above the doors was glowing bright white. Someone had been on the floor with him. Someone who had to know he wasn't alone. Murphy decided it was pointless to try and chase whomever it was by using the elevator. When it returned to gather up the detective, the person would be long gone. He looked for an alternate exit, a door that led to a set of stairs, but found none. He wondered how that passed a building inspection. Realizing there was nothing he could do about the other person he decided to investigate Katterwomp's office. He pulled a pair of latex gloves from another one of his coat pockets, slipped them on, and reached for the door handle. It was unlocked so he went inside.

"Were you in here when I arrived?" he asked the empty office. "And you left in such a hurry you forgot, or didn't have time, to lock the office door." Murphy looked around. The desk was clean as a whistle, the box of donuts that was there yesterday was long gone. He walked around the piece of furniture and stood where Katterwomp would sit. There was a slim center drawer which Murphy slid open. Pens and pencils, neatly arranged, sat next to a box of business cards. That was it. The desks other four drawers, two on each side, were locked. There was a black, wire wastebasket under the desk. The box, which yesterday held the pastries, was folded a few times and stuffed inside. Murphy pulled it out, unfolded, and examined it. He saw several blobs of what could only be excess, multi-colored frosting stuck to the top and the bottom but nothing else. Murphy poked at a pink glob and the sticky paste stuck to his gloved finger. He put it in his mouth.

"Strawberry," he said appreciatively, "and still pretty fresh."

He refolded the box and was about to put it back in the trash can when he noticed several small pieces of charred paper. He touched one and it disintegrated. Murphy recalled smelling what he thought was the remains of paper burning during his visit yesterday. It had to have come from this. Someone, Katterwomp he presumed, had taken a receipt, or instructions, or maybe even a note, ripped it into little pieces, and set it all on fire. But why?

Murphy Murphy and the Case of
the Commission on Cliches

Murphy hadn't brought any evidence bags but he did have another glove. He pulled it out held the opening as wide as he could and dumped the remainder of the ashes inside. He doubted a lab could do anything with the evidence but, he knew, you never knew. Setting the box back in the basket Murphy's eyes lit on another object. About a foot and a half from the edge, and around the other side of the receptacle, he noticed a small, unburned, square of white paper. He decided it must've fluttered away and landed out of sight, and the reach, of Katterwomp.

"Well, well, well. What do we have here?" Murphy kneeled on the carpeted floor, plucked up the paper, and looked at one side then the next. When he turned the piece over, he noticed the writing. "**ele**" and what appeared to be an additional sliver of a line was written in neat, black, letters.

"E.L.E.," Murphy said the letters out loud one by one. "Elle," he said next, pronouncing the first letter of the non-word with a hard "e". "Elle," he tried, this time with a soft "e". Murphy couldn't make hide nor hair of it and he had no idea if the piece of paper, and the writing it revealed, had any relevance to the case in general or the untimely disappearance of Roger James in particular. He slid the gloves from the wrist forward off his hand making sure the newfound clue remained inside the latex. If would have to do until he found an evidence bag. Then he removed his other glove and left the office making sure to close the door behind him. He stopped at door number three before leaving. He felt the outside of the wood. It was cool to the touch, no blazing fire on the other side. He thought again of his pop pop. He made his way out of the building and over to his car. The Escalade, as Murphy expected, was no longer in its space. He chastised himself for not getting a picture of, or writing down, the plate number.

"Rookie move," he said as he got in the Mercedes.

GRASPING AT STRAWS

"Are you serious!?" Murphy asked his friend Judith from his familiar perch on a Bar Flight stool. She stood, facing him, behind the bar. Murphy's gal Charlie was on the barstool to his right. His actor friend Matthew Laurance, decked out as Dr. Mel Silver, loomed above them all from a 65" television screen.

"As serious as a poutine shortage in Maniwaki," Judith said.

"I'm going to pretend that's English," Murphy said as Judith continued.

She had just informed him that google told her there were nearly a thousand words that began with the letters "ele". "From elegy to electroencephalographically," she added.

"Good grief," was all Murphy Murphy could think to say. *A thousand words* he thought as he remembered the slip of torn paper he'd discovered in Katterwomp's office. "That's a Herculean task."

"Maybe more like Theseus than Hercules," Charlie said touching his arm.

"What?" Murphy asked. Judith smiled.

"Theseus," the bartender said, "you know Poseidon's kid. The guy that enslaved the Minotaur. Not as strong as Herc but still quite the badass."

"That's the guy," Charlie nodded.

"You two," Murphy shook his head, "could you please speak the King's English as opposed to whatever Judith said a second ago and Greek Mythology."

"Okay," it was Charlie, "the *English* language has 26 letters."

"I know that," Murphy interrupted.

"But," Charlie continued ignoring him, "if I remember correctly the fourth letter on your little piece of paper had a straight line to it."

"It did indeed," Murphy wondered where this was going.

"So, you can immediately eliminate a, c, e, g, m, o, g, s, u, v, w, x, y, *and* z," Murphy nodded but Charlie wasn't finished. "Also, if you ask me, d is a stretch and so is f. I'd even argue n, p, and r are iffy."

"She's good," Judith said with admiration.

"The best," Murphy agreed.

Murphy Murphy and the Case of the Commission on Cliches

"So by my count we, and by that I mean you, are down to seven viable letters and they would be b, h, i, j, k, l, and t. So start there." She kissed Murphy on the cheek. "I'll have another Bloody Mary," she said to Judith.

Roger James remembered every detail of the minute he met his wife. The day, the time, the slight, warm, breeze, the way the clouds formed, moved, and changed in the sky. In fact, it was because of the clouds that the whole thing was possible.

His first peek at the sunrise gave Roger the feeling that the day would be a glorious one. He took his lunch to Paradise Park almost every day but it was a special treat on afternoons like that one. A brown paper sack contained a container of applesauce, a plastic spoon, two Dixie brand 1/8th fold disposable napkins, and six Ritz Cracker sandwiches. Three of them had peanut butter between the discs, two others had a square of cheddar cheese and a pickle, and the last one featured peanut butter and a pickle. That one was desert. He remembered that too.

He also carried a notebook and had two pens, one black and one blue, in a plastic protector inside his shirt pocket in case he needed to jot down some particulars with regard to the masses of water drops or ice crystals suspended in the atmosphere. You see Roger James was a card-carrying member of the Cloud Appreciation Society, a decades old organization with members in more than 120 countries around the world. Member number one was a genial Brit who convinced others that clouds deserved widespread and public gratitude. The club's manifesto was based on the belief that clouds "are unjustly maligned and that life would be immeasurably poorer without them." The charter implored members to "always live life with your head in the clouds."

So off he rambled to his favorite spot in the park. The slope was perfect allowing his 6'2" frame to get the best look at the sky and the treasures it held. When the ritual first began he would bring along a sketch pad and did the best he could capturing the images above. Then technology came to the rescue delivering the first camera phone and life as a member of the Cloud Appreciation Society improved greatly. As he had done hundreds of times before Roger James assumed his position on the grass. He pulled his latest phone from his pocket, then reached into the brown bag, grabbed a napkin, and selected one of the first five "Ritzwiches". It happened to be one of the cheese and pickle ones which delighted him.

A few wispy whites drifted through his field of vision but a rather large formation captured his attention. It looked like a dog on a mountain or maybe it was a cow surrounded by bales of hay, both were possible he remembered thinking. He picked up his phone to document the formation and post it to the CAS website. He knew if he was interested hundreds of other members would be as well. Then, all of a sudden, a whole new world came crashing around him.

Murphy Murphy and the Case of
the Commission on Cliches

Adalindis Katterwomp was in a rocking chair on the deck of his penthouse condominium. From where he sat, he could see almost all the way to the Pacific Ocean. It was his favorite spot to think, especially at sunset when the sky went from blue to pink to purple and the palm trees turned a deep grey in silhouette.

"The fat's in the fire now," he said softly to his cat, Back Seat Driver, who was perched on the deck's railing. He took a sip of gin. "I figured I might have me a decent stalking horse in that nosy detective but I had no idea the fruits of my labor would ripen so quickly." He looked down at the briefcase resting, opened, at his feet. $250,000 dollars in small, unmarked, bills stared back at him.

"That damn Roger James can be as slippery as an eel so I've got to mind my p's and q's." The cat yawned and jumped from the rail to Katterwomp's lap nearly spilling his drink. "Don't you worry Driver," he said petting the creature, "I'll meet the man at the appointed place and time and pretend to feather his nest with this," he gently kicked the case and took another gulp of Bluecoat. "But when he least expects it I'll turn the tables and go at him with hammer and tongs." The cat, perpetually uninterested, licked its paws.

"Once I've cooked his goose I'll beat a hasty retreat. Then I'll give that ol' goodie two shoes detective some cock and bull story as to how I got the book back and send him on his way." He swirled the last bit of gin around the melting cube of ice and raised his glass to

87

the remnants of the setting sun. "Here's to the best laid schemes," he proclaimed and finished off his gin.

Bonnie Willows certainly didn't intend to meet a man that day, let alone her future husband. It was just another day for the young lady who worked as the Director of Imaging and Radiology at one of the top hospitals in town. As a schoolgirl she discovered a *Little Golden Book* about Marie Curie during a field trip to the town library and couldn't put it down. She convinced both her teacher and the librarian to let her keep it. In exchange little Bonnie agreed to dust and straighten the shelves in the children's books section every Saturday for two months.

It didn't take long for her to discover other books about the 19th century Polish physicist and chemist. Through them she learned Curie was a naturalized French citizen who, in 1906, became the first female professor at the University of Paris. So she daydreamed about learning that language and moving to the City of Lights. In the meantime, she also found out that the scientist was the first woman to win a Nobel Prize and the *only* woman to earn that honor twice. She read Curie coined the term radioactivity and, in the early 1900's, discovered the elements plutonium and radium. Bonnie Willows also discovered Curie died in 1934 of aplastic anemia. It was the direct result of exposure to the work with radiation that made her famous. It all helped mold a young girl into a woman driven to excel in the field of Radiology. She earned her Bachelor of Science degree from the

Murphy Murphy and the Case of
the Commission on Cliches

University of San Francisco and a Masters degree from Thomas Jefferson University in Philadelphia. It all led to her current job and a midday walk in the park on a beautiful day.

Bonnie had been a cute girl and she blossomed into a beautiful woman. Jealous peers, looking for something to criticize claimed her nose was slightly turned up at the tip and a little too big for her face. At that moment that very nose was buried inside a book. This particular book happened to be **Advanced Neuroradiology Cases**. She was particularly engrossed by a chapter describing a case of acoustic schwannoma with post radiation therapy central necrosis. There was absolutely no way she could have seen or sensed the man, supine on the grass, doing something as unproductive as staring up at the clouds. She tripped over the body of Roger James and fell flat on her face, breaking her aforementioned nose.

It was love at first sight, at least for Roger. It took a little longer for Bonnie because her "sight" was impaired thanks to a swollen shut right eye.

"I'm so sorry," Roger said as he held Bonnie's hand in the emergency room. The bleeding had been stopped thanks to a nurse but they still waited for a doctor to tend to her sniffer.

"Why are *you* sorry?" she asked squeezing his hand, "it takes two to tangle."

"Tango," he corrected her.

"What?"

"Two to tango, not tangle," he explained. "The cliché is it takes two to tango."

"I could care less," she shook her head.

"Couldn't," he couldn't help himself.

"Couldn't what?"

"Care less," he looked at her hoping she wasn't about to break his nose with a right cross. "You said you *could* care less when I think you meant you *couldn't* care less. I mean if you *could* care less, you *would*." She stared at him but she didn't punch him.

"Good gravy Roger," she said instead, "you should write a book."

The doctor patched her up, prescribed some pain medication and sent them on their way.

"The swelling should go down in a few days," he had said. "If it doesn't you should see your doctor." She said she would, but she knew she didn't have to. They stopped for ice cream on the way back to each other's work and made plans for a dinner date by the end of the week.

A chance encounter blossomed into a romance. They were married within a year and happy parents a year after that. Roger and Bonnie named the baby girl Elena after his mother Elaine and Curie because Marie Curie was Bonnie's hero. Elena Curie James grew up to be a bright, inquisitive girl who shared both parent's passion for learning. Her subject of choice was animals. Big animals.

LET'S GET THIS SHOW ON THE ROAD

Courtney Cagley was busy filing the latest set of overnight detective reports when she heard a soft knock on the outer door. She thought the knock strange because she knew the door was open and people usually walked right in. She stood and turned toward the sound.

"Chief," she said surprised to be staring at David "Dud" Hill.

"Ms. Cagley," he said, "how are you on this fine day?"

"Doing well Chief," she answered not knowing quite what to say.

"Good. Is," the Chief of Police looked at the door to the inner office, "Captain Katrek in?"

"He sure is, sir," she said as she took a step toward her desk. "Let me just let him know you're here."

"No need," the chief replied with a slight smile, "why don't we just surprise him?" He headed for the door.

"Yes, why don't we?" Courtney parroted.

Murphy Murphy and the Case of the Commission on Cliches

The first thing the chief saw upon entering the office was an empty desk. Then from just to his right and out of his field of vision he heard the sound of a soft "ping". He turned and observed Captain Brian Katrek/Johnny "Mags" Maginnes casually stroking golf balls along an eight-foot strip of green carpet. A white Titleist went straight into one of the two holes at the end of the rug.

"Chief," Katrek said without looking at his visitor. He poured another ball into the cup.

"Nice stroke Mags," the chief complimented his captain, "how did you know it was me?"

"Two ways," Maginnes responded then pinged another ball toward the hole. "First, you're the only one who comes on in without knocking," the chief nodded.

"And the second way?" the boss asked.

"I heard you speaking with Courtney. These walls are paper thin."

"I can certainly see how you were named one of the top 100 detectives in **Policeman's Monthly**." Dud Hill walked over and stood next to his captain.

"It's a gift," Katrek replied without a hint of modesty. He made a fourth straight putt.

"It seems you can't miss with that thing," the chief said with admiration.

"It's the arrow, not the Indian," the captain said purposely misquoting a line he once heard famous golfer Lee Trevino say.

"New putter?" Hill asked.

"New to me," was the answer. He offered the club to his superior. "It's an original Ping 1A, the first putter ol' Karsten Solheim designed in his garage. It made the 'ping' sound that turned out to be the inspiration for the name of his golf club company. Go ahead give it a try." The chief did but unlike Katrek/Maginnes his putt came up inches short of the hole. "Dang, you broke it!" the captain laughed. Then the chief struck one more putt. This time the sound of the club striking the ball was just a little louder and the sphere rolled straight and true into the middle of the hole.

"Feels nice," the chief said, "If you don't mind me asking, what did it set you back?"

This time the trip into Southern California was made on a glorious day. A Santa Ana wind had blown through the area clearing the skies and leaving spectacular views from the San Gabriel Mountains to the Pacific Ocean. A brilliant sun shone down on the mass of humanity that never ceased to amaze Murphy Murphy. The aircraft descended over miles and miles and miles of homes, highways, and what he thought had to be millions and millions of humans.

"Is all of this LA?" Charlie asked turning away from the window and toward the detective.

"Depends on who you ask but technically no. There are dozens of communities that make up the greater Los Angeles area. Basically from east to west it's San Bernadino all the way to Santa Monica. North to south you could include San Fernando to Costa Mesa. You're talking about somewhere in the neighborhood of twenty million people."

"Sheesh," Charlie responded, "and more just keep coming."

"Yep," Murphy agreed, "75 degrees and sunny every day appears to be one heck of an incentive."

A few rows back and still in first class, Judith Colman looked at the same scene through a different window. This was her first time in Los Angeles and she found it hard to contain her excitement. She knew she was about to see iconic sights and famous people that, up until now, had only been larger than life images on television or movie screens. The only thing that tempered her enthusiasm was the fact that she missed her dogs.

"Could you please put your seat back all the way up?" she heard someone say. "Ma'am?" the someone touched her shoulder. Judith jumped. "I'm so sorry to have startled you," the flight attendant said, "but I need you to put your seat back all the way up. We're on final approach."

"Oh, sorry," Judith replied, "I didn't realize you were talking to me." She pushed the button to raise her seat back.

"First time?" the question came from her row mate. They were the first words he had spoken during the entire trip.

"Sorry?" she asked taking a good look at the man. Her first impression was that he had great hair. She thought he was good looking in a "comfortable in his own skin" kind of way.

"Is it your first time visiting El Pueblo de Nuestra Senora Reina de Los Angeles de la Porciunala?" She tried to place the accent and landed on Eastern European, maybe even Russian but his Spanish was impeccable.

"Sorry?" she said again feeling herself blush. "I only made it through high school Spanish and barely remember any of it." That made him laugh.

"No hay problema," he said. "It basically means the town of our lady Queen of the angels. Los Angeles."

"Oh. Nice. And yes, it's my primero visit." His mouth formed what she thought was a beautiful smile.

"Very good," he complimented her, "how long will you be here?"

"Not sure," she shrugged, "at least a week."

He bent over and reached inside a black leather Tumi backpack, extracted a business card and a pen. He turned the card over and scribbled something on the back.

"I'm Luca," he handed her the card. She noticed the front featured three abstract drawings of faceless heads. Each had a different hair style. There was a website and nothing else. She turned it over to find a ten digit telephone number. "My mobile," he said.

"Thanks. I'm Judith," she answered softly. She hadn't noticed the plane had come to a stop at the gate. A bell dinged and Luca rose to open the overhead bin.

"Do you have anything up here that I can retrieve for you?" he asked pulling out a jacket.

"Uh, yes," she stammered, "The green carryon." He grabbed it and set it in the aisle behind him. "Thanks, I have everything else down here." Holding tight to the card she reached under her seat.

"Well Judith, it was my pleasure to meet you," she saw him bow his head slightly. "I hope that if you have some free time in our fair city, you will give me a call. It would be my privilege to show you around." He smiled one more time and headed toward the exit door.

"Who was that?" Charlie asked when Judith had joined them a few seconds later. Speechless she simply showed Charlie the card. Luggage in tow the three of them headed out of the terminal.

"Did we rent a car?" Judith asked.

"Not this trip," Murphy answered, "the studio has arranged for transportation." As if on cue a middle-aged man in a black suit stood holding a sign with Murphy's name on it. "That's us," Murphy said getting his attention.

"Welcome to LA," the man said, "my car is right outside." He turned and they followed. The car turned out to be a white Tesla Model X, its gull wing back doors were wide open.

"Sit up front honey," Charlie said to Murphy, "the girls will climb in back."

"Wow," Judith said as she examined the interior.

"Nice car," added Charlie.

"If only it were mine," the driver answered wistfully. "Hotel or studio?" he asked Murphy Murphy.

"What do you think Doll?" he asked looking over his shoulder at Charlie.

"Let's go to the hotel first. That way we can check in, drop our stuff, and freshen up." He nodded. "is it the same place as last time?" she asked remembering the hotel in Malibu.

"Afraid not," Murphy said and saw he disappointed her, "but I'm sure the Peninsula is just as nice."

"Oh, it's *very* nice!" the driver interjected.

"You heard the lady," Murphy told him. "Hotel first."

"Very well, sir and by the way they call me Do It Up Brown and I'll be at your beckon call during your stay."

"Beck *and* call," Murphy corrected him. "Tell me Do It Up Brown do you happen to know a man named Katterwomp?" Brown considered the question for a moment.

"Can't say that I do," he finally answered, "but he sounds like a brass hat." A horn honked behind them. Brown looked in the rear view mirror and then started to pull out into the slow moving traffic. "This marvel of engineering tells me it should take about a half an hour, straight up the 405, so make yourself comfortable."

"Brass hat?" Charlie asked from the back.

"It's cliché for an important person," Murphy answered noticing a nod from the driver, "a big wig."

"There's water and snacks in the cooler if you're hungry or thirsty," Do It Up Brown informed them and they were off.

"Tell me more about that cute guy," Charlie turned her attention to Judith.

"Not much to tell," she answered honestly, "yet," she added with a smile.

"On the way over here I stuck my head in Murphy Murphy's office," the chief said not comfortably seated in a chair facing Captain Katrek. "But it was empty."

"He's on his way back to LA."

"Back?"

"Yes sir. He's been there and back a few times. Combining business with pleasure I think."

"What do you mean?" Katrek/Maginnes thought the chief looked upset.

"No big deal, Chief," he said reassuringly. "The pleasure part is that he's been hired as a consultant on a movie set."

"Murphy Murphy?" the chief asked. "*Our* detective Murphy Murphy?" he repeated. "What in the world? Are the making a movie about the 1973 cartoon **Grammar Rock**?"

"Very funny boss," the captain said because he thought it was. "Actually the movie is about the Serious Crisis case that he solved. Remember the missing girl's uncle?"

"Fake Uncle you mean." Katrek could hear a hint of anger in the chief's voice.

"Fake?" he asked.

"Yeah fake!. F-A-K-E," he spelled it out. I'm her real blood uncle. Her mom is my sister. Laurance is an uncle by marriage. The brother of the loser who married Chloe."

Murphy Murphy and the Case of
the Commission on Cliches

"Hang on while I log in to Ancestors dot com," the captain decided to poke the bear.

"Watch your tongue captain," the chief warned. "To quote one of my favorite authors, C. J. Box, 'this could get western real quick'."

"That's a 10-4 sir," Maginnes said sheepishly, "anyway then you know this Laurance guy is an actor and apparently he's got some sway out in Hollywood. Thanks to him this movie is getting made."

"And they hired Murphy Murphy as a consultant?" the chief asked, calm again.

"Indeed. He's there to make sure the portrayal of cops is accurate, as well as the story."

"And you just let him shirk his duties as a detective on this force?" Katrek couldn't tell if the chief was mad again or not.

"He had nothing going on but I made sure he knew if something came up this department took priority."

"At least you made that clear."

"Plus, I told him the folks making the movie had to identify him as a member of this police force in the credits," the captain said proudly.

"Well then there's a feather in your cap," the comment was sarcastic. "Geez Mags, nobody sits through the credits."

"I do," Maginnes admitted.

"So they're making a movie about our most famous case," the chief said talking as much to himself as the captain.

"And you know what that means?"

"We're going to be in it."

"Yep."

"I wonder who's going to play me? Probably Brad Pitt or Russell Crowe, or Hugh Jackman."

Yeah probably the captain thought. "I wondered the same thing but when I asked Murphy didn't know. He said he'd find out."

"Enough daydreaming," the chief sat up a little straighter, "what's the business part?"

"Sir?"

"You said he was out there on pleasure *and* business. What's the business?"

"Oh, yeah. He caught a case. Something to do with something called the Commission on Cliches and a guy named Katterwillie or Katerstomp. Seems a very important book has gone missing." He snapped his fingers, "it was Katterwomp."

"I remember now," the chief scratched his chin. A few months ago I got a call from this Katterwomp character asking for help. I gave him Murphy's name because I couldn't think of anything else. Never thought he'd actually follow through."

"Well, he did."

"So, what is my out of the blue suggestion costing this department?"

"Not a thing."

"How can that be? Resources, manpower, per diem at least?"

"Nada, zip, zero," Katrek assured the chief. "Every thing Murphy does, every minute he spends tracking down this book, every penny he spends, will be paid for or reimbursed by the United States Government. And, in addition to that, the movie studio is doing the same with all the expenses he racks up because of the film. Far as I can tell it's not costing the taxpayers of our fair city a dime."

"So, the only thing it's costing us is not having our grammar corrected every time we turn around."

"There is that," the captain conceded, "plus it has our detective working a case. Keeps him sharp." The chief nodded and leaned back in the chair, he steepled his fingers and stared out the window for a beat or two.

"Maybe we should change that," he said finally.

"Meaning?"

"As much as he can be a pain in the neck, I'd hate to lose Murphy Murphy to the big city. Let's spend a little of that taxpayer money and keep an eye on our famous detective. Make sure he's not garnering too much attention."

"I guess I still have a few contacts out there. I'll ask around and get somebody on it."

"No. You go."

"Me?"

"Sure, why not? You know LA and it's not like you don't have experience keeping track of Murphy Murphy. Besides you never know he may end up needing your assistance." The two men stared at each other and it didn't take long for Captain Katrek to come to the conclusion that this wasn't a suggestion.

"Can I take my golf clubs?" he asked resigned to his fate.

"Don't see why not," the chief said getting up and walking out the door.

"Courtney!" the captain yelled.

"On it, sir!" came the reply.

"Man those walls are really thin," the chief said as he headed out the door.

ALL IN A DAY'S WORK

The Peninsula Hotel was located at the intersection of Wilshire and South Santa Monica Boulevards in Beverly Hills. It was, indeed, nice. Murphy and Charlie were treated to a Beverly Suite and immediately took advantage of its King size bed. Judith was on a different floor and in a more modest Patio Deluxe room. She unpacked, used the bathroom, and plopped down on her own Queen mattress. She stared at the ceiling and thought about Luca.

Should she call? she wondered. *I mean, after all, he must have wanted me to. Why else would he have given me his card and gone the extra step by adding his cell phone number on the back?* She sighed then rolled over onto her stomach. Another thought entered her fertile mind. *Maybe he's a cad. Some good looking guy looking to prey on a stranger and add another notch to his bedpost.* She buried her face into her pillow and let out a scream. She went back to staring at the ceiling.

"What the actual hell Judith?" she said out loud. "Who are you? Your mother? A *cad?* Another notch on his bedpost? Good lord." She found the business card in her pocket and stared at it. *Just call the guy* she thought, *you're a big girl and can take care of yourself.* "Here goes nothing," she said grabbing her phone and punching in the numbers. It rang twice and went to voicemail. His voice was strong yet soothing, confident, she was prompted to leave a message. As he spoke, she steeled her nerves and then the beep came.

"Hey there Luca. This is Judith the first time visitor to LA that you met on the plane this morning. I hope I'm not being too forward but you did say to call. I'm at the Peninsula so, uh, give me a call back if you're so inclined. Thanks." She left her number even though he now already had it. She tossed the phone onto the bed. *"If you're so inclined!?"* she said to the phone. "What a dipshit," she scolded herself as she headed toward the shower.

She let the hot water cascade over her as she admonished herself again for acting like a lovesick teenager. She hoped her message sounded better to him than it had to her but she doubted it. She turned off the shower, toweled off, and got dressed. Jeans, ankle boots, and a Ralph Lauren American flag navy sweater. She picked up her phone. No voicemails but there was a text from Murphy Murphy. "Lobby at 1:30" was all it said. She eyed her watch and realized she was already five minutes late.

"Shit," she said and then she typed "on my way!"

Murphy Murphy and the Case of the Commission on Cliches

"Where to?" Do It Up Brown asked after they piled into the Tesla and the gull wing doors had closed.

"Universal Studios," Murphy said buckling his seat belt. "What should I call you?" he asked the driver, "Do it? Do it up? Mr. Brown?"

"Dub works," the driver answered. "It's my abbreviation for Do It Up Brown," he added proudly.

"And a darn fine one," Murphy complimented him, "Dub it is."

"There are a couple of ways to go," Dub announced, "but the quickest is going to be the freeway. About half an hour give or take a few minutes, up into the valley," Brown smiled.

"Then let's take the freeway," said Charlie. Murphy pulled his phone from his pocket and called Matthew Laurance. He picked up on the first ring.

"Go ahead caller," the actor barked.

"Hey Matthew, it's Murphy Murphy."

"Well I'll be," Laurance said, "this caller ID thing is *amazing* technology!"

"Try, for once, not to be a smart ass," Murphy told his friend.

"I'm sorry," the actor used his best robot voice, "I cannot comply with that request."

"Are you on set today?" Murphy decided to move on.

"I am but not on *your* set."

"Are you saying someone else actually hired you?"

"Now who's being the smart ass?" Laurance asked.

"Fair," Murphy replied, "sorry. What's the gig?"

"Pharmaceutical commercial," he answered. "It's a hemorrhoid medication and thank goodness I'm not required to pronounce the name of the drug. All I have to do is act like I'm in excruciating pain, pretend to speak to a fake doctor, and toss a tennis ball to a dog."

"Sounds like it will require all your skills."

"It's a living," Laurance answered, "and a pretty decent paycheck."

"We're on the way to the Universal lot," Murphy pivoted again. "They're shooting the scenes in the Gas Pump Lounge when I first interview the band."

"If I can swing by later I will but in case my thing runs long let's plan on dinner."

"Sounds good."

"Just you and Charlie?" he asked. "I'll make a rez at Davenport's. It's in Encino but that's going to be a lot closer for you guys than heading back toward Hollywood. Especially later in the day. I'll make it for four because I think my brother Mitch will want to join."

"Make it five," Murphy countered, "our friend Judith Colman is with us."

"Judith Colman from Bar Flight?" he asked excitedly. "*That* Judith Colman?"

"There's only one."

"Fabulous! I can't wait to meet her." Murphy turned to look at Judith who was grinning ear to ear.

"I believe the feeling is mutual," she gave Murphy a thumbs up.

"By the way," the actor added, "the Miso Chilean sea bass at Davenport's is to die for."

"Good to know," Murphy replied and said goodbye.

They rolled along looking out the window. Past the Getty Museum, through the hills and into the San Fernando valley. They saw an abundance of Teslas but everything from Prius's to Honda Civics to Lamborghinis, Porsches, and Ferraris joined them on the blacktop. Occasionally a Rolls Royce or Maserati zoomed past.

"This is unreal," Judith said as she stared out the window.

"Sadly, it's all too real," Charlie added with a shake of her head. Judith leaned over and touched her friend's arm.

"I called him," she said softly but not so softly that Murphy didn't hear.

"Luca?" Charlie asked. Judith nodded.

"Yep, Luca. Mr. business card."

"Atta girl," Charlie said proudly.

"Who did you call?" It was Murphy from the front seat. Both ladies looked his way and found him smiling.

"Judith made a friend," Charlie said and Judith punched her softly on the upper arm.

"That didn't take long," Murphy said.

"Guess I had a bee in my bonnet," Judith responded.

"Who is it?"

"No idea," Judith admitted.

"She met him on the airplane," Charlie offered the information then giggled.

"What does he do?"

"Geez Murphy," Charlie jumped in again, "who do you think you are, her Father?"

"Just a friend," Murphy defended himself.

"It's okay," Judith said.

"So, what does he do?" Murphy asked again.

"No idea," Judith repeated.

"Show him the card," Charlie urged her pal.

"The card?" Murphy asked another question.

"He gave her his business card and wrote his mobile number on the back," Charlie answered as Judith handed the card up to the front passenger seat. Murphy looked at three minimalist faces sporting three different hairstyles printed on fancy card stock. www.Luca.com was the only thing printed on it.

"Is this his business?" the detective asked.

"I don't know about his business but I do know that's his name. He told me."

"Maybe he's a mime," Murphy blurted.

"What?!" Charlie called out. "A *MIME*? Where in the world did you come up with that?"

"Well, none of the faces have mouths," Murphy was defiant. "Maybe they're all him. Maybe he's a street performer. A mime."

"And maybe he's the wonderful wizard of OZ," Charlie shot back.

"But he spoke to me," Judith was calm, "he never once pretended to be stuck in a box."

"A freakin' mime," Charlie shook her head, "You are a funny guy Murphy."

"It's *not* impossible," Murphy defended his observation.

"Hey that's Luca!" it was the driver. "Sorry I didn't mean to pry," Do It Up Brown apologized.

"No worries," Charlie said. "You know this guy?"

"Not personally, no," Dub admitted, "but a lot of folks around LA know *of* him. His face is plastered on a billboard overlooking Sunset Boulevard, right across from Chateau Marmont. He's practically famous."

"Famous for what?" Judith asked.

"Hair!" Brown said. "He's a hairdresser. 'Stylist to the stars' the billboard says."

"You're kidding," Charlie giggled again.

"You'd be better off if he was a mime," Murphy mumbled.

"I read in **People Magazine** he's Chris Hemsworth's guy," the driver was still talking. "Does his hair in movies."

"Even Thor?" Charlie asked. "His hair was magnificent in Thor."

"I don't know specifics," Brown admitted.

"Heaven help me," Murphy sighed.

Eventually Do It Up Brown took the Cahuenga exit off the 101 freeway then turned onto Lankershim Avenue and into the lot where he stopped the Tesla at a gate.

"Three guests to visit the Serious Crisis set," Dub said.

"Do It Up Brown as I live and breathe," the guard greeted the driver. "Long time no see."

"Hey there Money. How's it going?" he returned the greeting.

"Can't complain and even if I did my Mom wouldn't listen. Who do we have here?" he asked looking in the car.

"Mr. Murphy, Miss Carlucci, and Miss Colman," Brown pointed to each. "All here as guests of Mr. Ron Howard," he added.

"Very good," the man said as he went back into his hut. When he returned, he had a green card with a hole in one end and a white 8"x 11" white envelope in his hand. "Here's your parking pass Dub," he handed the card to the driver. "Just hang it on the rear-view mirror whenever you're inside. You can use the VIP entrance from now on."

"Appreciate you," Brown said taking the pass.

"Here are the credentials for your folks," he handed over the envelope. "Make sure you have them visible at all times inside these gates," he made eye contact with each of them.

"Will do," Murphy said. Charlie and Judith nodded.

"Head straight on James Stewart Drive, It'll take you right to Stage 22. That's where the Serious Crisis movie crew is working today."

"Got it," said Brown.

"Now, don't be a stranger Dub," the guard said tipping his cap and raising the gate.

"Promise not to, Money," Brown said rolling up the window and pulling forward.

"Money?" Murphy asked.

"Long story," was all Dub offered as a response.

"A hairdresser to the stars," Judith repeated from the back seat.

WHEN IT RAINS, IT POURS

There's an old saying, some might call it cliché, with regard to the behavior of children and their parents. Certain historians believe "the apple doesn't fall far from the tree" was first uttered as early as the 1500's. Different, but equally credible, folks contend the great poet Ralph Waldo Emerson was the first to say it in English. That was in 1889. Regardless of the etymology, the phrase fit Elena Curie James to a t.

It wasn't *what* the child, then young lady, then woman found interesting. It was the way in which she immersed herself in *what* she found interesting. Like her mother she sought out, then devoured and absorbed as much information as possible about her passion. Large mammals in general and pachyderms specifically. To that end **Dumbo** was her favorite childhood movie. By the same token she was certain the novel, *Water for Elephants* would be the book she loved best. But she was disappointed when she realized it was the story of two people falling in love and not about keeping elephants hydrated. She did realize the thing both stories had in common was the backdrop of the circus. The other thing the works of fiction described were the real-world implications of these magnificent animals in pain. She couldn't stand the thought of that and therefore knew that no matter how noble, she could never devote her life to a profession which centered around that pain. Her mother's life was medicine but she would not follow in those footsteps.

"What do you want to be when you grow up?" Bonnie James asked her daughter one night while reading the bedtime story, *Babar's Picnic*.

"I want to be like Hugo Schmidt," she said emphatically.

"And who," her mother asked while stroking the child's hair, "is Hugo Schmidt?" The question made the child sit straight up in bed.

"Mommy, don't you know?!" she asked. Bonnie shook her head. "Hugo Schmidt is *only* the greatest elephant trainer in the whole world!"

"Well, I certainly know who Hugo Schmidt is now," her mother replied with a smile.

The girl spent hours upon hours in the library reading books and watching movies about elephant training. She volunteered and then interned at the local zoo. When she had convinced her parents that this was more than just a passing fancy she talked them in to letting her go to the internationally acclaimed Elephant Conservation Center School in Thailand. It was there she studied the secrets behind training both Asian and African elephants. She also met Granderson Ossidy.

It didn't take long for her to learn everyone called him Grandi. It also didn't take long for her to become smitten. One day she asked another of the trainers how the man acquired the nickname.

"Granderson was one of the first and major proponents of non-violent resistance in elephant training," the man said. "He even wrote the book on it."

"Alright," she said, "but help me understand how that gets Granderson to Grandi."

"It may sound sacrilegious," he answered, "but you see non-violent resistance was the hallmark of the teachings of one Mahatma Ghandi. The same can be said of our very own Grandi."

"I get it," she said getting it. She thought it rather silly but she got it.

She made it a point to spend more time around Granderson Ossidy and each liked what the other saw. Before long her being smitten was reciprocated and despite the fact that he was a dozen years her elder, they fell in love. Eventually they returned to the United States and Grandi Ossidy asked Roger and Bonnie James for their daughter's hand in marriage. It was easy for the parents to see how happy Elena was so the request was granted.

"Universal Studios was founded and established way back in 1912."

"You don't need both," Murphy interrupted Do It Up Brown.

"Both what?" the driver asked.

"Founded *and* established," Murphy answered. "They basically mean the same thing so using them together in a sentence is the epitome of redundancy." Dub just looked at him.

"Don't mind him," Charlie offered from her back seat, "when it comes to grammar, he can be a bit of a stickler. Please continue Mr. Brown."

"Anyway," Brown got his thoughts back together, "Lon Cheney, Sir Laurance Olivier, Abbott and Costello and many, many more all walked this lot in the 20's, 30's and 40's."

"Cool," remarked Judith as she stared out the window. "And Jimmy Stewart too I presume."

"You presume correctly," Brown nodded. "In fact, the man this little street was named for was responsible for a major new breakthrough for actors at the time."

"Oh my god!" Murphy seethed. Charlie gave the back of his seat a gentle nudge.

"What happened?" Judith asked.

"Stewart's agent back then was a powerful guy named Lew Wasserman."

"The Last Mogul!" Judith blurted.

"So you saw that movie?" the driver asked turning to look at Judith.

"I sure did," she nodded.

"Then you know all about him," Brown turned back.

"I don't," added Charlie.

"Well, he was a formidable presence back in the day. Influential enough to strong arm the studio into agreeing to a contract for Stewart that gave the actor a share of the movie's profits instead of just a straight salary. It had never been done that way before and it changed the industry."

"*Fascinating*," muttered Murphy.

'Okay then, moving on," Brown moved on. "You're looking at more than 400 acres of land."

"The hits just keep on coming," Murphy said shaking his head.

"More than half," Brown ignored the rebuke and continued, "is taken up by the theme park that was added in the 60's. The section we're in now is where the sausage is made."

"I'm hungry," Charlie said.

"I'm sure they've got craft services all set up so there will be plenty to munch on," Brown replied as he pulled the Tesla to a stop. "Here we are, sound stage 22." They all piled out of the car.

"I'll disappear from view for a bit," the driver said with a wink letting Murphy Murphy know he had his number. "Just call me when you need me and I'll be back here in a jiffy," he added getting back in the car.

"What we may *need* is a different driver," not quite loud enough for Do It Up Brown to hear.

"Cut it out copper," Charlie said punching him gently on the arm. "I think he's cute."

"Just one more reason to get rid of him," Murphy said under his breath.

"This is *so* exciting," exclaimed Judith who hadn't heard any of the exchange. "Let's go!" and in they went.

"Oh my lord," Charlie practically gasped. "This is amazing. I feel like I just walked into The Gas Pump," referring to her club back home. They all stared at the set, which was an exact replica, right down to the bottles behind the bar.

"Well, hello there," a man said as he approached the trio. Each reflexively checked to make sure their credentials were around their necks. "I'm Connor Williams," he added extending his hand first to Murphy then the others. "I'm Ron's first assistant director, his right-hand man you could say. Been with him since **The Paper** in 1994."

"Michael Keaton was so good in that," Judith said.

"That and everything else," Williams replied with admiration. "You must be Judith."

"How did you know?" she asked. He just pointed to her lanyard and smiled.

"And Charlie," his eyes shifted to her but his smile remained. "And, of course, detective Murphy Murphy," he finally addressed Murphy. "It's a pleasure to see you again."

"Hello Connor," Murphy replied.

"Come on, let's get you situated. We're about to shoot the Murphy meets Charlie scene.

"Um, Connor," Charlie started, "Can I call you Connor?"

"Most certainly."

"Is there anything to eat? I'm suddenly starving."

"Of course," he smiled again, "right over there," he pointed to a long table filled with what appeared to be a variety of fruit and snacks. "Go grab something and then I'll take you to your seats."

They ended up in the director's chairs facing the set. They watched as a number of technicians and make up specialists moved in and out of their field of vision. Ron Howard stood right in the middle of the activity.

"All right everybody," the director called out. "Places please. I'd really like to get something memorialized before we all fart dust."

THE BIGGER THEY COME THE HARDER THEY FALL

If one was to look up "marital bliss" in the dictionary they might have seen a picture of Granderson and Elena Ossidy. To say things started swimmingly would have been an understatement. They poured themselves in equal parts into their work and their relationship despite, or maybe because, of the fact that Grandi was more than a dozen years Elena's senior. Together, they approached the local zoo about jobs as elephant keepers. The zoo director knew specialists of their quality were hard to come by and the public relations advantages of a husband and wife team on top of that was too good to pass up. She hired them on the spot.

Dreams were shared, children were discussed and life was good. Then one day Grandi was summoned back to Thailand. The Elephant Conservation Center School was in crisis and needed him. His loyalty dictated that he come when called. They assured him it was an emergency and once the ship was righted Grandi would be able to return to the United States. A month, maybe two at the most was all they required. Elena hated the prospect of him leaving but she knew if the shoe had been on the other foot she would have gone and Granderson would have supported that decision. She helped him pack, took him to the airport, and kissed him goodbye. Life was fabulous with him and she knew it would be less so without him but a month or two? She knew she could handle anything for a month or two. It never occurred to her that the husband she loved would never come back.

Elena had read somewhere that Australian Cattle Dogs had proved useful to zoos in helping train elephants so, to give her something else to take care of during Grandi's absence, she bought a puppy on the way home. She named the dog Timothy after the mouse friend in **Dumbo** and started taking it to the zoo every day.

Grandi Ossidy loved his wife and their life together but he had to admit the Kingdom of Thailand held a special place in his heart as well. He had lived in that part of Southeast Asia, on and off, for more than twenty years. He loved its mountains, forests, and the thousands of elephants that populated the country. But as much as he found he still loved Thailand he missed Elena more. He wrote her love letters once a week and called home every day. On Thursdays he would find a nice quiet spot to put pen to paper and tell his beloved how much he missed her. The spot on one particular Thursday happened to be at the base of a magnificent, fifty-foot tall, Malayan Dwarf coconut tree. As he settled his back against the tree's impressive trunk he looked up and allowed himself a chuckle. He knew the tree was called a dwarf but it had nothing to do with how tall the tree would grow. It referred instead to the size at which the tree would begin to produce fruit.

In his letter he professed affection for Elena and reminded her the days were counting down until the time they would be together again. He wrote that this would be the last time he would agree to such a separation, no matter the circumstances. If someone or something needed him again part of the deal would be they would tackle the issue as a team. He asked about Timothy and assured his wife again how excited he was to meet the pup. He told her about his elephants and wondered about the pachyderms he left behind in sunny Southern California. He made it a habit to end every letter to Elena with a poem so he set his pen and paper on his lap and stared off into the distance to think of just the right words.

In his peripheral vision he saw movement on the ground which drew his full gaze. He was alarmed to see, there among the dirt and leaves, a fearsome sight. It was a Chinese Redheaded centipede and it was crawling his way. He knew from experience the critters could grow as large as twenty inches long and this one, while not that big, was at least a foot. Grandi also knew the creature's front legs had, over time, adapted to become pinchers which contained a highly toxic venom. A bite from the beast *probably* wouldn't kill him but it would hurt like the dickens and Granderson Ossidy had zero interest in that. He remembered reading that the centipede was more likely to attack if provoked so he willed himself to sit as still as possible as he watched the insect approach.

Go away! He thought as if he could will the creature to stop and change course and the bug did stop when he thought it. His mind was so focused on what might slither his way he never heard, saw, or sensed the fruit from the Malayan Dwarf come loose and fall. The three and a half pound coconut travelled fifty feet straight down, at a speed of 38 miles an hour, in less than two seconds. Grandi's human head had no chance. The coconut connected, crushing his skull, and killing him instantly. His body toppled sideways landing on the centipede which bit him a couple of times for good measure.

NECESSITY IS THE MOTHER OF INVENTION

"Where's Domhnall?" somebody yelled.

"It's a little hard to film a scene involving the movie's protagonist when the actor portraying said protagonist is nowhere to be found," Ron Howard lamented out loud. Murphy, Charlie, and Judith sat, just off the set, mesmerized.

"What?" someone else asked.

"You need Domhnall to be present to shoot a scene involving Domhnall," the director simplified.

"Got it."

"Do you?" Howard asked. "Got it?"

"Aren't they just the cutest things ever?" A voice said from behind the three onlookers. They turned in unison to find Domhnall Gleeson standing there wearing his Murphy Murphy costume and an impish grin. "He's such a task master," he said of Howard as he looked at Murphy, then Charlie, then Judith. "I'm Dom," he said to the latter.

127

"Judith," she said back.

"The *bartender*!" he emphasized. "But not *our* bartender," he added with a wink toward Murphy

"In the flesh," Judith said feeling herself blush.

"Nice to make your acquaintance," he said with a slight bow. Then he turned his attention to Charlie and spoke to Murphy. "*This* is our bartender and she is gorgeous," he said. "Rebecca does not do her justice."

"Rebecca?" Charlie said to both Gleeson and Murphy. "I thought Brie Larson was playing me."

"Nope," Gleeson said matter-of-factly, "Rebecca Hall got the role and between us girls you're better for it." Charlie looked at Murphy who shrugged.

"Hollywood," was all he said.

"Indeed," added Domnhall.

"GLEASON!" Howard shouted having located his star actor.

"Gee whiz," Domnhall said with a smirk, "guy wins a couple of Oscars and he thinks he's the bees knees. Ta ta all, enjoy the show," he said to the group and headed for the set.

"Make up," the director said, "our wandering leading man most likely needs a touch up," he added.

"This is so damn cool," Judith said. "Thanks for letting me come Murph." Charlie nodded her agreement.

They spent the next several hours listening to dialogue and watching actors and actresses play out events that happened to them in real life. Charlie was beyond thrilled at the portrayal of her by the English actress Rebecca Ferguson.

"How does she sound so much like me and so little like her?" Charlie asked Murphy.

"She's an actress," Murphy answered simply.

"And a darn good one if you ask me," she said turning her attention back to the action.

Murphy also thought Gleason did a very nice job capturing what he was sure were his better qualities. They all watched Howard work inserting himself in scenes at what always appeared to be the exact right time. He gave his actors instructions or encouragement or ideas while still other times he just hung back letting the scene unfolded from beginning to end then shouting a simple, "from the top" if he wanted them to do it again or "print it" when he was satisfied. Charlie thought she recognized Paul Dano who was cast as the Serious Crisis manager, Jeff Giucigiu. She picked out Hallie Steinfeld who was Lyndsay Howlund and she knew Ving Rhames was Mo Mo Morrison because Murphy had told her. But she couldn't put a name to everyone's face.

"Who's that?" she asked Judith when another, different, actor arrived.

"That's Joe Keery," Judith knew.

"Joe who?" Murphy chimed in.

"Joe Keery," she repeated. Her friends just looked at her dumbfounded. "You two old fuddy duddies," she laughed. "He's in Stranger Things. He plays Steve. He was also in the Ryan Reynolds movie, *Free Guy*, recently."

"Means nothing to me," Charlie said with a shrug, "but I do like me some Ryan Reynolds."

"I think I remember Ron mentioning him," Murphy added, "he's DeMaio Turrell."

"Oh my god, is that Jack Black?" Charlie was on to someone else.

"Looks like it," Judith confirmed.

"Is he playing Gaston? He looks like he's playing Gaston," Charlie recognized the outfit as something her brother would surely wear.

"Must be a cameo," Murphy said trying not to sound snarky but unable to pull it off.

"I have to get a picture," Charlie said ignoring him and grabbing her phone. "He's going to be blown away."

"Not allowed honey," Murphy said putting one hand on her arm and pointing to a sign that read "no video or still photography allowed" with the other. Charlie shook him off and took the picture anyway.

"You're going to get us 86'd," Judith scolded her friend. Charlie quickly put her phone back in her jeans pocket. "I have to use the loo," Judith pivoted.

"I think I saw bathrooms outside," Charlie said.

"Be right back," Judith said and headed for the nearest exit.

THE SLINGS AND ARROWS OF OUTRAGEOUS FORTUNE

The phone call was unexpected, brief, and devastating. Elena went numb and didn't quite know how to react when the person from the Elephant Conservation Center School more than 8,000 miles away told her that her husband was dead because a coconut fell on his head. The reaction that ended up bubbling to the surface was a laugh.

"Oh I can assure you it isn't funny Mrs. Ossidy, not funny at all," the young man said. "A handful of people perish that way every year here in Thailand. One must be *very* careful when loitering under the palms," he added gravely.

"I wasn't laughing because it was funny," she countered. "I was laughing because of the absurdity of it all. A fucking coconut," she said and then she burst into tears.

Eventually arrangements were agreed to, the body of Granderson Ossidy was transported back to Los

Angeles and he was laid to rest in the dirt of Forest Lawn. Elena learned her husband had purchased an additional five million dollar life insurance policy and named her the beneficiary. This was in addition to the pair of three million dollar policies they had taken out on each other after getting married. There was also the decent sized nest egg Grandi had accumulated thanks to investments, savings, and royalties from his various writings. Elena had become a very sad, somewhat wealthy, woman overnight. She ended up also having to deal with a handful of, what she was certain were, scam artists claiming to be Granderson's long lost relatives. She fielded calls from people named Virtu, Fabul, Tortu, and Gener. To help alleviate any more stress she referred all those calls to her father's attorney and then changed all her Identification documents back to her maiden name.

She bought another Australian Cattle Dog, named it Dundee, and took them both when she went to live with her parents in their Los Feliz compound. The cattle dogs got along famously with James's Landseer, Cooper and Elena had always enjoyed her parents' company. There was more than enough room for everyone and she was now just minutes from work. Days turned into weeks that turned into months that turned into several years. One day she was enjoying a morning cup of tea on the veranda before work when her father approached.

"I'm calling a family meeting," he announced. "Tonight, after dinner."

"Roger, Roger," she said with a smile and took another sip of tea.

"So we have clearance, Clarence?" her dad said walking away.

"Depends. What's our vector, Victor?" she replied softly.

The warm Southern California breeze smacked Judith in the face. She hadn't realized how chilly it was inside the sound stage. She stood for a moment with her eyes closed and let the sunshine and warm wind caress her skin. *I could get used to this* she thought before realizing how much she would miss home and Bar Flight. She reminded herself to call Buck and check on the place. She opened her eyes, located the restroom trailer and walked that way.

When she had finished, she decided to have a look around before going back inside the sound stage. The narrower than normal street was even more constricted because it was lined with golf cars. Some had names attached, others appeared to be free agents. None had keys so a quick joy ride was out of the question. She couldn't help but notice a few small trailers with what looked like Hollywood stars attached to the doors. She stepped closer and saw one belonging to Domhnall Gleeson and another to Rebecca Ferguson. Her eyes wandered as she looked for additional trailers and stars wondering if Rebecca Hall also warranted such treatment. Murphy had told her she was the actress who had won the part of Judith Colman in the movie. Not seeing a "Rebecca Hall" star on a trailer door, she turned to go back to action and her friends. As she did, she noticed a tall man exiting the Ferguson trailer. She stopped dead in her tracks when she realized it was Luca.

THE TIP OF THE ICEBERG

Timothy and Dundee happily clambered into the back of Grandi's old 1973 Red FJ40 Land Cruiser. Elena had sent the vehicle, which, at the time, was little more than a bucket of bolts, to be restored by Resurrection Land Cruisers in Orchard City, Colorado. It ended up costing her an arm and a leg but two years later they sent her back a beauty. She climbed into the driver's seat, fired up the 3fe, fuel injected, straight 6 engine, and checked her watch. Normally, at this time of day, it took about ten minutes to get to her reserved parking space at work so she knew, even with a stop at Maru Coffee, she'd be among her elephant friends long before the gates opened to the eager public at 10. Nearly two million people visited the zoo every year and almost every single one of them wanted to see the 40,000 pounds of Asian elephant housed there under her care. There were three females and one male. At one time the zoo was also home to a bull African elephant but that seven ton beast was sent to a sanctuary, and subsequently died, long before Elena was hired. These days it was Bertha, Tina, Nugget, and

Sebastian that were free to roam the more than six acre exhibit.

Elena's days were spent mostly at her desk, the dogs at her feet, in a state of the art elephant barn that was the envy of zoos all over the world. It was her job to make sure the herbivores had enough food to eat and water to drink. That was no small task. Each elephant consumed more than 25 kilograms of hay, ten kilograms of straw and ten to fifteen kilograms of carrots, beetroots and feeding turnips. That was just for dinner. Three times a week they also enjoyed bushels of apples, bunches of celery stalks, and fennel. That was in addition to all the branches they could break up into bite-sized pieces and eat all day. To wash it all down Elena had to provide at least 100 gallons of water every 24 hours. It also fell upon the elephant keeper to ensure the 3 acres of sand in the exhibit was at least two and a half feet deep and rototilled on a monthly basis. The animals' mouths were inspected at least once a week and that chore included brushing their teeth and making sure Sebastian tusks were trimmed as were the girls tushes. Elena loved to make the kids who visited laugh by saying Berth, Tina, and Nugget needed their tushes trimmed. Then she explained that the tushes were just the female's version of tusks. All four elephants received daily pedicures to ensure their nails, cuticles, and foot pads were in excellent condition. Even though the animals constantly sprayed water on themselves and each other, weekly baths inside the barn were also part of the agenda. It was a big job, fitting because it had to be.

Twice a day, usually at 11 AM and again at 3 PM she supervised as the elephants and the dogs put on a little "show" for the patrons. Nothing fancy. Just some kneeling so the dogs could jump on their backs, lifting tree branches with their trunks, or doing an elephant jig. These were not circus elephants, although both Bertha and Tina had spent a good part of their early lives under the big top. Most elephants live between sixty and seventy years, so Elena knew there was still plenty of get up and go in her four friends.

Circus trainers were known to use tools called bull hooks to train their elephants and keep them in line. It was simply a long metal rod with a hook attached that is used to poke, prod, and hook the animal persuading it to do what the trainer wants. Animal rights activists had been protesting this technique for years. Elena knew about bull hooks and was even aware that some zoos still used them. She did not but she did use her dogs and that too was not without controversy. She had studied elephant attacks on humans in US zoos. She found they were rare, and almost always involved the much larger African variety of the animals. The last time was in the early 2000's at a zoo in Pittsburgh when a female African elephant called "M" fatally attack her keeper of six years. Elena knew her four were far gentler but she was trained to never lose sight of the fact that they were wild animals. Big, wild, animals.

The dogs helped keep them in line. It never ceased to amaze her how a twenty pound canine could control an animal as big as an Asian elephant but they did. The school children who visited on field trips seemed to love the dogs as much as the pachyderms, constantly asking to pet them or rub their bellies. But the dogs also attracted protesters and PETA fanatics. Those people showed up with signs and strident voices demanding the zoo send the pups, and Elena, packing. She was constantly grateful the demonstrations fell on deaf ears in the administration building. Elena and the dogs even went so far as to train Sebastian to spray the eight gallons of water he could store in his trunk on the harpies. Over time their numbers dwindled and eventually they stopped showing up altogether.

"That's the 'Martini Shot'!" Ron Howard exclaimed. The words were met by a round of applause from the cast and crew. "We're back tomorrow, oh nine hundred for the scenes with the band at The Gas Pump Lounge. Somebody make sure Bruhl is here ready for work!"

"Don't tell me they're all going to have a martini now," Charlie spoke to Murphy, "and who's Bruhl?" Conner Murphy overheard.

"Bruhl is Daniel Bruhl," he answered the second question first. "A hell of an actor but rumor has it he's fond of the wormwood if you know what I mean."

"I don't," Charlie said honestly.

"Absinthe in its purest form," Murphy answered for the first assistant director. "It is said it has hallucinogenic properties. Van Gogh loved the stuff. That and the oils and turpentines in his paint."

"What?" Charlie seemed incredulous.

"Story for another day," Murphy patted her knee.

"And the crew isn't about to get hammered on the spot," Williams continued. "Although, some of these folks definitely will. But 'martini shot' is movie director lingo for the last scene of the day."

"I thought they said, 'that's a wrap'," Charlie countered.

"Very good, Charlie," Connor complimented her, "but that phrase comes at the very end of the final scene of the entire movie."

"You're awfully quiet," Murphy said to Judith.

"She has been ever since she got back from the bathroom," Charlie looked at her friend. "Is everything okay?"

"I saw Luca," she said as an answer.

"The mime?" Murphy asked.

"He's not a mime!" Charlie slapped Murphy on the knee.

"Maybe they're making a Marcel Marceau movie somewhere on the lot," he ignored Charlie's rebuke and referenced the famous French actor.

"You're nonsensical *and* ludicrous," Murphy opened his mouth but Charlie stopped him with an index finger. "Don't you dare tell me that's redundant because *I know*!" Murphy shut his mouth. "You saw Luca?" she turned back to Judith.

"He was coming out of Rebecca Ferguson's trailer. Oh god! Do you think he's sleeping with her?" Before Charlie could offer an answer Connor Williams laughed out loud. They turned to look at him. He held up both hands as if in surrender.

"I apologize for eavesdropping again but I couldn't help but set the record straight before your imaginations ran completely unchecked."

"We're all ears," Murphy said.

"I'm sure you did see Luca and he was, no doubt, exiting Ms. Ferguson's dressing room."

"But?" Judith asked.

"No but. It's just that he's one of the best hair stylists in Hollywood, maybe all of LA. He's worked with Ron before, well actually with Chris Hemsworth who worked with Ron on **In The Heart Of The Sea**. Anyway, both Rebecca and Joe Keery, who has fabulous hair by the way, asked Ron if he'd bring Luca on board for them. As far as I know he's not sleeping with either one."

"So he's really not a mime," Murphy said and they all laughed, Judith maybe the loudest.

Just then Murphy's phone buzzed. He grabbed it and looked at Connor Williams to see if it was okay to answer it.

"All good," he said, "the set is dark for the day."

"This is detective Murphy," he said because he had recognized the number.

"Ahh, my favorite flatfoot," Adalindis Katterwomp said. "It would be a shot in the arm, and I don't mean maybe, if you were to tell me you're in LA."

"Oh how I've missed you," Murphy deadpanned.

"And I you," Katterwomp returned the sentiment.

"As a matter of fact, I *am* here in Los Angeles."

"That's the best of all possible worlds," the commissioner squealed with delight. "Then I implore you to come like greased lightning to my office for a heart to heart. That way we can put the finishing touches on this entire escapade."

"Has something happened?"

"Indeed something has," Katterwomp answered, "and it's a dilly!"

"That's certainly intriguing," Murphy said, "but unfortunately I am otherwise occupied for the rest of the day."

"I'll just have to tough it out until tomorrow then. Shall we say 11 o'clock?"

"I'll be there," Murphy ended the call before his ears could be bombarded by more cliches.

"Mister Matthew!" the maître d' came out from behind a podium, "welcome back to Davenport's my friend."

"It's been too long, Matteo," Laurance said as the two hugged, "way, way too long." They separated.

"And Mister Mitchell too," he had noticed the actor's actor brother Mitch. "Double the pleasure."

"Hello Matteo," Mitch said smiling, "how's the lovely Angelica?" he asked after the man's wife.

"More beautiful than ever," the man said, "Grazie, Mister Mitch for remembering. Now come, everyone, we have the best table in the house ready for you. Please follow me." The group obeyed. When they arrived at the table, they noticed cocktails in front of two of the places, what Matthew assumed was a Woodford Reserve neat for him and a Negroni for Mitch. "I didn't know the other three drink preferences but if you'll kindly give me your requests, I'll make sure they are delivered forthwith." Charlie, Murphy, and Judith ordered up. "Enjoy your meal," Matteo said and turned on his heel without writing anything down. The drinks came as promised and the group settled in to consider the menu.

"Are you busy tomorrow?" Murphy asked Matthew.

"That depends," he said.

"I got this strange call from this Katterwomp character earlier today."

"The cliché guy?"

"That's the one. He wants me to come to his office tomorrow, hinted that my services may no longer be required."

"Interesting."

"I thought so too."

"What time?"

"He said 11 but I'd like to get there a little earlier than that."

"I can make that work," Laurance said as a waiter approached.

"Has everyone decided or do we need a few more minutes?" he asked.

TAKE UP THE CUDGELS

It took a handful of phone calls for Johnny "Mags" Maginnes to find out where Murphy Murphy was staying. The first one was to his former employer, and Chief Hill's sister, Chloe. She was a well-known casting director in town and Maginnes asked her if she knew where Universal would put up VIP guests. She gave him several options including the Hilton and the Sheraton near the studios which he immediately discounted. He did call Shutters on the Beach, the Hotel Bel Air, the Waldorf, and the Beverly Hills Hotel asking to be connected to Murphy's room. Having no success, he moved on to the next spot on his list, The Penninsula, and hit paydirt.

"Gotcha," he said as he disconnected and headed for the rental car counter to pick up his BMW 4 series, which he had gotten for a sweet law enforcement officer discount.

"I'll start with the grilled California artichoke," Judith said, "and the chimichurri skirt steak."

"How would madam prefer her steak cooked?"

"Medium please," she answered.

"Of course," the waiter said unable to hide his disdain.

"And for you miss?" he quickly moved on to Charlie.

"I'd like the roasted beet and burrata salad to start and, because Matthew recommended it so highly, I'll have the miso Chilean sea bass for my entrée."

"Excellent choices," the waiter was clearly pleased.

"*Excellent choices*," Judith muttered.

Murphy ordered French onion soup and a rare New York strip while Matthew and Mitch both duplicated Charlie's order.

"Oh," Matthew stopped the waiter before he left, "I'll have another one of these," he said holding up an empty crystal glass. "Mitchy's driving," he announced to the table. "And," he turned back to the waiter, "could you please send Matteo over."

"As you wish," the waiter said. Murphy thought some of the color had drained from the man's face. Moments later the maître d' was back.

"Is something not to your liking Mister Matthew?" he asked Laurance.

"Two things Matteo," he replied.

"I'm all ears."

"First the bourbon is very much to my liking. What is it because it doesn't taste like the Woodford Reserve that I usually drink when I'm here."

"That's because it isn't what you normally drink here," he answered. "It's a specialty bourbon from a small distillery in Colorado Springs, Colorado called 291. We were fortunate enough to procure several bottles of both their barrel proof single barrel and small batch Colorado Rye. I'm glad it meets with your approval and I'll happily bring a bottle over for your inspection."

"That won't be necessary," the actor said.

"What's the second thing?"

"I'm well aware all waiters and most people prefer their steak cooked on the rare side," Laurance winked and smiled at Judith. Across the table she couldn't contain a blush. "But there *are* some that like it a little pinker."

"Say no more," Matteo left the table again.

They enjoyed the rest of the meal and each other's company. They did see Roberto wait on other parties but he never made it back to their table. Two bottles of Cayuse God Only Knows 2013 Grenache, courtesy of Davenport's, did make an appearance.

"I'll pick you up at 10," Matthew said as he climbed into the passenger seat of his brother's Audi e-tron.

"Why don't we just have Do It Up Brown drive us," Murphy retorted.

"Do It Up what?"

"Not what, who. Do It Up Brown is the driver the studio assigned us while we are here. Might as well put him to work *and* he drives a Tesla."

"Well that seals the deal," Laurance said.

"Good night, Mitch," Murphy said to the brother.

"Thank you for the wonderful meal," Judith said from behind the detective.

"Did I buy?" Laurance shot a look at Mitch.

"That you did brother Matt, that you did."

"Damn good thing hemorrhoid commercials pay well," he said and they drove away.

"You two have a date tomorrow?" Charlie asked.

"Just a little unfinished business."

"Then Jude and I are going shopping," she smiled at her friend.

"I thought you'd never ask," Judith said.

"And just maybe we'll get our hair did," Charlie added.

Dinner at the James hacienda that night was an entirely different animal. Baby back ribs on the grill slathered in Big Mama's Soppin Sauce, home-made broccoli salad, ice cold Dos Equis beer, and plenty of napkins.

"How was your day, honey?" Roger asked his wife as he peeled off a chunk of pork and slipped it to the canine garbage disposal that was Cooper the Landseer Newfoundland who was sitting nearby. A glop of soppin sauce landed on the big dog's chin.

"Somebody is going to need a bath tomorrow," Bonnie remarked.

"Somebody needs a bath every other day," Elena added.

"My day was normal except for one interesting case," Bonnie said dishing more broccoli salad onto her plate.

"Interesting how, mom?"

"Well, a woman came in with a spatula stuck down her throat." Roger spit out whatever was in the bite he was chewing.

"That qualifies as interesting," he said wiping his mouth. The dog pounced on the morsel.

"It seems she was cooking and suddenly couldn't catch her breath. She thought something was in her throat so she grabbed a spatula and jammed it down her pie hole to dislodge whatever she imagined was in there."

"And it got stuck?"

"It sure did," Bonnie nodded, "luckily her daughter was visiting and rushed her to the hospital. We x-rayed her throat and an ER doctor removed the kitchen tool. We never did find out what hampered her breathing in the first place."

"Nothing that happened in my day, week, or month could ever compare to that," Elena admitted. "Now as a tribute to the head of the household and a card-carrying member of the commission on cliches let's get down to brass tacks," the daughter deftly changed the subject. "What's the purpose of this family meeting?"

"You have either purposely or inadvertently hit the nail on the head young lady," Roger congratulated his daughter. "This meeting has everything to do with the aforementioned commission."

"Don't tell me that baboon Katterwomp is finally stepping down and you're going to take his place. *Your* rightful place at the head of the commission," Bonnie proclaimed.

"Hear! Hear!" Elena chimed in.

Roger and Bonnie James raised Elena in a loving environment. She was adored but not spoiled, cared for but not coddled. They believed and taught their daughter to understand that hate had no place in a reasonable world. Despite that Elena James *hated* Adalindis Orval Katterwomp. She knew him to be a self-centered, unapologetic, know-it-all, a bombastic blowhard and a boor. But everyone who met the man knew that. Elena also knew the man was in love with her mother but none of that was her reason for loathing him. She was convinced the man was a creep and a pervert.

Elena was never certain it wasn't a nightmare but she had a vivid recollection from when she was a little girl. Her parents had thrown a party for some friends and the guest list included Katterwomp. The drinking, eating, and merrymaking went on into the night and Elena went to bed. What felt like hours later she woke up awash in a feeling of dread. She opened her right eye a slit and was certain she saw the sillhouette of a man standing in her doorway. She knew it wasn't her father and sensed it was Katterwomp. The figure took several silent steps into her room and Elena squeezed her eyes shut praying he would go away. The stench of the man's cologne mixed with body odor was overpowering and it was all she could do not to scream. Then, as if in answer to her hasty prayer, she hear her mother call out from the bottom of the stairs. The intruder receded much quicker than he had entered and the little girl felt a wave of relief wash over her. Tears sprung from her eyes bringing with them an uncontrollable anger.

She never told her parents. She never told her husband. She never told a soul.

"I appreciate your support," James replied, "but I am not going to tell you that. In fact, it's quite the contrary. I've decided to step away from the commission, give Adalindis the *Dictionary of Cliches*, and wash my hands of the entire ball of wax. I'm just so tired of the drama and his petty games. When I started, I really believed we had good intentions and I'm quite certain that's no longer the case."

"That was my second choice," his wife said as she rose to give her husband a hug.

"So, I wrote and sent him a note to tell him I was finished but, of course, I had to have a little fun at his expense."

"How so?"

"I added a bit of intrigue thinking A-OK would appreciate it. I told him to meet me at the elephant exhibit in the zoo at 11 PM sharp and to come alone."

"How mysterious of you," Bonnie complimented her husband.

"Why the elephant exhibit?" Elena asked.

One, because I know someone who has the keys so we'll have easy access and two," he looked from his daughter to his wife, "the baboon exhibit is currently closed for repairs." Both Roger and Bonnie looked at their daughter who, at that moment, appeared to be lost in thought.

"Dear," Bonnie asked, "did you hear your father?"

"Oh, mom, I just remembered something," Elena said ignoring Bonnie's question. "I had a prescription refilled recently. Could you pick it up for me tomorrow?"

Of course, dear," she nodded. "I'll be happy to."

"Group hug!" Roger practically demanded.

They all shared a laugh and then held hands as Roger James outlined his plan to meet Katterwomp and hand over his letter of resignation and the book.

A WHOLE NEW BALLGAME

After a morning stretch and a shower Murphy and Charlie left the hotel in search of breakfast. The concierge recommended The Farm because the food was good and they could walk. They exited the hotel on to Santa Monica Boulevard, crossed Laskey, Wilshire, and then strode hand in hand eleven short blocks to Beverly. It took them all of nine minutes. Once inside Murphy ate huevos rancheros while Charlie opted for the homemade granola and yoghurt. Murphy sipped Egyptian chamomile tea and Charlie ordered a decaf Americano to go. They walked back the way they came never noticing the blue BMW.

Maginnes pulled up to the Peninsula valet and asked him to park the beemer right out front so he could easily get to it.

"I'll have to check with my manager," the kid had said, "we normally don't park rented BMW's in front of the hotel," making it sound like the car was a 10 year old Honda Civic.

"The only thing you have to check is this," Maginnes replied pulling out his badge. He contemplates being a hard ass but decided on a more conciliatory approach, "I'm working a case and would really appreciate your help."

"No problem officer," the valet acquiesced, "I'll just leave the keys on the dash."

"Good man," Maginnes had said getting out of the car. He made his way to a window seat at the Starbucks across the street. A few minutes and a half a cup of Pikes roast later he watched as Matthew Laurance pulled up to the hotel in a 1957 blue Chevy Bel Air convertible. "That baby should be easy to tail," he said to the steam rising from his cup.

Twenty more minutes passed before Maginnes recognized Charlie Carlucci and Judith Colman coming out of the revolving door. They looked extremely happy as they strolled away, the police captain figured, in the direction of Rodeo drive. Almost immediately his detective and the actor came out of the hotel too.

Here we go, the former private investigator thought as he got up, went outside, and prepared to retrieve his car. He noticed a Tesla SUV parked next to the BMW but it started to pull away and drove to up the entrance as soon as Murphy and Laurance arrived. They both climbed into the vehicle.

"Shit! Change in plans," Mags said as he lowered his head and jogged across the street.

"You must be Do It Up Brown," Matthew said as he buckled his seat belt.

"The one and only."

"Well, thank goodness for that. Could you imagine two people in this world named Do It Up Brown?"

"You can call him Dub," Murphy said from the back.

"That simplifies things," the actor said. Brown checked his mirrors.

"Where to Mr. Murphy?" he asked.

"5931 West 18th street," Murphy said from memory. Dub punched the address into the GPS, checked the mirrors again, and put the car in drive.

"I forgot to tell you," Laurance turned in his seat and addressed Murphy Murphy, "I spoke with Lyndsay and she said Serious Crisis was at the Greek on Wednesday night. They're playing with Twenty One Pilots."

"The Greek?" Murphy asked, "and what's a Twenty One Pilots?"

"The *Greek Theatre*? It just might be one of the more famous amphitheaters in the world and Twenty One Pilots is an alternative rock band. Haven't you heard the songs, *Heathens*, or *Stressed Out*? I believe that one won a Grammy."

"Only if Mozart recorded them."

"You are hopeless," Matthew said. Murphy shrugged.

"Get the tickets. It will be great to see them all again," Murphy said looking out the window at another picture perfect Southern California day.

"We're already on the list." Laurance turned back around as Do It Up Brown made a left turn onto Park Way. "Hey!" the actor shouted. "Park is one way and it's not the way you're going. Are you trying to get us killed?"

"We're being followed," the driver said in response looking in his rear view mirror. "Blue beemer, rental, had to make sure."

"Who do you think you are, James Bond?" Laurance asked.

"And how do you know it's a rental?" Murphy wondered from the back seat.

"Sticker on the lower right of the windshield. My kid worked a summer at STIX Rental Cars and said they all have to have them."

"Back to you being Bond," Matthew continued, "why do you think someone is tailing us?"

"Besides the fact that he followed me the wrong way on a one way street?"

"Well yeah, besides that."

"That same car was parked next to me out front of the hotel and now it's behind me."

"You said he," Murphy piped up.

"White guy, not young, behind the wheel. It looks like his hair is either slicked back or pulled into a ponytail."

"That's very observant of you."

"It's why I make the big bucks detective. What would you like me to do?"

"First I want you to get off this one way street, then drop us off at our destination, and keep your eyes peeled."

"10-4", the driver said hanging a right on Canon. Seconds later the blue BMW did the same thing.

"This is just one of the things I love about hanging out with you Murph," Laurance spoke up.

"What's that?"

"Never a dull moment."

A pair of thumbs quickly tapped out a text message, *The time is nigh Katterwomp. We'll both soon get what we want. Remember, the elephant exhibit, 11 PM sharp, the gates will be unlocked. Come alone.* James put the phone back on the desk.

Murphy Murphy and the Case of
the Commission on Cliches

The commissioner heard his own phone ding alerting him to an incoming missive. He picked up the device and read the words. Twice.

"Don't you get your knickers in a knot old friend," he said. "I'll meet your demands and come dressed to kill, literally. Then you'll never darken this hallowed commission's door again." Then he replied to the text with one of his own, *I'll be there and we can let it all hang out* and hit send. Katterwomp noticed the time and decided he had a little more than an hour to get ready for detective Murphy's visit.

Just minutes later Do It Up Brown pulled up to the kiosk at the Los Angeles Center for Enriched Studies and rolled down the window.

"Help you buddy?" a different, more rotund, uniformed man asked.

"I actually have all the help I need," Brown replied, "and I also have detective Murphy Murphy. He's expected." He rolled the passenger window down so the guard could see inside. Murphy offered a little wave.

"And who is this?" he pointed at Laurance.

"I'm Sal," Matthew said before either of the other two could answer, "Sal Amato," he added recalling the character he played in **Eddie and the Cruisers**.

"He's with me," Murphy said.

"Go ahead," the fat man shook his head, returned to his shack, and lifted the gate.

"Sal, huh," Dub said, "sounds like a gangster name."

"You got a problem with that," the actor said in his best Brooklyn accent. They all laughed.

Maginnes watched the exchange from down the block. He had no idea what the Los Angeles Center for Enriched Studies was or why Murphy and Laurance were there. It didn't look like he'd be able to find out on this visit. He decided to call an old friend who happened to be the head golf professional at Wilshire Country Club to see if he could wander over and hit a few balls. After some small talk and an okay, he engaged the transmission and rolled past the entrance of the center. He hoped the two men would be at least an hour inside and if not, he'd catch up with them again at the Penninsula.

THE POINT OF NO RETURN

"What the heck is this place?" Laurance asked as Murphy Murphy opened the door and they entered the building.

"Good question," Murphy answered. "I'm still not exactly sure. I do know the level below us is where the Commission on Cliches is headquartered."

"You mean there really is a physical Commission on Cliches? You weren't yanking my chain?"

"Never. And yes, surprisingly there actually is." Laurance shook his head at Murphy's answer.

"My hard-earned tax dollars at work," he said. "So, that's downstairs but what about up here?"

"It seems to be some sort of school for budding sports announcers and, quite frankly, the reason I wanted you to come along."

"Go on," the actor urged.

"You consume a lot more sports television than I do."

"A pangolin consumes a lot more sports television than you," Laurance offered.

"Fair," Murphy conceded, "but my point is you consider yourself a connoisseur of the stuff, especially the commentary."

"Why? Because most of the nonsense they spew drives me right to the mute button on my remote?"

"Precisely," Murphy nodded. "I brought you here because it would appear this is one of the places young men and women come to learn how to drive you bonkers."

"Thanks. And to think I could be on Rodeo Drive looking for Robert Downey, Jr. with the girls."

Outside the building the guard stuffed the remainder of an Entenmann's Mini Crumb Cake into his mouth. After chewing and swallowing he reached his pudgy hand into the pocket of his pants leaving a smidge of white powder on the material. The act took some effort because the trousers had, over the past several months, become at least a size too small stretching the fabric to a near breaking point. After a few moments longer than should have taken he extracted a business card. His phone was in his back pocket because he could no longer get it to fit in the front one. He grabbed it as well and punched in the number on the card. A trickle of sweat, from the effort, rolled down the side of his face. It took four rings for someone to answer.

Murphy Murphy and the Case of
the Commission on Cliches

"Is this line secure?" he practically whispered.

"As secure as a screen door on a submarine," a voice answered in a whisper of its own.

"Good. Good," the guard said proving, without a doubt, he was both dense and dense.

"I'm guessing there's a reason for this call."

"You told me to alert you if I saw anything surreptitious."

"Suspicious," James corrected him.

"What?"

"You mean suspicious."

"*I do?*"

"You really are a wazzock aren't you?"

"Thank you," the guard responded thinking it was a compliment. "Just doing my job." If a head shake could make a sound the fat man would have heard it emanating from the other end of the phone.

"Is Katterwomp up to something?" James wanted the guard to get to the point.

"He *has* been a bit more active lately, coming and going a lot but that's not why I called."

"So, why did you?"

"There was just a detective here, Murray, I think he said his name was."

"Really?"

"The facts are inconvertible."

"In*contro*vertible."

"Huh?"

"God, never mind. I can't believe I'm saying this but good job. Let me know if there are any further developments and rest assured there will be additional compensation for this."

"10-4," the guard said, "and don't you think I deserve a little more money too?"

"Astounding," James said.

"Over and out," the guard replied and the line went dead. James immediately made another call.

"Go," a man's voice said.

"We may have a problem. Apparently, there is a detective sniffing around Katterwomp. I'm told his name is Murray."

"First or last?"

"Unclear."

"Told by who?"

"Whom, and it's not important."

"Badge number?"

"Don't have it."

"You're making this really easy on me, aren't you?"

"Figure it out. Remember you owe me."

The informant, whose given name was Andrew Rosenberg, just happened to be an old James family friend. He grew up with Elena and his parents were both members of the Cloud Appreciation Society with Roger. While Elena's sun revolved around animals in general and elephants in particular Rosenberg, who went by Rosie, was fascinated by policemen and grew up wanting to protect and serve. He was accepted into the LAPD Academy on the earliest possible date as a twenty year old, went through a six and a half month process, and came out a police officer at 21. He worked patrol for the requisite four years with an eye always on earning a detective shield. Rosie accomplished that feat a week after his 27th birthday. He started in the Juvenile Division but eventually was tabbed to join the team in Robbery Homicide.

Rosenberg's career was in full bloom but then trouble bubbled up in the form of a pay to play scheme involving some of his colleagues. He was subsequently caught up in an Internal Affairs investigation. Even though Andy wasn't involved in the actual racket he wasn't without guilt. His initial alibi would have meant coming clean about an illicit affair with the wife of a lieutenant in the Gang and Narcotics Division so he turned to his old friends the James's for help. Around the family dinner table Roger insisted Andy end the tryst and then Bonnie and Elena came up with a plan. They supplied him with the story that Rosie had been serving as a chaperone on his off hours for various charitable organizations bringing children to the elephant exhibit at the zoo. Since IAB already had little, if any, evidence that he was as intimately involved in the caper as his co-workers they bought the excuse hook, line, and sinker and cleared Rosenberg of any wrong doing. While he untangled himself from the romantic entanglement, all parties felt he still owed Roger, Bonnie, and Elena James for his freedom.

"I'll do this and when I do that debt is paid in full, understood?" Rosie was starting to get angry.

"Any records will be destroyed and the entire matter will be forgotten," James assured him.

"Agreed. Now what was this detective's name again?"

"Murray."

Charlie and Judith were still on Rodeo Drive at that exact moment. Bags from Ferragamo and Ralph Lauren in hand, walking out of Alexander McQueen.

"I want to stop in Geary's on Rodeo and look at a watch for Murphy," Charlie said. His birthday is right around the corner."

TIME TO KILL

Like many of the retail outlets on the famous street, Geary's on Rodeo had a guard posted inside the door. A tall, burly guard. This one gave the ladies an almost imperceptible nod as they entered.

"The minute Buck decides to retire I'm coming back and convincing *that* guy to come work for me at Bar Flight," Judith exclaimed.

"I'm sure he'll drop everything to stand guard at your door for the chance to eat Lou and Gail's cooking. I mean anything has to be better than this hell hole."

"What are we looking for? Judith asked ignoring her friend's comment.

"Something nice," Charlie said looking around.

"Is there anything *not* nice in here?" Judith asked.

"Doesn't look like it." They both took in displays featuring products from Patek Philippe, Rolex, Baccarat, Gucci, and many more. Judith marched up to one.

"This watch is lovely," she remarked pointing to a Patek Grand Complications with a blue face.

"It's a *timepiece*, a salesperson had suddenly appeared. "And it is lovely, isn't it." Charlie came over to look.

"It's exquisite," she said, "and it better be for $100,000."

"*American money*!?" Judith said nearly choking on the amount. The salesperson smiled surely having heard similar reactions dozens of times a day.

"Are they all that expensive?" Judith whispered to the woman.

"Oh no dear," she answered," most are less. In fact, only two of the models we carry cost more."

"More than a hundred grand?" Judith was incredulous, the woman merely nodded.

"You know what they say," Charlie joined the conversation, "if you have to ask how much it costs you can't afford it."

"You know what *I* say?" Judith responded. "If you spend a hundred grand or more on a watch you've got more money than sense." That made the salesperson chuckle.

"Come on Mr. Burns, let's go look at the Rolex display," Charlie said gently grabbing her friend's arm.

"Who's Mr. Burns?" Judith asked.

"Tell me you don't watch The Simpsons without telling me you don't watch the Simpsons," Charlie chided. Judith used her sleeve to cover up her Timex as they walked to the next set of timepieces. The salesperson followed closely behind.

"You two are a hoot," she said. Charlie was drawn to an Oyster Perpetual Day/Date with a bright blue dial.

"What do you think?" Charlie asked Judith.

"Wow! It's beautiful," she said. I also like the one next to it with the lighter blue face."

"That's an ice blue dial," the woman had made her way behind the display and was reaching for Charlie's choice. She handed it to her. Charlie gave it a once over and passed it on to Judith.

"Holy cow," she said, "it's heavy."

"This piece is white gold with a matching bracelet," the salesperson said, "we also offer it in platinum. Charlie knew changing the precious metal would also change the price to the tune of tens of thousands of dollars.

"I'll take this one," she said taking the watch back from Judith.

"Very well," the woman nodded appreciatively, "may we gift wrap it for you?"

"Of course," Charlie gave her the Rolex.

"Man," Judith said touching her friend's arm. "Happy Birthday Murphy Murphy."

"The Gas Pump Lounge had a record year," Charlie said with a shrug referring to the club she co-owned with her brother. She handed over her credit card.

Murphy looked at the Casio on his wrist and confirmed they still had a few minutes before the appointed rendezvous with Katerwomp. He and Matthew strolled down the hallway. The scene was more like the first time he visited than the last. There was an energy to the place and several classrooms were in use. They approached one and cracked open the door.

"Does making a putt on the last hole of the day really make lunch or dinner taste better?" a female student asked. The teacher, a rather short, dark haired man put his hands on his hips.

"Well, McCrane," he started.

"McCabe," she corrected him.

"Whatever. The point is it doesn't make a hill of beans of difference." Both Murphy and Matthew noticed an accent.

"Australian?" Murphy whispered a question. Laurance shook his head.

"South African," he assured his friend in his own low voice. The teacher droned on.

"This particular phrase is one of the staples of golf broadcasting," he chastised his student. "In fact, it may just be *the* gold standard. If someone on the announce team doesn't use it at least twice a telecast it would qualify as malpractice."

"Can I kill that guy right now?" Laurance asked.

"Come on," Murphy turned and continued down the hall. A door three classrooms down was wide open. Murphy peered in and saw the same professor he had met before. Hair slicked back, feet up on the desk, colorful socks peeking out from the bottom of cuffed slacks. "You gotta meet this guy," Murphy said to Laurance, "I think you'll like him." They entered the room.

At the other end from the professor two students sat, headphones on their heads, watching a golf tournament on individual monitors. Each was intermittently pecking away on a laptop.

"You lost?" the question came from the professor.

"Hello again," Murphy said, "we met the other day."

"I remember."

"What are they working on?" Laurance asked pointing to the students.

"Final round of the Arnold Palmer Invitational presented by Mastercard."

"Why?"

"Because I'm making them."

"What's the assignment?" Murphy added.

"I asked them to identify and document every cliché and stupid thing the announcers say."

"Seems like that could take all day," Murphy replied.

"I actually gave them a week and *that* won't even be enough."

"Good thinking," Laurance added. The teacher stared at him.

"Have we met?" he asked the actor. "You look familiar."

"He's an actor," Murphy jumped in, "you may have seen him on tv." The man considered it for a moment then snapped his fingers.

"I know. You're Benjamin Gold from Dawson's Creek." Murphy thought the man might as well be speaking in tongues. Laurance just smiled.

"Close but that's my brother Mitchell," he said.

"The lawyer from **The Hand that Rocked the Cradle**," he tried again.

"Once more, my brother."

"A pair of twins then," the professor said.

"That's too many," Murphy corrected him. The teacher turned his attention to the detective. "You see a pair of twins would be four people," Murphy went on undeterred, "quadruplets in essence."

"I know that" the man responded. "I was just checking to see if you were paying attention."

"He's always paying attention to redundancies," Laurance piped up. "It's kind of his thing." Murphy nodded.

"Are you here to see Katterwomp again?" the teacher changed the subject.

"We are. In fact, we should go."

"Nice to meet you," Laurance said. "Good luck with your students. I wish more of them were in here than over there," he pointed toward the previous classroom.

"You and me both," he said as Murphy and Matthew turned to leave. "I know," the teacher added, "you're Richard Mathers from LA Law," knowing that was another character played by Mitchell, not Matthew, Laurance.

Matthew raised his left hand and offered up the middle finger. They exited and turned toward the elevator.

"You were fabulous in Eddie and the Cruisers," they heard the compliment, followed by laughter, from the classroom.

"You're right," Matthew said to Murphy, "I like that guy."

STICK YOUR NECK OUT

After trying on shoes at Jimmy Choo, looking at sunglasses at Persol, and window shopping at Prada, Louis Vuitton, and Hermes Judith and Charlie found a bench, took a load off, and enjoyed a few minutes of people watching.

"Have you thought anymore about Luca?" Charlie asked Judith.

"Not for," she looked at her watch, "twenty seconds," Judith admitted. "I'm acting like a high school sophomore crushing on the senior quarterback. It's a little embarrassing."

"It's not embarrassing at all," Charlie assured her friend.

"Thanks."

"Call him."

"Right now?"

"Why not? You got something better to do? Call."

"What would I do without you?" she admitted and plucked her phone from her purse.

"Would you like some privacy?" Charlie asked.

"Nope. I'd actually welcome the support," Judith found the previous call to Luca and punched redial.

"Hello," she heard his voice and, for a second, considered hanging up.

"Hey there," she said instead.

"Judith? Is that you?"

"It is."

"What a delightful surprise. I'm so happy you called back." *That accent* she thought as she felt her heart pound a little harder. "How are you?" he asked.

"Good. Real good," she sputtered, still trying to calm down.

"*Where* are you?" he asked, "sounds busy."

"Rodeo Drive," she answered, "spending money I can't afford to spend," she added. *Why did I say that* she chastised herself?

"Rodeo Drive will do that to a person," he commiserated. "That's why I shop at the Men's Warehouse," he chuckled.

"You do?"

"No." This time she laughed.

"I think I saw you yesterday," she changed course.

"Really? Where?"

"Universal Studios. Near the sound stages."

"You were there? Why? What were you doing?"

"Watching them make a movie about me and my friends," she answered. "It was surreal."

"You're kidding? The Ron Howard film?"

"That's the one," she said. "You were coming out of Rebecca Ferguson's trailer."

"Great hair," he said, "but not as good as the other one's. That Keery kid is blessed."

"Funny," she said.

"Why didn't you say hello?"

"Honestly it caught me a little off guard and I wasn't a hundred percent certain it was you."

"Fair enough. I accept that explanation. I'm disappointed but accepting."

"I'll make sure I approach you the next time I see you. I'd hate to disappoint you twice."

"How about tonight?" he lobbed out the question.

"How about tonight what?" she lobbed back.

"How about tonight being the next time you see me?" he waited for an answer. He didn't have to wait long.

"Sure. Yeah. Of course."

"Great!" she thought he sounded genuinely excited. She smiled and stole a glance at Charlie. She was smiling too. "I hate to sound unchivalrous but would you mind meeting me somewhere?"

"I guess not," she thought the request was a little strange, " as long as it's not some spooky, out of the way place."

"Not at all," Luca assured her, "do you have a pen?"

"I have a great memory," Judith replied and he gave her the address. Judith said it out loud and Charlie entered it in her phone.

"Say around seven o'clock?" he asked.

"See you then. Ciao," she added. *Why did I say that* she asked herself for the second time.

"Au revoir ma Cherie," he said in fluent French and hung up.

"You're blushing," Charlie said.

"Do you think it would be alright if I borrowed Do It Up Brown tonight?" she asked.

"I'll make sure it's alright," Charlie answered.

Murphy and Matthew took the elevator and Murphy punched 3.

"What's on 2?" the actor asked.

"Absolutely nothing," Murphy replied, "in fact, there is no 2. It's a mare's nest.

"A what?"

"Mare's nest," Murphy repeated. "An illusion or disappointment. Mare's, as horses, don't make nests."

The door to the commissioner's office was wide open but Murphy Murphy knocked on it anyway. Katterwomp was standing in a corner of the room his back angled mostly away from the door. Murphy could still see that he was staring at his phone. He jumped at the sound of the knock. Quickly recovering, he stared at the two men in the doorway and then stole a glance at his wristwatch.

"Detective," Katterwomp said, "you're early." At that rebuke Murphy checked his own wrist and the trusty Casio told him it was 10:59.

"By one minute," he said.

"I aim for pinpoint accuracy," the commissioner commented.

"I'm sure you do," Murphy said with a shake of his head. At that the man approached his visitors.

"Please, without further ado, come in. Come in," He waved an arm toward the inside of the office. "And who, might I ask, have you brought with you? I hope he's not a wolf in sheep's clothing."

"This is my friend Matthew," Murphy answered as Katterwomp turned and walked toward his desk. The two guests followed and sat in chairs facing the commissioner.

"Detective Murphy," Adalindis said after plopping down, "I won't mince matters. This investigation is closing up shop." Murphy opened his mouth to speak but Katterwomp silenced him by putting an index finger in the air. "I don't want you to think you were weighed in the balance and found wanting. Your work has been all to the good so I will pay the piper and dole out the agreed upon sum."

"But," Murphy started but he was interrupted again.

"Now, now detective, don't try and change my mind. I'm packing it in." Through his peripheral vision Murphy could see Matthew Laurance staring at Katterwomp, open mouthed.

"Amazing," the actor said.

"I'm not sure I understand," Murphy said. "What happened?"

"This happened," the commissioner said handing Murphy a typewritten note. The detective took in the words.

My dear Adalindis the note began, *you know you have always been a tower of strength for me personally and a man among men professionally.* Laurance also read the words looking over Murphy's shoulder. *That is why it pains me to say I must do an about face and resign from your wonderful commission. Elena, my daughter, is marrying a man born to the purple and wants us all to blaze a trail and move to the land of milk and honey, the South of France. You can imagine it came as a bolt from the blue so I am hopeful you can show us the milk of human kindness and wish us Godspeed.*

I didn't mean to stir up a hornet's nest but I have the book and I've made some necessary edits and eliminated redundancies to make sure I return it to the commission Simon Pure. Therefore, you shall receive it quick as a cat.

Here's mud in your eye,

Your friend Roger.

"That's quite a note," Murphy said after reading it a second time. Laurance nodded in agreement.

"And it's no cock and bull story," Katterwomp agreed taking the paper back.

"So then, all is forgiven?" Murphy asked.

"I'd be a fibber McGee if I said I wasn't as mad as a wet hen, that's for certain. But now it's water under the bridge. Forgive and forget. After all, blood is thicker than water."

"I'm happy to stay on the job until the book is actually in your hands," Murphy offered.

"What a good Samaritan you are but that won't be necessary my good man. It's not going to go haywire; Roger James is true blue. He won't resort to any monkey business. Now, as much as I am enjoying our little brain trust, I'm going to give you the bum's rush." Taking the hint both Murphy and Laurance rose and went to, and through, the door, Katterwomp followed close behind. "Be of good cheer," he said as he closed himself inside the office.

"That was extraordinary," Matthew said as they entered the elevator. "I'll tell you what if I'm making a Sleepy Hollow sequel *that guy* is my Ichabod Crane," the actor went on. "And the use of cliches! Just sensational. If I didn't hear it with my own ears, I wouldn't have believed it."

"He's unique," Murphy replied, "but there *is* something you shouldn't believe."

"What's that?"

"The silly note."

"What do you mean?" the actor asked.
"I mean I'll bet you dollars to donuts Roger James
didn't write that," Murphy said as the elevator doors
opened and the men walked out.

"So, who did?"

"If you ask me."

"I just did ask you," Laurance broke in.

"Katterwomp did," Murphy answered. "This whole
thing stinks to high heaven."

"I guess that means you're not shutting down the
investigation."

"On the contrary," Murphy said, "I'm just getting
started." They left the building and reunited with Do It
Up Brown.

"Gentleman," the driver said as he put the Tesla in gear
and drove, "the BMW is back."

"Did you happen to get a plate number?" the detective
asked. Brown reached behind him and handed Murphy
Murphy a post it note.

TIME AND TIDE WAIT FOR NO MAN

Back at the Penninsula Hotel Murphy Murphy, without pressure from Charlie, gladly gave the okay for Judith to "borrow" Do It Up Brown for the evening. But the consent came with one condition. He needed Brown for an errand before that. His word, and the fact that Charlie had made reservations at Cha Cha Cha, was more than enough incentive. A quick search on his laptop revealed the rental car agencies in Los Angeles that offered BMW sedans so with promises to return in plenty of time the detective and the driver headed out. Armed with his badge and a license plate number Murphy stood in line at the rental car counter waiting his turn, which finally came.

"Reservation?" the woman said without looking up.

"Hello," Murphy said, "I'm detective Murphy Murphy and I would like to speak to your manager." That made her look up.

"That would be me," she said after more than a momentary stare. "Can I see some identification?" Murphy obliged by showing her his badge. "What can I do for you?" she asked.

"I need to know who rented a blue BMW sedan, license plate 6MCJ277," he answered. "Please," he added.

"That's an easy one," she said quickly."

Why's that?

"I was the one who rented it. Coincidentally he was a cop too."

"You don't say," Murphy said.

"He had a badge that looked an awful lot like yours."

"You don't say."

"I *do* say and I *did* say."

"My apologies," Murphy was sincere.

"No problem," she smiled, "give me just a sec Hon." She tapped away at her computer. "Here it is," she said triumphantly, "his name is Maginnes."

"You *don't*," Murphy started and stopped. The woman behind the counter raised an eyebrow. "You've been a huge help Miss," he looked at her name tag, "Carol Kusama. I can't thank you enough and I'll make sure to send a note of appreciation to your company."

"It's Mrs. and you're welcome but don't bother."

"Why?"

"I've worked for this company for fifteen years and I can assure you they could care less." Murphy shook his head and left without correcting her.

Judith practically jumped into the Tesla's front seat.

"My," Do It Up Brown looked impressed, "you sure have a pep in your step. And you look fantastic."

"Why Mr. Brown are you flirting with me?"

"Would it do any good?" the driver asked. They both laughed. "Where to?"

"I think I have a date," she responded.

"The hairdresser to the stars?" Brown wondered. Judith's reddening face answered his question.

"Could you please take me here?" She handed him the piece of paper on which Charlie had written the address.

"You're going to The Improv?" he said looking at the piece of paper.

"Is that good?" she asked.

"It is if you like comedy clubs," he said and off they went. It took them about 25 minutes because of traffic but finally Brown dropped Judith off at the corner of Melrose and Kilkea. "You have my number, call if you need me," he said as she exited.

Inside the club she approached a young looking girl wearing far too much make up and far too few clothes. Judith disliked her immediately.

"Welcome to The Improv," she practically sneered, "do you have a reservation?"

"Uh, yeah, I think so," Judith answered.

"You *think* so?" she scoffed.

"I'm meeting someone," Judith said trying her best not to punch the girl in the nose.

"Of course you are. Last name?"

"Actually, I don't even know his last name," Judith said realizing she never asked.

"Maybe it's Underwood," the girl offered up a contemptuous smile.

"Good one," Judith said catching the reference to the Carrie Underwood song. "I just know him as Luca." The girl's smile disappeared as her mouth dropped open.

"You're with Luca?" Judith thought she sounded both envious and incredulous.

"Well obviously not at the moment, Einstein," Judith got a shot of her own in, "but that's definitely the plan."

"Follow me," the girl said reluctantly as she turned and led the way. The girl sat Judith at a prime table marked "reserved", handed her a menu and stomped off. A waitress appeared and Judith ordered a shot of tequila and a beer. She looked around for Luca. A few minutes passed and the waitress brought the drinks. *I hope this guy doesn't stand me up* she thought then chuckled. The idea of being stood up in a standup comedy club tickled her funny bone. She downed the shot as the lights dimmed.

"Ladies and Gentlemen, welcome to The Improv LA's best and most famous comedy club," a man's voice boomed. Still no Luca Judith lamented. "We've got another outstanding show for you tonight featuring Tom Dreesen," she heard both mild applause and a few groans, and Erica Rhodes". That name was greeted by applause and a few whistles. "So, enjoy the show and please tip your waiters and waitresses," he implored. "Without further ado to kick things off please welcome to the stage, making his Improv debut, Lukos Lukoceau." Most of the audience, including Judith, clapped their hands.

The curtains opened and a spotlight lit the stage. After a brief pause into it walked Luca. Judith gasped as she saw he was dressed in black pants with black suspenders over a white and black horizontally striped shirt. He wore white gloves on his hands, a black beret on his head, and his face was painted white. Elaborate makeup, including a big, black tear completed the picture. He took a few cautious steps and his face took on an amazed look as he pretended to be trapped in a box.

"A *MIME*?" someone behind her shouted, "you've *got* to be kidding me? A *freaking mime*!?!" A few people shushed him. Judith couldn't contain a laugh.

"Oh my God," she said softly, "he *IS* a mime."

"I was wondering how long it would take you to discover I was out here," Johnny "Jack" Maginnes said after answering the phone.

"Honestly, you didn't make it very hard," Murphy Murphy responded.

"Not for a world famous detective, that's for sure."

"Why *are* you here and more importantly why the cloak and dagger approach?" Murphy asked ignoring the jab.

"The Chief wanted to make sure you weren't being recruited by the LAPD. The amateur James Bond tactic was my idea. You weren't supposed to know I was spying on you."

"I'm not and I did," Murphy said.

"Touche," Maginnes replied, "and I'm glad to hear it." An uncomfortable moment passed as the captain thought his detective might hang up on him.

"Well, now that you're here I could probably use your help," Murphy said instead.

"I'm happy to serve," Maginnes said finding himself relieved. "What's up?"

"It's this darn Commission on Cliches," Murphy answered, "there's something fishy in Denmark. I can feel it in my bones."

"I see what you did there," Maginnes congratulated Murphy. "Sounds like you don't like the color of his money."

"That's an understatement," Murphy said hoping to stop the nonsense."

"Should we put a tail on the guy?" Maginnes took the hint.

"Not if it's done as clumsily as you did it," Murphy got another dig in.

"Flattery will get you nowhere," Maginnes tried again.

"Maybe you could enlist your friends at the LAPD," Murphy didn't bite. "Surely they'll know enough not to follow the guy the wrong way down a one-way street."

"Let me get right on that," the captain responded. "And don't call me Shirley."

"Thanks for coming," Luca had lost the beret, cleaned off the makeup, changed clothes, and joined her at the table. "The pizza is actually pretty good here and I see you already have a beer." A couple approached the table.

"Excuse us," they said. Luca turned. "We just wanted to say we thought you were really good," they looked at each other. Luca guessed they were in their 50's. "It's been a while since we've seen a mime act."

"Thank you," Luca said and they left.

"You were *really* good," Judith concurred. Luca smiled at her. "That climbing part was very convincing. I could actually picture a rope."

"So, do you want to split a pie?" Luca asked.

"Sure," she said.

"Did you like the haircutting scene?"

"Is *that* what that was?"

"I'll take that as a no," he shook his head. "I probably ought to remove that from the act. The audience burst into a raucous laugh as the comedienne on stage told a joke about a drive-in movie theatre.

"They seem to like her," Judith said pointing to the stage.

"That's Erica Rhodes," he said without looking, "she's super funny."

"Can I ask you why you wanted to be a mime? Seems like a lost art."

"That's exactly why!" Luca said a little too loudly.

"Ssshhh, ssshhh, ssshhh," someone at the table admonished him. Luca ignored the person.

"A while back I was watching an old movie channel on TV and **Silent Movie** came on."

"The Mel Brooks comedy?"

"Precisely. I was curious and after a short time I found myself sitting there fascinated by it."

"It is brilliant," Judith agreed.

"It was more than that." The waitress appeared and took their order.

"You were saying?" Judith prompted him. He thought for a moment.

"I'm around *movie* stars all the time. They're mostly nice but believe me they *love* talking and their favorite topic is usually themselves. Between you and me, most of them are pretty boring and, as far as I'm concerned, only a few of them can act. So, I was in awe as I was watching Mel Brooks and Marty Feldman and Dom DeLuise."

"And Bernadette Peters," Judith added.

"Of course," Luca acknowledged. "Anyway, I'm watching all these great actors and thinking could any of today's stars be in that kind of movie today? A movie where none of them says a word."

"Except Marcel Marceau," she offered.

"Except Marcel Marceau," he repeated. "The world's most famous mime has the only spoken line in the entire movie and it's just one word."

"*Non*," Judith said in her best French accent.

"I couldn't stop laughing and for some reason it made me want to learn more about the man and his craft."

"So you did." Luca just nodded.

"Did you know pantomime used to be a huge form of comedic entertainment?" he didn't give her time to answer. "In Europe, during the 1800's, Joseph Grimaldi was one of the world's most popular entertainers and he was a clown." He said it with admiration. "Then Etienne DeCroux brought the discipline into the 1900's." Judith could tell Luca was on a roll and couldn't help but notice the excitement in his voice. "Marcel Marceau learned from him."

"You really did do a deep dive."

"I'm sorry," he said sheepishly, "am I boring you? I do tend to go on and on." She shook her head as an answer. "Fast forward to Shields and Yarnell," he continued.

I've heard of them."

"In the seventies a lot of people had. They appeared on television programs hosted by Red Skelton, Sonny and Cher, Johnny Carson, and The Muppets. They even had their own variety show on CBS. Robert Shields was a street mime in San Francisco when he was discovered by none other than Marcel Marceau."

"Full circle," Judith added. Then the pizza came.

"Shields and Yarnell got married in 1972 but divorced 14 years later."

"All good things come to an end," Judith said before taking a bite of pizza.

"That was pretty much the end of the road for the art. They were the last great mime act." He sounded sad.

"Until you," she said hoping to cheer him up.

"You're too kind but that's highly unlikely," he said.

"Why?" she asked as someone else approached their table. It was a twenty something kid in a hoodie.

"Stick to cutting hair billboard boy," he said and walked by.

"The world seems not to have the patience anymore," Luca lamented.

THE SHOW MUST GO ON

Another sun rose on the nearly 20 million people that called the greater Los Angeles area home. Shockingly to those who lived there it promised to be another 77 degree, sunny, day. Over breakfast together, the James family made plans to face the day. Bonnie was off to her patients and the hospital, Elena said it was her one day a week, 20 minute, bus ride to her elephants at the zoo, and Roger claimed to have errands to run.

Murphy Murphy and Charlie Carlucci were still lounging in their Peninsula hotel King size bed. Holding hands, Charlie's right leg laid languorously over Murphy's left. Both had their eyes closed but neither slept. Smiles graced their faces. Judith, on the other hand, spent most of the night and early morning up, walking with, sitting beside, and talking to Luca. They shared their thoughts on everything and anything that came to mind. She happily discovered they had many things in common including a love for dogs, a dislike of perfidious people, and tacos. But she also sadly realized during the early morning hours that there were too many things that would forever be a barrier to

195

any type of serious relationship. He loved LA and said he would never want to live anywhere else. He also wasn't much of a sports fan and, despite professing a love of movies, he had never seen **Eddie and the Cruisers**. To make matters worse when she offered to see it with him he told her his life would actually be quite complete if he never saw the darn thing at all. In the end they mutually agreed they enjoyed each other's company but friends, potentially very good ones, was all the future held. He left after a long, purposeful, hug. She returned to her room alone, set the alarm for an 8 AM studio call and, fully clothed, fell on top of the bed and into a deep sleep at 4:30.

Adalindis Orval Katterwomp snored like a locomotive. He dreamt of ivory towers, a bevy of beauties, eager beavers, and a bull in a china shop. The head of the commission on cliches slept like a man without a care in the world.

"Nice work Domnhall," Connor Williams shouted, "you too Matt," he added. "That dialogue is some of my favorite in the entire film," he commented on the Beachwood Café scene they had just finished shooting. "That Kamens did a heck of a job with the screenplay."

"You're full of compliments today," Gleeson responded, "could you sub for the tyrant Ron Howard more often?" The entire crew gave that a hearty laugh.

"Very funny," Williams, the first assistant director who was running the show on this day, agreed. "Okay now, let's take 15 and get set for the Murphy Murphy Maginnes confrontation. That means we need Serious Crisis!"

Murphy, Charlie, and Judith sat in the same director's chairs but in a different part of the sound stage. This time they were also joined by Captain Maginnes.

"This is wild," he said. Just then Matthew Laurance wandered over.

"What did you guys think?"

"I think," Murphy was the first to react, "that they could have found someone more convincing to play the Matthew Laurance character."

"You see, smartass, in the movie business," Laurance shot back, "it's sometimes necessary to go with the actor that is cheaper in cost."

"I think the whole thing is fantastic," Maginnes, still wide eyed, interrupted the back and forth. "I'll never watch a movie the same way again." Everyone, except the actor, nodded in agreement. "But I will admit," the police captain wasn't finished, "I *was* hoping to get Ron Howard's autograph."

"I'm pretty sure you have to buy the book he just wrote with his brother Clint to get one of those," Matthew poured a little water on Maginnes' fire. "Just wait until you see yourself in action," the actor immediately tried to cheer the cop up, "Danny Bruhl is one good actor."

"Places everyone!" it was Williams.

"This way folks," a young woman with her glasses perched on her head and a clipboard in her hands had suddenly appeared beside Murphy Murphy. "Let's all head over to the other set. "Graham," she addressed a young blonde man who was clearly a lackey, "grab these chairs and follow me." He obediently did as he was told. Across the room Joe Keery, Trace Adkins, Hailey Steinfeld, and the rest of the make-believe band took the stage. Daniel Bruhl, wearing a wig pulled into a ponytail, stood off to the side. He was dressed in cargo shorts, a Hawaiian shirt, white knee socks, and sandals.

"Is *that* supposed to be me?" Maginess asked pointing at him. Murphy just laughed.

"Do we need to do a run through?" Williams asked the actors, "does anyone feel like they need to get the lip synch timing down?"

"We *can* sing, you know," Trace Adkins baritone boomed at the first assistant director. For emphasis he waved his arm acknowledging his fellow bandmates. "Lip synch is for the talent challenged," he added. Joe Keery and Hallie Steinfeld nodded in unison.

"Fair enough," Williams said, "but this is what Ron wanted." The actors just stared at him. "Ok, what if we do it both ways?" he hoped that would appease them. The last thing he wanted was to have an extended conversation that would delay the shooting of the scene.

"Do we have *just* the music track?" he yelled asking no one in particular.

"We do," someone shouted back.

"I guess that works," the country singer, playing Big Joe Lionns, acquiesced.

"Perfect," Connor was relieved. "Places everybody!"

"Can we talk?" Maginnes touched Murphy Murphy on the arm just before the music started blasting through the speakers. Murphy recognized the tune as *Ascend Up the Ladder* one of the Serious Crisis's biggest hits.

"Let's go outside," he said.

A gloved right hand lifted the keys to the refurbished Toyota Land Cruiser off the rack near the back door to the James home. The left hand, also gloved, held an envelope. Moments later the fifty-year-old "brand new" SUV cruised past multi-million dollar mansions. James noticed Rooney Mara walking her dogs and gave a little wave thinking *has she been in anything good since **The Girl With the Dragon Tattoo**?* After turning left onto Commonwealth, it was about a twenty minute drive to the destination.

The portly guard pulled another piece of red licorice from a tub he had purchased on sale at Office Depot. He bit off half the stick and made a mental note to be sure and put in for the full amount when he filled out his expense report. *If they're going to be persimmons* (he meant parsimonious) *with my pay, I'll nickel and dime them to death.* He also knew no one ever really looked at the receipts. He was gnawing away on piece after piece of candy and looking at an Only.fans website on his five-year-old tablet when the old, red Toyota came rolling down the entrance road.

James had no intention of stopping or even slowing down for that matter. The V-8 engine propelled the Land Cruiser along at a steady 25 miles per hour as it approached the kiosk. The gloved right hand reached over to the passenger seat. James grabbed the envelope and in one smooth motion sent it sailing through the wide open window.

The Falstaffian rent-a-cop barely had time to look up from the jiggling body parts on his screen before a white envelope filled with twenty, fifty, and one hundred dollar bills sailed through the door and smacked him on the side of the head. It fell to the ground and he labored to climb off his stool and pick it up. Before tearing it open he noticed writing on the outside in big, block, black, letters.

LOSE MY NUMBER

By the time the guard looked back down the entrance road the Toyota and its driver were long gone.

James pulled over to the side of the road on South Crescent Heights Boulevard and hit redial on the burner phone.

"Go."

"Any news?" James asked.

"We're a little impatient, aren't we?"

"*We* are. What did you find out?"

"Not much," Rosie answered.

Andy had access to the LAPD database and pored over the detective files. He came up with a handful of Murrays, first name and last, on the payroll. He knew one was in Internal Affairs because this particular Murray, Murray Schwartzman, had tried to bust Rosie's balls during the investigation. He secretly hoped it was him but knew immediately it wasn't. The IAB guys wouldn't ever work on anything that wasn't part of going after another cop. A second Murray was part of COMSTAT which was basically statistics and analysis, a desk job while a third one worked in the Juvenile Division. So unless this Katterwomp character was a child molester or a gang banger he was a dead end. There was a fourth but he was looking at twenty-seven days until retirement which meant he was doing nothing more than sitting on his behind counting down the hours. He relayed all this information to James.

"Is that it?"

"There was one more Murray," Rosenberg said.

"And what is he doing?"

"Well, *he* isn't doing anything because he is actually a she, Abigail Murray in Robbery Homicide. Gender precluded me from digging any further. Sorry."

Five Murrays none with even a remote reason to interact with Katterwomp James thought. "Thanks for checking." "The tub of goo guard probably got the name wrong," James said to himself even though it was loud enough for Rosie to hear. "Anyway, tomorrow is Wednesday," James added.

"What difference does the day of the week make?"

"It makes all the difference in the world." James hung up. Twenty minutes later the Toyota slowed as it cruised along West 6th street. The area had seen an unprecedented spike in homelessness and James thought it the perfect place to dispose of the burner. The phone went flying out the driver's side window and skittered along the sidewalk until it bounced off one of a dozen or so cardboard boxes and came to rest. The Toyota sped up. After all what difference did it make if there were still minutes left on the device, who was a homeless person going to call?

"Is that Vin Diesel?" Maginnes asked as he watched a golf cart pass by.

"Could be," Murphy answered. "They are making more movies than just ours around here."

"I did read about another **Fast and Furious** movie coming out," the captain said nodding.

"That must be it," Murphy said. *Whatever that is* he thought. "What did you want to talk about?"

"I reached out to a buddy, former LAPD now out on his own."

"Great."

"Guy's name is Christopher Henley. He said he'd be happy to keep an eye on your Katterwomp character for a few days, see what bubbles up."

"I believe he's *our* Katterwomp now," Murphy countered. "And what did you tell this guy?"

"Just that this bird is a person of interest. Trust me, my guy doesn't ask a lot of questions."

"He's just happy to be back in the game?"

"Something like that," was the answer Maginnes gave. "Anyway, I asked him to meet us for a drink this evening at 5:30 at the Club Bar in the Penninsula."

"Let's go back inside," Murphy said. "I want to see how they're going to portray our first meeting."

"Me too," the captain agreed. "They better get it right."

"And what, exactly, would be right?"

"Me handing you your lunch."

"Is *that* how you remember it?" Murphy asked as they both made for the sound stage door.

The rest of the day was unremarkable if you could call watching a movie being made, having lunch with Kevin Bacon, Ving Rhames, and Joseph Gordon Levitt (he was playing Serious Crisis drummer Herbie Albanese) unremarkable. Meanwhile eight and a half miles as the crow flies away Serious Crisis was going through a sound check for the first of their two gigs at The Greek Theatre. They were scheduled to take the stage after Twenty One Pilots and while the show was supposed to start at 7:30 the two-man led American alternative hip-hop band from Columbus, Ohio was notorious for being late. Serious Crisis knew they probably wouldn't start until after 9 PM. The Greek had a hard curfew at 11 PM so they had that going for them. On the way back to the hotel from the set Murphy told Charlie and Judith they

would be going to the Greek the next night and the band
would love to see them all.

"Did you know the idea for a "Greek theatre", Do It Up
Brown used air fingers quotes when he said the words
'Greek theatre', "was the brainstorm of a wealthy Los
Angeles landowner named Griffith J. Griffith."

"I like the place already," Murphy Murphy said. "You
can always trust a man with two first names."

Brown chuckled and then related the entire story. He
told them Mr. Griffith donated 3,000 acres of land to
the city of Los Angeles in 1896 that led to the creation
of Griffith Park. "Today it's more than 4,000 acres and
includes the Los Angeles Zoo, The Griffith
Observatory, The Museum of the American West and,
of course, The Greek Theatre," the driver imparted the
knowledge.

He went on to tell the story of how Griffith left money
in his will to create the venue and a canyon site was
chosen because of the acoustics. He added the
cornerstone was laid in 1928 and the building was
dedicated two years later on September 25th. He added
the first shows were operatic concerts and were free to
the public.

"Except the first two rows of seats," Brown said with a
smile, "they cost a buck. The capacity in the '30's was
4,000 souls," he added. "Today it's 5,900."

"Fascinating," Murphy said because he thought it was. It also helped kill the time on the ride back to the hotel.

"Lots of famous people have played there, right?" It was Judith.

"The best of the best," Brown beamed. "Sir Elton John, Springsteen, Pearl Jam, Crosby, Stills, Nash, and Young, Jackson Browne, Wilco, Los Lobos, Neil Diamond, and so many more."

"What about movies?" Charlie wanted to know.

"Those too," Brown nodded. "The delightful **Bye, Bye, Birdie** with Ann Margaret and Dick van Dyke and the less delightful **Get Him to the Greek** starring Jonah Hill and Russell Brand were filmed, in part, there.

"And I read somewhere the scene with Bradley Cooper and Lady Gaga singing *Shallow* for the **A Star is Born** remake was also shot there," Judith chimed in.

"I wouldn't doubt it," Do It up agreed. "By the way do I get to see the show tomorrow night too?" he inquired inviting himself.

"Sure, why not?" Charlie answered for Murphy, "Can't imagine one more of us would make any difference."

"I'd sure prefer that," Brown said with a smile, "to sitting in the Tesla in the parking lot."

Murphy Murphy and the Case of
the Commission on Cliches

"Can you text Giucigiu," Charlie spoke to Murphy, "and tell him to add Mr. Brown to the list?"

"On it," Murphy, who knew Giucigui was the band's manager, nodded and tapped out the request on his phone.

The remainder of the drive was made in relative silence. Brown turned right onto Sunset, The Laugh Factory on the corner serving as a landmark. The mile and a half on the boulevard sent them past some of Los Angeles's most famous hotels including the Chateau Marmont, the Standard, the Mandarin, and the Jeremy. They were going in the wrong direction to see Luca's billboard.

"Is this the fastest way?" Murphy said after an audible sigh.

"Tesla says it is," Brown looked straight ahead, "and Tesla don't lie."

They continued through intersections at La Cienega and San Vincente before turning left on Doheny. A little more than a mile on Santa Monica Boulevard was still ahead.

"By the way," Judith piped up again. "We have a dinner reservation at Maude tonight."

"We?" Charlie asked.

"Maude?" Murphy also had a question.

"Don't ask questions," Judith admonished them both. "It's Luca's treat."

"Well then," Charlie started.

"Don't go there," Judith cut her short, "we're just friends and he knows I'm leaving so he wanted to treat us to dinner."

"You're leaving?" Murphy was surprised.

"Friday," she said with a nod. "I've got a bar to run, remember?"

"So, back to dinner tonight," Charlie brought the conversation back.

"Yep. 7 o'clock. Luca says it's a 15 minute walk from the hotel. Oh, and Murphy?"

"Yes?"

"Luca is, in fact, a mime."

"Wwwhhhaaattt!?" Charlie blurted. Murphy just smiled.

"And if you bring it up before he does," Judith continued looking at the detective, "I swear I'll stab you in the eye with a fork."

"Understood," was all Murphy added.

"You said 7, right?" Charlie asked, Judith nodded. "I guess that means we have some time," she looked at Murphy and smiled. He smiled back.

"Maybe *you* do," he said, "I've got a meeting with Johnny "Jack" Maginnes."

"Well, aren't you lucky."

JOHNNY COME LATELY

After a quick pit stop upstairs Murphy jumped in the elevator and texted Maginnes that he was on his way. The captain met him when the elevator doors opened. They walked into The Club Room a little before the appointed meeting time. The room was mostly bar and it was impressive. Made out of a rich wood, it was fronted by at least a dozen chairs waiting for butts. Murphy let out a little whistle.

"I read in the hotel brochure that this bar is made out of California Birch," Maginnes said. "They must have let them build it before the tree huggers got wind of it."

Several bottles of various liquors were perched, along with a variety of glassware, on shelves behind the bar. The room was softly lit thanks to at least a dozen lamps mounted on walls and columns. Murphy counted several tables, each with a small candle perfectly placed in the center. The carpet was thick and lush, bordering on spongy, and like the rest of the room it was luxurious. On the opposite end from the entrance was a wood burning fireplace, logs and kindling waiting for a match. The room smelled like cedar smoke, bourbon, and money.

In the very left, back, corner of the room a man sat at one of the cloth-covered tables. Save for the bartender, Murphy, and Maginnes, he was the only other person in the place. Murphy thought that a little odd considering happy hour had already started. Figuring it had to be Maginnes' man Henley, Murphy allowed himself a closer look. The man's hair was blonde, short and stuck straight up from the top of his rather round head. He wore a not new in years blue sports coat over a white dress shirt which was open at the collar. From a distance, and Murphy would discover even up close, it was impossible to tell how old he was. He couldn't see what type of pants Henley had on but the detective could see one shoe poking out from under the tablecloth. It appeared to be a well-worn Nike sneaker. Henley looked down at his drink as if looking for answers in the liquid then grabbed the glass and took an impressive gulp. He closed his eyes clearly savoring the cocktail.

"That's my guy," Maginnes said on approach.

"I figured." The man set his glass back on the table and looked up.

"Katrek!" he said greeting the captain.

"Hello Chris," Maginnes responded, "Maginnes works too," he added. Henley looked at him like a third eye had suddenly popped up on Maginnes's forehead. "It's my given name," the captain said shrugging.

"No kidding," Chris said and looked at the detective. "You must be Murphy Murphy." The detective gave him an almost imperceptible nod. "Is that *your* given name?"

"It is."

"Well, alrighty then," he took another sip, "I like parents with a sense of humor."

"I assure you," Murphy countered, "a sense of humor had absolutely zero to do with it."

"What are you drinking?" Maginnes attempted to change the subject.

"It's one of their signature drinks," Henley went with the flow, "they call it My Buddy Bolden."

"What's in it?"

"Bruichladdich scotch, Talisker 10, lemon, honey, and ginger."

"Wow!" Maginnes said. Murphy saw him actually lick his lips. "Is it as good as it sounds?"

"Better be," Henley said swirling what was left in the glass around a single, large, crystal clear, ice cube, "for twenty-two bucks. I told the barman I was meeting a couple of guests so this is on you," he raised the glass

Murphy's way then brought it to his lips and poured what was left in it down his throat.

"Shocker," Murphy said.

Have a seat fellas," Henley waved an arm as an invitation, "let's get this party started". Suddenly the bartender appeared.

"Can I get you gentlemen anything to drink?"

"I'll have one of those," Maginnes said pointing to Henley's empty glass.

"And I'll have a refill," Henley added.

"For you sir?" the bartender asked Murphy Murphy.

"Jameson. Neat."

"Of course," the man said, "and will this be a room charge?"

"It will," Murphy answered and gave him his room number.

"Very good Mr. Murphy," the barkeep said and walked away.

"How did he know my name?" Murphy asked.

"Good business," Maginnes replied, "the guy knows every name associated with every room number. It gives it the personal touch."

"I think it's creepy," Murphy settled in.

"Thanks for meeting us, Chris," Maginnes said.

"No worries and call me Kip."

"Not Don?" Murphy asked. Henley theatrically slapped his knee with his hand.

"Wow, you know detective, you're the first one who came up with that," Henley said without humor. "No, not Don."

"Why Kip?" it was Maginnes who asked. Henley looked away from Murphy and at the captain.

"When I was a little my kid brother couldn't say Christopher. It came out 'Kip kup er'. Kip stuck, I guess." The drinks came and the men touched glasses then took sips.

"Mmmm, that's tasty," Maginnes said.

"So, fellas," Kip after a sip of his own, "what can I do for you?" He asked even though Maginnes had already filled him in. Murphy didn't like that but decided it was just one more thing about the guy he didn't like. The detective laid out the plan with Maginnes filling in any gaps.

"When would you like me to start?"

"As far as I'm concerned you've already started," Murphy said with a nod toward Henley's cocktail.

"First thing tomorrow morning would be great," Maginnes interjected. Murphy handed him a piece of paper on which he had written Katterwomp's name and title as well as the address for the Commission on Cliches.

"9 AM should be early enough," Murphy said.

"Perfect," Kip said then he turned his attention to the bar. "My good man," he said a little too loudly, "uno mas por favor." The bartender nodded. Murphy hadn't even seen the man drain his glass.

"And I'll take the check," Murphy added.

YOU GET WHAT YOU PAY FOR

The fire crackled and popped. Adalindis Katterwomp sat with his back to it. The heat from the flames warmed him as he put pen to paper.

My Precious Bonnie, he wrote.

You have been the apple of my eye for what seems like a coon's age. I know you think your heart belongs to Roger but now the time is ripe for me to fill this aching void and bring an end to this eternal triangle. I'm finished chasing rainbows and am prepared to promise you cakes and ale.

It was one of at least a hundred letters of affection he had written to a happily married woman who had never once shown any interest in a man other than her husband. But Katterwomp paid that no mind. He had first laid eyes on Bonnie Willows James at a cocktail function for the commission on cliches. The fact that she was clearly in love with her husband on that, and every subsequent, occasion at which he had observed her didn't stop him from pursuing a lost cause. The torch for her, which he still carried, was lit.

Murphy Murphy and the Case of the Commission on Cliches

He had actually mailed the first few dispatches directly to the object of his affections and even summoned his courage and approached her at one social gathering hoping to arrange a romantic rendezvous. She stopped him short responding that would happen "when hell freezes over." Rebuffed and now burdened by this unrequited love Katterwomp did a slow boil. Such that subsequent letters were shredded, set ablaze, or secreted away in various dumpsters and trash bins around the city. He even cut two of them up into tiny pieces and chewed then swallowed them with his morning juice.

But he also kept the ones he felt were particularly entrancing. Those went into a 1954 Superman cartoon lunch box which he had purchased at auction for $16,452. It was paid for with taxpayer money, of course. The treasure trove of love letters currently rested in the box at the bottom of a locked file cabinet in his office.

I am now, as I've always been, head over heels for you he wrote a final line or two. *A little bird told me the main impediment to our being together will soon vanish into thin air.*

Your tower of strength,
Adalindis

He admired his handiwork and then poured himself another glass of Taylor's Fladgate 1863 Single Harvest

Tawny Port. *Tomorrow I'll be in the catbird seat* he thought and he propped his feet up and sipped.

Dinner at Maude was delightful. The food was delicious, the conversation stimulating and no one was stabbed in the eye with a utensil. After a pleasant stroll back to the hotel and a nightcap Murphy, Charlie, and Judith were all in their rooms ready for bed. Nobody had to be anywhere the next day. Ron Howard had given the cast and crew the rest of the week off and Murphy Murphy was at the mercy of a scotch whiskey loving, private eye friend of Captain Maginnes for information about Katterwomp and his commission on cliches. Judith had informed them she was going to Malibu on Wednesday, so Charlie and Murphy would be on their own. The detective wanted to shop for records while Charlie wished for a Chinese chicken salad from Joan's on Third. They agreed that both could be accomplished when the sun came up. All that was left was snuggling, making love, and going to sleep.

An atypical, unfriendly looking, overcast day, complete with intermittent drizzle, greeted the inhabitants of and visitors to the City of Angels on Wednesday.

"Oh gross," Charlie said after throwing open the curtains. "I thought it never rains in California," she said turning to her detective boyfriend.

"Only in the warped mind of Albert Hammond," Murphy said climbing out of the bed. "Wanna shower with me?" he said as he padded toward the bathroom, "by the time we're clean and dry the rain will have stopped."

"I thought you'd never ask," she followed shedding what little sleepwear she wore along the way.

The last time Murphy was record shopping in LA he purchased vinyl at Amoeba Records, Record Jungle and stopped a robbery at Rockaway Records. This time he hoped to avoid petty criminals while patronizing establishments including Mount Analog, Atomic Records and The Poo Bah Record Shop. One was in Pasadena, another in Burbank and Mount Analog, widely considered LA's best, was on Figueroa street in Highland Park. It was also the closest to Joan's on Third so that's where the record shopping began.

Murphy had been correct. The precipitation had ended and the clouds were beginning to break when their Uber arrived. He was on the hunt for a copy of *Klemperer Conducts Mozart/Symphonies* but was disappointed to find out Mount Analog only had it in an SACD format. Murphy Murphy didn't want a CD. The extremely helpful salesperson did point out the store was in possession of a used copy of *Orchestre Hewitt Mozart Symphonie OG Fr* and Murphy was thrilled to find it in excellent condition. It was a little more than the vinylphile wanted to spend but it would certainly be a welcomed edition to his already impressive Mozart collection.

Charlie brought to the detective's attention that the store also had a copy of *Classical Kids Perform the Best of Mozart* but Murphy Murphy didn't find that revelation particularly amusing. In the end she added a still unopened *The Wild, the Innocent and the E Street Shuffle* by Bruce Springsteen, Sanford and Townsend Band's *Smoke from a Distant Fire,* Post Animal's *Forward Motion Godyssey,* and *Albert Hammond's Greatest Hits,* because of the conversation that morning and the fact that she was surprised the record even existed, to their haul. By the time they left the store it was time for lunch.

Mr. Katterwomp had spent a fitful night. Tossing and turning and finally giving up the ghost and getting out of bed just after 5 AM. He paced around his house for an hour before deciding to go to the office and pace around there. Beating the guard to work he parked the silver Escalade in his usual spot and went inside. Ten minutes after entering the office and settling into the chair behind his desk he was snoring.

Nine o'clock came and went but at ten minutes after 10 AM Kip Henley rolled up to the address he was given by Murphy Murphy the evening before. He was running a little later than promised because without the detective picking up the bar tab the private eye found it necessary to move from The Club Room at the Pennisula Hotel to the much more modest Tiki Ti Lounge. He knew the scotch was watered down but after three My Buddy Boldens a couple of weakened

Murphy Murphy and the Case of
the Commission on Cliches

Cutty Sarks was just what the doctor ordered. He turned off of 18th and on to the entrance way to the Los Angeles Center for Enriched Studies. Before approaching the guard kiosk Henley checked his watch, *10:12* he thought to himself, *right on time*. He rolled down the window of his ten-year-old Prius and rolled to a stop waiting for the guard to come out. He watched as a comely brunette came out of the little building. She had long legs, a slim waist, and Henley couldn't help but notice she filled out her rent-a-cop uniform top quite nicely. He also thought she looked a little mean which made her all the more attractive.

"Hello Toots. You're sure easy on the eyes," he said smiling what he thought was his most appealing smile. "What's a good-looking dame like you doing in a joint like this?"

"Nice try Bogie," she didn't smile back, "I gotta tell you that's the first time anyone's ever called me Toots. What do you want?"

"It's a term of endearment," Henley smiled again. "Did you like it?"

"No. It's not," the guard remarked, "and not even a little."

"Hey now," he raised both hands as if in surrender, "I think we got off on the wrong foot."

"No *we* didn't."

"I meant no disrespect," he tried again.

"Could have fooled me," the guard said, this time she did smile. "But I'm willing to give you another chance. What do you want?" she asked again.

"I may not be Bogart but I am a private investigator," he dug his credentials out of the glove box and showed her. "I've been tasked with keeping an eye on someone named Katterwomp. Can you do a working stiff a solid? Is he here?"

"Full disclosure?" she started to answer, "today is my first day on this job. The guy that preceded me didn't bother to come to work today so I got the call."

"What a coincidence," he stopped her, "it's my first day too."

"Apropos of absolutely nothing," she rebuked him. "Anyway, the notes I was given do indicate an Adalindis Katterwomp does have an office here and he drives a silver Cadillac Escalade which," she pointed down the road, "happens to be parked right there."

"What kind of name is Adalindis Katterwomp?" Henley was bemused.

"Pretty sure it's Paluaian," she said with a straight face.

"Makes sense," he said with a nod.

"Does it?" she asked then said, "his car has been there since I arrived at 6:20 this morning."

"Interesting," Henley said rubbing his chin with his right hand hoping it made it look like he was interested.

"I can't tell you for certain that means *he's* here or just his car is here."

"Good point," Kip said. "I'll just have to hang out here with you and find out."

"Finding out is *your* job but it's my job to tell you your job has to be done somewhere other than on this property."

"Fair enough," he conceded. "How about I buy you a drink later as a thank you?"

"That's certainly an intriguing offer," she said.

"I sense a but."

"*But* you're not my type."

"You're afraid I'm too much of a good thing?"

"Something like that," she walked back to her booth. Henley took his time watching her retreat then he wheeled the Prius around to the exit side of the kiosk. The guard held out her left hand, a slip of paper was between the first two fingers. Kip stopped and grabbed it. He saw a phone number.

"I'm Chris by the way," he said. "I don't even know your name."

"Hi Chris by the way," she said, "I'm Lauren Bacall."
He didn't believe her.

EAGER FOR THE FRAY

Elena James worked her dogs as they performed their daily dance with three of the four elephants. She loved how smart the canines were, the pachyderms too. Timothy, was slightly smaller and a little more aggressive, than the other Australian Cattle dog, Dundee. Elena surmised it was because early in their time together Dundee had gotten a little too close to the big elephant Bertha and found out an Asian elephant's trunk can launch a 40 pound dog a decent distance. She whistled and clucked commands as Timothy darted around and between the three elephants. Most times the giant mammals went wherever they wanted to go but when Timothy was around it was a different story.

Katterwomp woke with a start and a stiff neck. Sleeping upright in his office chair had a tendency to end with that result. He wiped a glob of drool from the side of his mouth with a shirtsleeve, got out of the chair and stretched. He hemmed and hawed about what to do next. A check of the cuckoo clock on the wall revealed he had several more hours before his date with destiny and Roger James.

"I'm within an ace of everything I've always wanted," he said quietly to the tiny bird that had appeared from within the clock. He picked the latest missive to Bonnie off his desk and deposited it in the Superman lunch box with the rest, locked the cabinet, and put the key back in its hiding place inside the clock on the wall. "But James is not just any Tom, Dick, or Harry," he prattled on to no one since the bird had retreated. "I'm not going to be able to wing it tonight." A thought occurred to him so he grabbed his car keys and left the office. "Forewarned is forearmed," he said as the elevator doors closed.

Kip Henley had pulled off to the side of the road on 18th street and he was trying to come up with ways to get into the good graces of the security guard. It was just about lunch time so he wondered if it might be a good idea to bring her something to eat. *Maybe Lauren Becall would like a Carl Reiner dog* he was thinking of his go to order from Pinks. A nine inch hot dog with mustard and sauerkraut. As his stomach rumbled the silver Cadillac SUV pulled out onto the street.

Katterwomp had made up his mind that his best course of action would be to scope out the situation at the L A zoo. The guard at the kiosk waved as he passed but the head of the commission on cliches was too busy tapping out a text to notice.

Roger,

Murphy Murphy and the Case of
the Commission on Cliches

I am trying to crack the code and figure out why our meeting must happen at the zoo tonight at 11. And the elephant exhibit to boot. I haven't got a clue. Please explain.

While he waited for an answer, he pulled one of his favorite CDs from a case attached to the sun visor, **Change in the Weather** by The Montana Band. He slid the disc into the slot and put track number one on repeat. **The Shoe is on the Other Foot Tonight** started to play. Then his phone dinged indicating the answer he was waiting for had arrived.

If you want the book you'll be there. The gate off Zoo drive near Australia House will be unlocked.

"He seems to be getting too big for his britches," Katterwomp said of his adversary. The song played on. "It's clearly time to knock him down a peg." He reached for the knob and turned up the song. Katterwomp pulled on to the entrance ramp for the 10 Freeway going east and merged into traffic. Henley, in the Prius, was five cars back.

Charlie and Murphy walked hand-in-hand through the Storrier Stearns Japanese Gardens in Pasadena. Atomic Records held no treasures so they came and went without a purchase.

"Babe?" Charlie had asked as they left the shop.

"Yes, my love."

"Do we really need to go to The Poo Bah Record Shop?" Charlie wondered after they had gotten in the Uber.

"We don't *need* to do anything," was Murphy's answer. "What would you like to do?"

"A park would be nice," she answered, "as you predicted it has turned out to be another lovely day."

"A park it is," he squeezed her hand.

"Storrier Stearns is nice," the Uber driver had said.

The Japanese gardens had been there since the 1930's and featured bridges, ponds, a 25 foot waterfall, and a winding riverbed shaded by oaks and sycamores. The most impressive part of the park was the authentic Twelve Tatami Mat teahouse.

"I've made an executive decision," Murphy said as Charlie sipped from a beautiful porcelain cup.

"What's that?"

"I think it's time to go home," he said. Charlie smiled. "I mean," he continued, "LA is nice and all but it seems I'm no longer needed by the commission on cliches. There's a ton of work to do at the precinct that I've neglected for too long and when you stop and think about it how much movie sausage making can two people stand?"

Murphy Murphy and the Case of
the Commission on Cliches

"Ron Howard does seem to have everything under control," Charlie agreed, "and Matthew is here in case something comes up." Murphy nodded. "Besides, Gaston reminded me he booked Tame Impala to play at The Gas Pump this weekend. They're selling out arenas these days so this is a tremendous get and I'd love to see them."

"I'd *hate* to be the reason you missed *that*!" Murphy said, "what's a tame impala?"

"Why it's a domesticated, diurnal, medium sized antelope found in eastern and southern Africa silly."

"Well played," Murphy congratulated her.

"Or it's a psychedelic rock band from Australia. I can't remember which one Gaston booked. You really need to get out more my dear."

"I *am* seeing Twenty-two Pilots tonight," Murphy said in his defense.

"Twenty-one," Charlie said with a punch on the arm for emphasis.

"Twenty-one, twenty-two, whatever it takes," he said.

"Okay Michael Keaton."

"Let's get the check. I'm going to see if we can get on the same flight as Judith."

"That would be fantastic."

"Speaking of Twenty-one Pilots," Murphy got it right, "we should get back to the hotel and get ready for the show."

"I'll order up another Uber," Charlie said.

"Your boy is on the move," Kip was talking to captain Maginnes.

"Where to?"

"He just took the exit for the 134. Looks to me like he's either going to the Griffith Park Observatory or the zoo."

"Or the Harding Park golf course," Maginnes said from memory.

"This is Katterwomp I'm following," Henley said, "not you."

"Fair point," the captain admitted. "Stay with him and keep me posted."

"You got it."

Katterwomp was indeed headed for the zoo. He turned onto Zoo drive, a road that circled the facility. Henley was well aware that the traffic had thinned considerably so he peeled off, parked and waited. Thirty minutes later he was still sitting there.

"This guy is either enjoying the penguin show or I lost him, "Kip admitted to Maginnes on the phone.

Murphy Murphy and the Case of
the Commission on Cliches

"I guess head back to the commission on cliches and see if he turns up," Maginnes suggested which made Henley think of the security guard again.

"Great idea!" he said a little too enthusiastically.

IT'S ALL GREEK TO ME

"I'm going to miss you folks," Do It Up Brown said to the group, "even you detective Murphy." They had gathered at Katsuya on San Vicente in Brentwood. Dinner had been arranged, as a thank you, by Ron Howard and the studio. "I just hope when you're back in town you ask for me," the driver added. Dishes of yellowtail jalapeno, steamed edamame, and spicy tuna with crispy rice were brought to the table.

"Chef Uechi has prepared a special feast for you," the decidedly non-Japanese server announced.

"I hope Robata vegetables are included," Charlie said.

"But of course," the girl assured her. "Now, what about cocktails? We have some delicious specialty drinks as well as an amazing selection of sake." The group, except for the driver took advantage of the offer. Brown ordered a Diet Coke.

"Giucigui suggested we arrive at the Greek between 7:30 and 8," Murphy told everyone. He looked at Do It Up and continued. "He said to go around to the artist entrance, they'll be expecting us."

"I know exactly where that is," he replied.

"Why doesn't that surprise me," the detective said as the waitress brought the drinks.

Dinner at the James house was again quite a bit more pedestrian, pizza and beer was on the menu. Three pies from Wood were being picked up by Elena while Bonnie and Roger sipped from glasses. A mug for her, a tulip for him. On Roger's 50th birthday Elena had purchased two Kegerators for the home's outside dining area. One was always ready to dispense Guinness for him, the other rotated between pilsners, ales, and porters. Currently Bonnie was enjoying a Montauk Wave Chaser IPA. Elena had prepared both drinks. Her mother had run the errand Elena had asked her to run and now both knew there was room for an extra ingredient in Roger's beverage. Just a pinch of the sedative Xylazine would put Roger down for the count. Mother and daughter knew just how much to include because Elena had used the unorthodox medication when sleep was elusive during the earliest days after Granderson's death. Elena delivered the drinks to her parents before leaving to fetch the pizzas. Roger always marveled at his daughter's ability to execute the perfect Guinness pour.

The evening meal for Adalindis Katterwomp consisted of him, alone, sitting in a booth at a restaurant called A Fine Kettle of Fish. A basket of deep friend cod pieces and chips was on the table, getting colder by the minute. He glanced at his watch and knew he still had several hours before the meeting with Roger James. The commissioner had no idea how he would occupy the time between now and then.

"I feel like a cat in a burlap sack," he said to the French fries as he waited.

A couple dozen feet away Kip Henley sat at the bar nursing a Miller Lite. His back was to his quarry but he could see every move Katterwomp made in the mirror behind the bar. So far those moves consisted of ordering his food and not eating it.

"You don't have a chicken dish on the menu," he said to the woman behind the bar. She shook her head. "A burger?" he asked.

"We have a tuna burger," she offered, "it's really good."

"I can't imagine," he mumbled.

"Dude," she took a step closer, "you're in a restaurant call A Fine Kettle of Fish. What in the world did you expect?"

"I've eaten at a Steak and Ale before," he answered, "and they have both chicken *and* salmon on their menu."

"We are *not* Steak and Ale," she huffed.

"Clearly," he said before taking another glance at the menu. "how's the clam chowder?" he asked.

"Better than Steak and Ale's," was her answer.

"Geez, sensitive," he whispered then ordered a bowl.

Henley had lost Katterwomp earlier in the day but picked him back up when the man returned to the building complex on 18th street. While the commissioner was inside, he made another run at the guard in the kiosk. She was just as non-committal this time as the last. He still had her phone number on the piece of paper in his pocket but he was afraid to call it for fear of being connected to a massage parlor or worse, an insurance agency. Katterwomp had been inside for several hours so Henley had plenty of time to reposition the Prius giving him a good look at the silver Escalade. As the sun started sinking in the western sky Adalindis exited the building and walked quickly to his SUV. Henley could see a briefcase in his right hand. The case currently sat at Katterwomp's feet inside the booth, the man fidgeted with his hands alternating between wringing them and drumming his fingers on the table. They never reached for a piece of fish. Henley felt he was looking at a man with a lot on his mind. He took the time to update Maginnes on the situation.

"Katterwomp is currently not eating his dinner at a seafood joint in West Hollywood," the captain read the text out loud. Across the table Murphy Murphy listened.

"I've been doing some thinking," Murphy said to his boss, "and I'm not sure it's wise to continue to expend resources keeping an eye on this character."

"It was your idea," Maginnes reminded him.

"I know cap but that was then and this is now."

"That was then was only 24 hours ago."

"Again, true but think about it," Murphy took another sip of sake as he thought about it. "I'm no longer technically involved in the case, a case that was only mildly interesting in the first place *and* we're going home on Friday."

"I'm staying for a few more days," Maginnes submitted.

"Why?"

"I'm not as convinced as you that Katterwomp is harmless," he said despite the fact that he firmly believed Katterwomp was harmless. He wasn't about to tell his detective that he had a tee time at the very exclusive Los Angeles Country Club on Friday and one at Sherwood Country Club on Saturday.

"I'm betwixt and between," Murphy lamented. "I hate to leave a case unsolved, but I just can't come up with a good reason to give a rip about the commission on cliches and its silly little book any longer," Murphy saw Maginnes nod.

"I'll call Henley off," he said, "but I'm still hanging around for the weekend."

"Suit yourself," Murphy responded as Maginnes tapped out a text.

Henley had laid his phone on the bar and was about to dump a small bag of Westminster Bakers Company oyster crackers into his steaming bowl of chowder when he got the notification.

Mission update Maginnes had typed *You are now 10-42.*

The private eye knew that was cop code for a policeman ending his assignment or tour of duty. He stared at the message for a few seconds lamenting the fact that a decent paycheck for doing a lot of nothing was going away, then another text appeared.

Your check is in the mail.

"It's *your* dumbass," he remarked to the phone then he pulled a wad of cash out of his pocket, peeled off a twenty and tossed it on the bar. He glanced one last time at Katterwomp still sitting in the booth, his dinner uneaten, then pushed his stool back from the bar and stood.

"I'm off to In 'n Out Burger," he announced to the bartender and walked out into the Southern California night. He still had almost a week's worth of per diem in his pocket and a pretty girl's phone number, so he thought *what the heck*. He dialed the digits and waited.

"This is Lauren," the voice announced.

Do It Up Brown parked the Tesla inside the gate right next to Matthew Laurance's Bel Air. Murphy, Charlie, Judith, and Maginnes climbed out of various doors and were greeted by Serious Crisis manager, Jeff Giucigui. The actor was alongside.

"Looking good Guice," Charlie said giving the man a hug.

"Feeling good Charlie," he offered a peck on the cheek. "How's Gas?" he asked referring to her brother and his college friend, Gaston.

"Good as always," she said.

"Glad to hear it," he then turned to the rest of the group. "let's get going," he said as he started to walk away, "there are a lot of people excited to see you."

They walked past several tractor trailers, a couple of portable power generators, and a satellite tv truck before getting to the first of the band's buses. Murphy saw a few familiar faces from the case and waved to Jimmy Dimsum and Olive Green as they were busy bringing instruments and other paraphernalia out of the fancy motor vehicle. Murphy noticed another, unfamiliar roadie crawling around the belly bays. He was lanky, had long blonde hair pulled back in a ponytail, and wore a Paul Cherry Band hoodie.

"Who's that?" he asked the manager.

"New guy, Brian Hammons," Jeff said. Goes by Hammer."

"Everybody goes by something," Murphy replied. "Where's Marty Kaufmann?" He asked about another member of the Serious Crisis road crew who Murphy once considered a solid suspect in the case that involved the band a few years before.

"Marty's gone," was all Giucigui offered.

"He left? Or you fired him?"

"His idea. About seven months ago he got a job offer from a magazine specializing in Scotch whiskey and golf called *Peat and Pars*." Murphy recalled the man had been a writer for a golf magazine based in Orlando, Florida before pulling up stakes and reinventing himself as a roadie. "Writing, drinking scotch, and playing golf," Giucigui continued, "three things he decided he liked better than schlepping gear and tuning guitars."

"MURPHY!" a female voice screamed. The entire group stopped and turned toward the sound in time to see Lyndsay Howlund barreling toward them. "It's soooo good to see you!" she said skidding to a stop right in front of the detective. She threw her arms around him. "Hi Uncle Matt," with her face buried in Murphy's chest she also acknowledged her actor uncle.

"You too Lynds," he hugged her back. "How are you?"

"You know, I fall down, I rise up. No harmful injuries."

"Good to hear," Murphy said although he didn't think any of what Lyndsay had just said was good to hear.

"And look!" she held her hand out palms down. "I stopped biting my nails forever and ever!"

"That's great news."

"Come on you guys," Lyndsay put her hands down and backed away from Murphy, "DeMaio, Big Joe, and Chuckie Gruber are all waiting on the bus."

Roger James stood at the sink rinsing off the dinner plates and putting them in the dishwasher. Elena and Bonnie sat in front of the television watching *Love it or List it*. Cooper lay, belly up, on the floor between them. Dishes in their place James started the appliance and yawned. He walked back into the living room and addressed the girls.

"Suddenly I'm bushed," he admitted, "I've got a little time before my rendezvous with Katterwomp so I'm going to go grab forty winks."

"Okay dear," Bonnie said absentmindedly.

"Will you make sure to wake me if I'm not up by 10?" he asked his wife.

"Sure. Sure," she waved a hand his way then turned to Elena, "do you think they are going to love it or list it?" she asked her daughter.

"Detective Murphy! My man!"

"Hello Big Joe," Murphy gave the band's bass player a handshake.

"Can I pour you a glass of wine?" the big man asked. Murphy shook his head. He was still pleasantly buzzed thanks to the top shelf sake.

"I'd love a glass," it was Judith.

"Coming right up, Joe said grabbing a red plastic cup and a half-filled bottle of red. "Excuse the elegant stemware," he laughed. "This is our Lionn's Den Pinot Noir," he proudly displayed the bottle, label out. "It's getting rave reviews."

"Your winery?" Judith was impressed.

"My *grapes*," he corrected her, "we've teamed up with a great boutique winery called Kosta Browne in California. I am the proud owner of twenty acres of prime mineral rich land in the Russian River appellation. It's great soil for growing Pinot grapes."

"Good for you Joe," Murphy congratulated him. "How's business?"

"It would be a lot better if Joe didn't suck up all the profits," DeMaio Turrell, the band's front man, gave his bass player grief.

"He's literally correct," Joe said as he took a gulp.

"Hello Walter," Murphy used the Turrell's given name. "You're looking well."

"Thanks man," he nodded, "I'm taking care of myself," he said before taking a long hit off a vape pen. Turrell and Chuckie Gruber were the band's original founders putting the group together in Chicago.

"Where's Herbie?" Murphy asked after the drummer.

"Is that *Mags!?*" Turrell looked at the police captain before taking another vape hit.

"It is DeMaio," Maginnes answered, "good to see you."

"You look like a cop," Turrell said releasing a plume of smoke.

"Herbie is in the other bus," Lionns answered Murphy's question. "he's bending John Gordon Leavitt's ear about drumming. Probably showing him his new whip."

"Joseph," Murphy corrected him.

"Who picked Trace Adkins to play me?" the bassist had moved on to the next subject. "Not that I mind, I mean I like Trace. It's just why couldn't it have been Tim McGraw?"

"Beggars can't be choosers," Laurance chided him.

"Says the guy who gets to play himself." Joe took another sip from his cup. Laurance simply shrugged.

"How did you find out about the cast?" Murphy wondered.

"I read **People**," Joe was unashamed.

"And a bunch of them came to last night's show," Lyndsay added. "It was crazy cool to be in close proximity to so many movie stars." Murphy bit his tongue.

"Okay kids," Giucigui had stuck his head in the door, "let's get you guys to your seats the Pilots are about to go on."

"Can't we just watch from backstage?" Judith asked.

"Sure," Turrell answered, "if you want to stand up the entire time, not see very much, and get distorted audio."

"Party pooper," Judith admonished him.

"Is Mo Mo around?" Murphy asked about the group's blind audio engineer Morris Morrisey.

"No, he's a square," Turrell deadpanned.

"That joke wasn't funny the first hundred times you told it DeMaio," Lionns said shaking his head.

"Bullshit Big Joe!" Turrell shot back. "It's big time and you know it." He added a laugh.

"I'm sure Mo Mo is wandering around somewhere," Gruber got things back on track.

"If he hasn't stolen another golf cart," Big Joe added before finishing off what was left of his wine.

"He's probably chatting up some groupies somewhere trying to get a date," Turrell had to have the last word.

"No dates tonight," the manager interrupted.

"I guess *you're* the party pooper," Judith said.

"Not usually," Jeff shrugged, "it's just that we've got to hit the road right after tonight's show. We're expected in Las Vegas first thing tomorrow morning because we're filling in for Aerosmith at the Park MGM. Four straight nights and it's the first time we've been there so I want to make sure everything is just right."

The group heard a roar of applause coming from a sold-out crowd. Twenty-One Pilots had taken the Greek Theatre stage. The bass riff that begins the song, *Jumpsuit* drifted through the bus's open door.

"Showtime," Giucigiu said with childlike excitement. A mere five miles from the roaring crowd everything was quiet at the L A zoo's elephant exhibit. For the time being.

THE CHICKENS COME HOME TO ROOST

Twenty-One Pilots had delivered a rousing set so when the song, *Trees*, came to its electronic end, the roar from more than five thousand fans was deafening.

"Those guys are fantastic," Judith said.

"Not really my cup of tea," Murphy replied, "but they're talented for sure."

The group of six had watched most of the opening act from excellent seats in Section A, Row E. The sushi from earlier in the evening had little staying power so Charlie and Murphy shared Santorini Volcanic nachos and truffle fries from a surprisingly good concessions menu. Judith opted for more Lionn's Den wine. Big Joe had given her a bottle to take to her seat. At one point Do It Up Brown and Maginnes went to stand stage left. The driver admitted he had never seen a rock and roll show from that perspective. After a 45-minute pause it was time for Serious Crisis to perform. The crowd, if possible, seemed even more amped up.

"Hello Los Angeles!" DeMaio Turrell announced the band's presence. The audience reacted appropriately.

"How about another round of applause for our friends Twenty-One Pilots!" Lionns had joined Turrell at the microphone. "Big Joe! Big Joe! Big Joe!" chants reverberated through the grounds. Lionns took a deep bow.

"Thank you to the general public who bought tickets and to our invited guests who didn't!" Lyndsay Howlund spoke into her microphone and with that Herbie Albanese banged his drumsticks together counting the band into their opening song. It was the band's first number one hit, *Ascend Up the Ladder*.

Do you wanna box?" the waitress asked Adalindis Katterwomp. He looked at her then his food as if seeing both for the very first time.

"I'd rather wrestle," he said just loud enough for her to hear.

"*Excuse me*?" she asked, clearly offended. A-OK just stared at her. "Cat got your tongue all of a sudden?" she asked staring right back.

"My apologies," he said feeling his features soften, "you have every right to chew me out. That remark was insensitive by a long chalk."

"You're weird," she said before dropping the bill on the table and walking away.

Katterwomp suddenly realized he had killed several hours sitting in the booth wondering if he would chicken out or grab the bull by the horns. He considered that to be the burning question. He decided to brazen it out and proceed with the plan. He paid the check with one of the one hundred dollar bills from the briefcase and left the restaurant. He figured it would take somewhere around 45 minutes to get to the zoo and that would put him there before the agreed upon time.

"The early bird gets the worm," he said getting into the silver SUV and starting the Escalade. He pulled out of the restaurant parking lot unaware that James was already waiting for him.

"We want you all to give a shout out to the Fire Marshall," Turrell spoke to the crowd. Rivulets of sweat rolled down both sides of his face. "He's given us the okay to break curfew by a few minutes so we're going to play a little more for you guys." Murphy Murphy couldn't imagine the audience had anything left to give but he was wrong.

"We've got a new record currently being completed," Lyndsay spilled the beans. "It's called **Populated with People** and this will be the first single, *Looking Back in Retrospect*". Murphy stood stage right in awe of the amount of redundancies that emanated from the young lady. Lyndsay gave him a wink as she sat down at her keyboard and played the first few chords of the new song.

A-OK duplicated the route he had taken earlier in the day. The zoo drive was relatively well lit thanks to strategically placed dirty streetlamps emitting a slightly spooky yellowish hue. A three quarter moon provided additional illumination. A few stars were also visible thanks to a crystal clear night and a healthy amount of separation from the bright lights of the country's second largest city. The big silver gas guzzler rolled quietly toward Katterwomp's pre-planned stopping point. He lowered the driver's side window and listened to the night. An owl hooted in the distance. A-OK also heard what he believed to be monkeys chatter in response. There was also a roar but the commissioner had no idea from which type of big cat it had come.

"Why did I go along for this ride?" Katterwomp asked himself. "I should do an about face and pave the way for a more advantageous encounter." He saw Australia House in the distance and all second guessing stopped. *I might as well make a virtue out of necessity* he thought as he pulled the car to the side of the road and parked. Katterwomp opened the glove box, pulled out and put on a pair of Uplander shooting gloves, then extracted his fully loaded Smith and Wesson M & P Shield EZ 9MM pistol. He thumbed off the safety so he wouldn't have to remember to do it later and got out of the car.

"One more, one more, one more," the crowd screamed as one, but from the side of the stage Murphy felt like they were finally losing a little steam. Still, dots of light from thousands of phones lit up the amphitheater. It was close to 11 PM so Murphy knew the show was coming

to an end. Just then Chuckie Gruber led the band out as
Serious Crisis took the stage for an encore.

Katterwomp walked past the Tom Mankiewicz
Conservation Carousel, the gun in one hand the
briefcase in the other. He knew the Treetops Terrace
was just ahead and so was the Elephants of Asia
Exhibit. He was on tenterhooks following the paved
walkway and proceeded as quietly as possible although
he wasn't sure why. He was certain there wasn't
another human on the grounds save for maybe Roger
James.

"I hope you're ready to meet your Waterloo you old
sod," he whispered as he thought of his adversary. He
tightened his grip on the gun. Grunting noises
interrupted his soliloquy, briefly startling him, before
he realized they were coming from the fenced in Congo
Gorilla Reserve on his left. He was just yards away now
from where he wanted to be.

"Okay. Alright. Okay. Just one more," Gruber told the
audience. "What do you want to hear?" He knew he had
made a mistake as soon as the words left his mouth.
Shouts of *"Fewer In Number"*, *"Unintended Mistake"*,
and *"Commute Back and Forth"* filled the night.
Gruber just laughed. "How about *Difficult Dilemma* he
offered as DeMaio Turrell played the songs first notes.

The gate to the elephant exhibit was unlocked as
promised. A-OK wasn't sure if that meant his adversary
had arrived before him or just arranged earlier in the

day for the coast to be clear. Not caring he stepped into the area and stopped. His rather pronounced proboscis was assaulted by smells of grass, dirt, and a musty scent which he assumed came from piles of elephant dung which he noticed. He made a mental note not to step in any of them. He also was sure he got a faint whiff of honey in the air. Katterwomp was slightly surprised he found none of it unpleasant. He avoided the poop and made his way toward a large tree.

"That's far enough!" a sinister, electronic, voice commanded. Startled, Katterwomp stopped dead in his tracks.

"Roger?"

"Don't talk!" the voice boomed.

"Why the bag of tricks, old friend?" A-OK asked.

"I said don't talk!"

"Wait a second, your voice sounds familiar. Are you supposed to be Darth Vader?" Katterwomp couldn't help but give a little giggle. James had indeed purchased a voice altering mask on the internet to add to the intrigue.

"I guess you're going to just keep on talking," James said, "and it's Kylo Ren, not Darth Vader."

"In the long run it makes no difference. Now it's time to fish or cut bait," Katterwomp raised the briefcase. "I came prepared to offer just compensation. I get my book back, you get the money and a one way ticket out of town. Now, where's the book?"

"The best laid plans as they say my old friend. I'm not going anywhere. Now, what's that in your other hand?" the voice of Kylo Ren asked knowing the answer.

"I see you kept your eyes peeled," A-OK said with a certain amount of appreciation. "It's just a little insurance."

"Insurance my foot," James rasped through the mask. "There's only one reason a man brings a gun to a book exchange."

"You're right, of course," Katterwomp admitted. "I've come to settle old scores."

"You know you never fooled anyone you dunderhead. You wore your disdain for me and your obsession for Bonnie on your sleeve. But you could never pull that particular rabbit out of your hat because you always had your head in the clouds. So, put that in your pipe and smoke it!""

"You'd know about having your head in the clouds, Roger. You and that silly cloud society. But you're off base, my Bonnie will see the error of her ways," Katterwomp countered. "As soon as you've met your maker."

"No. She won't!" James roared. "Your delusions of grandeur are going in one ear and out the other. They're nothing but a pipe dream! I intercepted your sophomoric love letters. Bonnie never saw them. She's head and shoulders above your station. Your chances with her were always as scarce as hen's teeth."

"ENOUGH!" the commissioner screamed back. "Your arguments are as dull as dishwater and equally useless." Katterwomp tried to fight back but James was on a roll.

"Despite never laying eyes on your childish attempts at romance Bonnie knew you were a creep the minute she met you and she still thinks you're a creep today," James continued his verbal assault. "She knew what you were up to. We *all* did."

Katterwomp didn't counter the claim this time. His mind raced. Something about what James said made him think. *What did he mean 'we all knew'?* he wondered. *Why would the man say 'we all knew'? and not "I knew", or Bonnie and I knew"?* Then it hit him like a bolt of lightning.

"Elena?" he asked, "Heavens to Betsy, is that you child?"

"It's time to slay the green eyed monster!" was the answer from behind the mask.

The next thing Katterwomp heard was two short, sharp whistles. The kind a person makes when they put their fingers in their mouth. That was followed by three loud "clucks". Somewhere nearby a dog yipped. Then Katterwomp felt 300 pounds of Asian elephant trunk blast him from behind. The briefcase flew a few feet in one direction, the pistol went the other way and the man hit the ground face first. The only thing that provided any cushion to his fall was his great big beak which broke on impact. A piece of a front tooth also chipped off and Katterwomp swallowed it. Blood and snot blended then seeped into the dirt.

"Help me!" he tried to shout through the pain, but the words came out a muddle. "I surely have one foot in the grave and am about to kick the bucket," his plea became a whimper. Five tons of pachyderm pressed down on his back squeezing out what was left of the man's breath and crushing the life from his body. James approached and removed the mask.

"Your life wasn't worth a plug nickel," James said staring down at the man who, thanks to hubris and a scam, had bilked the American taxpayers out of millions of dollars. The elephant stepped off and James stroked its trunk before gathering up the briefcase filled with cash and the gun. The only thing that remained was calling off the dogs.

THERE'S MORE HERE THAN MEETS THE EYE

The concert was long over and the gang had split up. Do It Up Brown shuttled Judith and Maginnes back to Beverly Hills while Murphy, Charlie, and Lyndsay accepted Matthew Laurance's invitation to join him at his Hollywood Hills home for a nightcap. Howlund got the go ahead only after agreeing to let Jeff Giucigiu pick her up when the band was ready to depart for Las Vegas. She threw a fresh change of clothes and her toothbrush in a duffle bag planning to shower at her uncle's.

"I made Basque burnt cheesecake in my new portable pizza oven and I need someone to help me eat it," the actor had sweetened the invitation. "It goes great with a Louis Royer XO cognac."

"Or a glass of chilly, cold milk," Lyndsay said.

"Or that."

The ride into the hills was relaxing. The Chevy's top was down so a nice breeze caressed everyone in the car. Laurance had cued up Southside Johnny and the Asbury Jukes and played it loud. The cheesecake was as good as promised so Charlie got the recipe after convincing Murphy Murphy they needed to purchase a portable pizza oven. Freshly showered, Lyndsay passed on the cake.

"It's an actual fact that cheesecake makes you fat," she said grabbing a fistful of Oreo Thins cookies to enjoy with her milk.

"I really need to sponsor you in 'Redundancies Anonymous'," Murphy told her.

"I imagine that would no doubt be therapeutic treatment," Laurance added much to Murphy's dismay.

"Could you two revert back to talking English," Lyndsay said before dipping another cookie into her glass.

"More cognac, please," Murphy lifted his snifter.

"That will be your last and final refill darling," Charlie joined in on the fun.

"You too?" Murphy shook his head. Everybody but Lyndsay laughed.

Eventually the singer's phone rang as Giucigiu called to say the caravan was ready to roll. He let Lyndsay know he'd be out front of Laurance's house in less than half an hour.

"I'm happy to order up an Uber for you two," the actor offered Murphy and Charlie, "or you can hunker down for the night here. I'm told the bed in my guest room is quite comfortable."

"That's a completely unanimous opinion," Lyndsay finished her glass and wiped the milk moustache off with her arm.

"That's a nice offer Matthew," Murphy began then looked at Charlie.

"Unlike your niece we aren't equipped with a change of clothes or a toothbrush." Murphy nodded.

"I completely understand," the actor said reaching for his phone and opening up the Uber application. A few seconds later he announced a car would be there in 12 minutes.

They said their goodbyes, wished each other good luck and safe travels. Laurance promised to get to The Gas Pump Lounge and Bar Flight in person one day and Charlie said she'd hold him to it. After a round of hugs, they went their separate ways. It was close to two in the morning when Charlie and Murphy finally slid into bed. They fell immediately to sleep. Three hours later Murphy's phone rang.

"You going to answer that?" Charlie asked in a sleepy voice.

"Let it go to voice mail," Murphy growled and rolled over. But the call didn't go to voice mail. After 15 seconds the phone started to ring again. Murphy grumpily got out of bed and grabbed the offending device.

"What?"

"Sorry to wake you detective," it was Maginnes.

"You don't sound all that sorry."

"You're right, I'm not," he admitted. "Have you seen the local news this morning?"

"You know you just woke me up," Murphy was still angry, "so, no."

"Turn on the TV. Channel 2. Then call me back."

"Why don't you just tell me what the heck is going on?" Murphy asked but his superior was already gone.

The detective went into the other room, found the remote and turned the television on to Channel 2. He had the volume all the way down so he couldn't hear what the news anchor was saying but he could read the graphic on the lower third of the screen.

Body found at the Los Angeles Zoo it read. Murphy hit redial on his phone.

"Why is some dead guy worthy of interrupting my beauty sleep?" he asked, still fuming.

"It's not just *some* dead guy. It's Katterwomp," Maginnes informed him.

"What's the emergency?" Charlie called from the other room.

"Looks like I'm not going home Friday after all," Murphy answered her.

"Honey!" Bonnie James called out. "Roger!" ROGER!!! Wake up!" she dropped the remote and rushed to the bedroom. Her husband layed on his side snoring peacefully, hands, seemingly in prayer, under his left cheek. Bonnie noticed a slight smile on his lips. Knowing there were now more important things than her husband's beauty rest she shook him awake.

"Roger James open your eyes," she commanded. He did.

"Bonnie. Darling," he said rolling on to his back and stretching both arms above his head. "I was just having the most wonderful dream about you and me."

"That's nice dear," she replied and smiled. "Slept well I take it?"

"Like a dead guy," he said stretching again. "Like a dead guy," he repeated.

"Speaking of dead guys," Bonnie retorted.

A TOUGH NUT TO CRACK

Murphy spent the next day and a half gathering as much information as he could about Katterwomp's untimely death. Most of the particulars of the peculiar passing came from accounts in the LA papers, local news, and a few online stories. National outlets including the New York Times, The Washington Post and The Wall Street Journal ignored the story apparently having no idea that this specific agency subsidized by the federal government had even existed. Let alone that its commissioner had perished under suspicious circumstances at the LA Zoo.

The detective put Charlie and Judith on an airplane home, kissing one of them goodbye. Since the studio was no longer picking up the tab for his lodging, he accepted his friend's generous offer of the guest room at Casa Laurance and moved his body and belongings there. He tried to assure the actor that he would do everything in his power to not be a pain in the butt and was informed that that ship had already sailed.

"It's comforting to know that even though Katterwomp's ticker has stopped his legacy of cliches remains unshackled," Murphy had said.

"Try not to get your nose out of joint," Laurance responded.

Murphy had decided early on that this was no accident so, as was his practice, he started a crime book. Compiling any and all information he could gather about Katterwomp, the Commission on Cliches, and the man's closest associates leading up to the moment of his death. The bizarre circumstances surrounding the night at the zoo also went into the book. At the same time, he huddled with Maginnes to explore ways to wrangle their way into the investigation. His boss still had contacts within the LAPD and he promised to exhaust every avenue to exploit those.

Both men wondered if or when Murphy might be questioned by the local authorities, but neither could be certain the cops knew or even cared about Murphy's ties to deceased. Sitting at a small desk in Laurance's guest bedroom, Murphy jotted down the things he knew about Adalindis Orval Katterwomp and what could have led to his final exit. The fact that Katterwomp's body was found in the elephant habitat at the zoo was especially interesting to the detective. *Why was he there? Did he die there or did he die somewhere else and was dropped there to confuse the police? Murder?* Murphy underlined the word three times. These were all questions that popped into Murphy's mind and then

he added another one, *does the book of cliches have
anything to do with it? Roger James?* And more lines
went under the name.

He knew he needed the LAPD's help, or more
specifically the county coroner, to answer many of the
questions so those would have to wait until Maginnes
could come through. But nothing was stopping him
from tracking down Roger James or finding out more
about the book. He picked up his phone and punched in
Maginnes's number.

"Hello Murphy," Maginnes answered on the third ring.
In the background Murphy heard what sounded like
golf balls being struck. "What's up?"

"I need to get into Katterwomp's office at the
Commission on Cliches. Any ideas?"

"One. Maybe."

"I'm all ears," Murphy said.

"Isn't that a cliché, detective?"

"Is it?"

"Not important," Maginnes admitted. "Remember our
friend Kip Henley?"

"How could I forget?"

"Good point," Maginness admitted again, "anyway I
think he might have an in over there."

"Give me his number please?" Murphy requested. Maginness did and Murphy dialed.

"Who dis?" was all Henley said when he answered Murphy's call.

"Who dis is not English," Murphy replied.

"Hello Detective Murphy," Kip said, "how's it hangin?"

"Since this conversation has started out in such a scintillating way I'll cut right to the chase. Maginness told me you might have a way to get me into the Commission on Cliches building. I need to get in there."

"Why? What has that weirdo done now?" Henley asked of Katterwomp.

"He died."

"Oh geez. Damn. When?"

"Sometime Wednesday night," Murphy answered.

"No kidding?"

"Just for the record, it's not my normal practice to kid about people dying."

"Big of you. What time Wednesday night?"

"What difference might that make to you?" Murphy wondered.

"Well depending on the TOD, that's time of death by the way."

"I know what TOD stands for," Murphy interrupted. Henley ignored him and kept talking.

"It might mean I was one of the last people to see him alive. If not the last."

"Did you kill him Kip?"

"What!?! Of course not. Why would you say something like that?"

"Well, you just said you might have been *the* last person to see Katterwomp alive. If that's true it just stands to reason that you did the deed." Murphy smiled, enjoying yanking the guy's chain.

"It was a figure of speech, detective. I didn't mean it liberally."

"Literally." Murphy corrected him

"That too," Henley agreed.

"Relax Kip," Murphy gave up the rouse, "I know you didn't kill the guy but why do you think you may have been one of the last people to see him alive?"

"Not over the phone," Henley demanded.

"Alright, whatever. Tell me about your in with the commission."

"I'm getting to know one of the guards."

"The fat guy?" Murphy asked. "Frankly I didn't see him as your type."

"A different guard thank you. And trust me *she* is not a fat guy."

"Can you meet me over there in an hour?" Murphy listened to Henley's suddenly muffled voice. "Hey what time do you go to work today?" he thought he heard.

"Make it two," Henley was back loud and clear.

"Why am I not surprised?" Murphy asked more of himself than Henley and he hung up. Two hours was just fine with Murphy. It gave him extra time to find out more about Roger James and work on the entrée to the LAPD. To that end he called his boss back.

"What now?" Maginnes barked.

"That's the question I was about to ask you," Murphy shot back. "Any progress on getting us involved with the Katterwomp case?"

"Maybe."

"Do tell."

"I found out the chap who caught the case is a dick named Scott McCarron."

"He's not a nice guy?"

"Not that kind of dick Murphy, a detective and a good one. Decent golfer too."

"Fascinating but what does his golf game have to do with anything?"

"Long story short. McCarron once won the department golf tournament 7 out of 10 years and six in a row."

"Impressive," Murphy said unimpressed.

"Damn right it is," Maginnes continued. "Do you know who the guy was that stopped that six straight streak?"

"How would I possibly know that?" Murphy asked.

"Because you're talking to him," Maginness said proudly.

"I think I liked you better when you were Brian Katrek," Murphy chided. "Anyway, I'm still struggling to find the relevance."

"It's relevant because in addition to being a good detective and a hell of a golfer Scott McCarron is damn good at carrying a grudge."

"You're kidding right?"

"Not even a little and that, my friend, could be a problem for us."

BEGGARS CAN'T BE CHOOSERS

Scott McCarron leaned back in his chair and steepled his fingers in front of his face. He was a decorated, seventeen year veteran of the force who had recently started seeing younger, less experienced, detectives "catching" the higher profile, much more interesting, cases he used to get. McCarron had solved his fair share of notable cases, chalking up big wins early in his career. He'd even been named "Detective of the Year" in an internal popularity contest as recently as a half a dozen years ago. But then he ruptured an achilles tendon in a pickup basketball game and lost his longtime partner, and best friend, to retirement. The injury took longer than expected to heal resulting in McCarron figuratively missing a step on the career ladder. That and his new partner, while good, was nowhere near as competent as his old one. He unsteepled his fingers and rubbed his forehead with his right hand.

Karen Free had come to be his new sidekick thanks to a program that fast tracked women and people of color in the department. McCarron inherently didn't have a problem with the initiative. In fact, he relished the opportunity to mentor someone the way he had been mentored. But so far the partnership had its ups and downs. The precinct had taken to calling the team "McKaren" which he actually thought was better than the early alternative of "Scott Free". He mused that no one dedicated to catching criminals wanted that particular moniker.

At this very moment Karen Free was in the middle of a City of Los Angeles mandated twelve week maternity leave so McCarron was working the case of someone named Adalindis Orval Katterwomp, mysteriously found dead in the middle of the Elephants of Asia exhibit at the zoo of all places, by himself.

"McCarron!" the desk sergeant yelled over the incessant buzz of the precinct. "Incoming!" Scott knew that meant he was about to get a phone call transferred from the desk. It was 20/80 that it would be anything meaningful and the detective dreaded the 80 per cent. His phone rang. He took a deep breath and answered.

"Detective McCarron my name is Murphy Murphy," the voice on the other end started in. "I am a fellow LEO who might be able to assist with your current investigation."

"Excuse me," McCarron was momentarily dumfounded, "can you repeat your name again?"

"Oh, not you too," Murphy lamented, "I'll happily repeat my name but you should know adding 'again' to your request is redundant. I'm detective Murphy Murphy."

"And detective Murphy Murphy how could you possibly know on which investigation I am currently at the present time working?" McCarron didn't even try to conceal his anger.

"Why couldn't it be anyone but this guy," Murphy said mostly under his breath before answering the question.

After hanging up with one current detective, McCarron immediately called a former one.

"Go for Maginnes," the now captain answered.

"Hey sandbagger," McCarron used a derogatory golf term reserved for players who claim a higher handicap than their skill level would dictate. It was a ruse used by some to ensure victory in tournaments.

"Gee whiz Mac, hold a grudge much?" Maginnes answered his old friend. "You still got the yips?" he asked referring to McCarron's inability to make short putts under pressure.

"Nah," he replied, "went to the broomstick putter a while back. Now I make everything."

"That's what anchoring will do for you pal," the captain said basically accusing his colleague of cheating.

"What the hell do you want?" McCarron asked, clearly angered by the conversation.

Murphy Murphy and the Case of
the Commission on Cliches

"Keep your powder dry big fella," Maginnes said with a chuckle, "you called me."

"Oh yeah," Maginnes could hear McCarron take a deep, cleansing breath. "Who the heck is the Michael Murphy character? He asked.

"The guy that wrote *Golf in the Kingdom* or the one who sang, *Wildfire*?"

"Neither wise guy. The detective."

"That's Murphy Murphy. He's one of my best *and* he can help you with the cliché guy case."

"The what guy?"

"The dead guy at the zoo. Cliché guy. The vic, Katterwomp, was head of the Commission on Cliches."

"The what on what?" McCarron was dumbfounded.

"Good grief Scotty you really do need our help. I'm in town for a few more days but I can make sure Murphy stays as long as you need him. Care to meet up?"

"I'd rather take a honey bath and hang out with a pack of grizzlies."

"It's a sloth," Maginnes replied.

"What's a sloth?

"A group of grizzly bears, dummy. You said pack but a group of grizzlies is called a sloth. Do you want to know why?" McCarron had already hung up. Then he immediately hit redial on Murphy Murphy's number.

"Meet me at the zoo in twenty minutes," he said after the detective picked up.

A smiling Murphy agreed and then called Kip Henley to reschedule. His next call was to Do It Up Brown and they worked out a deal for the man to drive Murphy around LA for the foreseeable future. He convinced Maginnes to approve the expense. Brown arrived and the two headed for the zoo arriving before detective McCarron. The driver agreed to wait in the car while Murphy went inside. He plopped down in a chair outside the zoo's CEO and Director and waited for the LAPD man to arrive.

Ten minutes later a man in a gray pinstripe suit entered. His hair was neatly coiffed, his shoes recently shined. The man's square jaw and smallish ears framed a handsome face. Murphy wasn't sure whether or not he was detective McCarron or a guy hired to play him on TV. Either way, Murphy stood to greet the newcomer.

"You must be Murphy," McCarron said without extending his hand.

"And you McCarron," Murphy replied as he did extend his.

"Nice to meet you, I think," McCarron shook it.

"Likewise."

"Let's get one thing straight," the LA man said still holding on tight to Murphy's right hand, "let me spell this out in detail." Murphy bit his tongue. "I'm bringing you in as a consultant, pure and simple," Murphy nodded, "and I'd appreciate it if you treat your role in this investigation accordingly. I just don't want you operating under a false pretense."

"You're the boss," Murphy acquiesced, "but can there ever be a 'true pretense'? he added. "Can I get a look at the crime scene?" Murphy quickly moved on.

"Don't see the harm in that but first let's go inside and speak to Miss Gable-Davis," McCarron said, the pretense question forgotten.

Bethany Gable-Davis sat behind her desk. A large, framed poster that read, *"Please Don't Feed the Animals. They'll Become Dependent and Will Soon Want Cell Phones"* hung on the wall behind her. Murphy thought she looked like she hadn't slept in days. Her eyes were red from crying.

"Welcome gentlemen," she managed a weak smile, "please sit down. I assure you the zoo and everyone employed by it will do everything in our power to assist at every level."

"Thank you, Ms. Gable-Davis," McCarron spoke. "We won't keep you long. I just have a couple of questions."

"Of course, officer."

"Detective," Scott corrected. "I'm Detective Scott McCarron and this is my uh," he paused in search of the right word, "associate Detective Murray."

"Murphy," Murphy said. Gable-Davis looked his way.

"Murray Murphy," she said. "What an unusual name or is it Murphy Murray?"

"Neither Ma'am," Murphy replied. McCarron chuckled.

"I realize you are responsible for the zoo in its entirety," the LAPD detective steered the conversation back on the right side of the road.

"I am," she said.

"But who, specifically, handles the elephants?"

"That would be Elena Ossidy," Gable-Davis responded then added, "she's wonderful."

"I'll need to speak with her," McCarron said while writing down the elephant keeps name in a notebook. "Where can I find her?"

"She called in sick. I'm sure you can appreciate how distraught she must be." Gable-Davis looked at the two detectives for any sign of sympathy. Seeing none she soldiered on. "After all one of her babies involved in such a horrific accident."

If it was, indeed, an accident thought Murphy.

Murphy Murphy and the Case of
the Commission on Cliches

"I'll need her information," said McCarron.

After exchanging a few more pleasantries and gathering the information he needed McCarron led Murphy Murphy to the crime scene. The space was impressive and Murphy took a few moments to snap some pictures with his phone. After wandering around the entire exhibit, he met McCarron at the spot he deduced must have been where A-OK met his demise. The dirt around a taped off area representing the commissioner's body appeared to be unmarred, almost unnaturally so thought Murphy.

"One set of footprints in, none out," he said out loud.

"Stands to reason since he didn't walk away from an elephant attack," McCarron spoke.

"Quite a few elephant tracks too but nothing I wouldn't expect," Murphy added. "And there was clearly plenty of blood." Murphy squatted near McCarron to get a closer look at the circle of dried blood that had formed in the dirt. Then he gazed at the surrounding area, "there are a few spots that could have been altered over there," he pointed, "but it's hard to say."

"Altered as in swept clean? McCarron asked. Murphy shrugged. "Why does an elephant attack a human being?" McCarron said mostly to himself.

"Why does a human being wander into an elephant exhibit at the zoo?" Murphy countered with a question of his own.

"Drunk or on drugs?" McCarron asked.

"Knowing what I know of the man neither is likely," Murphy said.

"I'd like the photos you took sent to me," McCarron changed the subject. Murphy punched in his LAPD counterpart's cell phone number and complied. "So how did you know the deceased and what do you know about Asian elephants?" Scott asked.

"They're big. But not as big as their African cousins," Murphy answered the second question first. "And it's a long story," He said responding to the first. Out of the corner of his eye Murphy spotted someone in a green jumpsuit shuffling around the perimeter of the complex. He tapped McCarron on the shoulder and pointed in the man's direction. McCarron stood and both detectives approached the interloper. As they got closer Murphy noticed the man was older and looked like the character Grady from the long ago TV series *Sanford and Son*.

"Excuse me!" McCarron said with authority. Grady stopped in his tracks. Murphy noticed a stick in the man's hand but realized he wasn't a threat. Just a guy picking up trash. The man picked up his stick showing the detectives a pointed end with an empty peanut bag stuck to the tip.

"Who are you two and what do you want?" Grady asked. Both McCarron and Murphy reached for their shields. Scott spoke.

Murphy Murphy and the Case of
the Commission on Cliches

"Police," he said. "Detectives McCarron and Muncy."

"Murphy," Murphy said.

"You here about the dead guy?" the custodian asked.

"We are," McCarron answered. "Did you know him?"

"Can't say that I do," he replied.

"Did," corrected Murphy Murphy.

"Did what?" Grady asked looking at Murphy.

"Not did, do. You said, 'can't say that I do' when you should have said 'can't say that I did'. The man is dead so it would be 'did'."

"Really?" McCarron looked at his colleague. Murphy shrugged.

"Sorry, can't help it," the detective said.

"Try harder," McCarron scolded then turned his attention back to the janitor. "Were you working the day in question Mr…?"

"Grady," the man said.

"No way," Murphy muttered.

"Were you working the day in question Mr. Grady?" McCarron picked up where he left off.

"In question of what?" Grady asked.

"The day the man died?" McCarron clarified.

"I work every damn day," Grady lamented. "Nobody picks up none of their trash anymore." McCarron held a finger in front of Murphy's nose.

"Don't you dare say it," he commanded. Murphy nodded.

"Were you here that night?" McCarron pressed.

"No sir. I clocked out at 5 PM and that's what I did that night. You can check my timecard."

"No need for that," Scott admitted. "Are there cameras? A security guard?" he asked.

"Both," Grady said, "but one don't work and the other don't care." McCarron made a mental note to ask Gable-Davis about both. "Besides," Grady kept talking, "Who breaks into a zoo? What they gonna do steal a hippopotomouse?"

"Mus," Murphy couldn't help but correct him.

"I mus what?" Grady asked.

"Not *you mus*," Murphy said. "You said hippopotomouse, it's hippopota *mus*."

"Maybe the big ones are," Grady said chuckling then turned away and started picking up more trash.

"That was interesting," Murphy said but McCarron was already walking away. Murphy hurried to catch up.

Murphy Murphy and the Case of
the Commission on Cliches

"You said your story about how you knew our vic was a long one."

"I did," Murphy replied.

"Good, because you can tell it to me on the way to the coroner's office." Murphy called Do It Up Brown and told him they were leaving. He said he'd reach out later if, or when, he needed him.

IT'S A SMALL WORLD

Throughout the course of his life and career Murphy Murphy had formed different opinions about some of the folks who made their living off dead people. Specifically, morticians and coroners. The former, Murphy believed, were capitalists pure and simple. People die and there's business in that. From what Murphy could glean a lucrative one at that. He didn't begrudge the mortician his right to earn a living off the poor souls who no longer lived but he saw it for what it was, an occupation.

A coroner or medical examiner in Murphy's mind approached their work with a purer motive. He found every one of them, at least the ones he had dealt with, to be curious about the science of death. They were interesting and interested participants in helping solve the mysteries around how and why someone left the earthly bonds. The L A County coroner was no exception. But he was different.

Scott McCarron had sat behind the wheel of his Chevy Tahoe gobsmacked for the entire ride as Murphy brought him up to speed about his knowledge of all things Adalindis Katterwomp. Scott kept coming up with questions to ask but had no idea where to start so he just listened and drove. In addition to not asking a single question he failed to warn Murphy Murphy about the man they were soon to meet. Los Angeles County Coroner Brobdingnagian Leviathan Yee.

McCarron flashed his shield in front of everyone he felt needed to see it as they went through the entrance, the recesses of the building, and into the lab. Murphy knew what was coming but he was still taken aback by the blast of cold air that hit him in the face. The smell was another, separate matter. A mix of medicine, bleach, stale air, and death also greeted the cops, but both were used to that too. A gurney was placed in the middle of the room. On it a bright, white sheet covered what had to be the body of Adalindis Orval Katterwomp. Next to the gurney sat a small table filled with all sorts of medical examiner tools. A silver metal stepstool was on the ground. The gurney and the tool table were also familiar to Murphy, but he couldn't remember ever seeing a stepstool, metal or otherwise, in this type of setting. He wondered why it was there. He didn't have to wonder long.

A whooshing sound accompanied the opening of a set of metal doors at the other end of the room and in walked Dr. Yee. Murphy almost laughed out loud. The man couldn't have been taller than five feet (4 feet 10 inches Murphy would later learn) with a bald head, coke bottle lens glasses, and a lab coat that reached all the way to the floor. It had the effect of some otherworldly creature floating into the room.

"Hello Brob," McCarron said.

"Bob," Murphy thought he echoed. The little man looked at the L A detective, then locked eyes on Murphy. Through the glasses the peepers looked to be the size of Kennedy silver dollars. Yee broke off the gaze and looked back at McCarron.

"Scott," he acknowledged the man with a voice so deep Murphy was caught off guard again. "Hello person I have never seen before in my life," he said to Murphy without looking away from McCarron. Then he did. "It's Brob," he said, "two 'b's', like Bob, one at the beginning and one at the end but there is an r right after the first b. You failed to include that." He kept going. "My friends call me Brob, other people sometimes refer to me as Levi because my middle name is Leviathan. You, person I have now know for 2 minutes, can call me doctor."

"It's an honor doctor," Murphy said with a slight head nod.

"Don't lie, person I have known for 3 minutes now. It's unbecoming."

"Brob," McCarron interrupted in an attempt to save his counterpart, "this is my colleague detective Murphy Murphy." Murphy smiled to himself at the fact that McCarron finally got his name correct. "Murphy,"

Scott continued, "this is Brobdingnagian Leviathan Yee the Los Angeles County Medical Examiner."

"Very interesting name," Murphy offered. "If I'm not mistaken it's from Gulliver's Travels. The name given by Swift to the land where everything was huge in size. And, of course, Leviathan is self-explanatory."

"You are correct," Yee replied, and Murphy thought he saw the small man give the smallest of smiles, "the young man I just met 4 minutes ago who I will now call Murphy."

"If I might ask, why did you decide to become a medical examiner?" Murphy couldn't help himself. Yee gave him a long look.

"I got tired of dunking on all my teammates and opponents on the basketball court," he said with the straightest of faces. "Science seemed more interesting to me than athletic domination. I wanted to learn why things are the way they are. Shall we get started?" And he did by climbing up on his stepstool.

Bonnie and Roger James sat at their table in the breakfast nook. She looked at him, he looked at his English muffin.

"This is terrible," he said.

"You toasted it yourself," his wife responded.

"Not the muffin Bon. Katterwomp. I can't believe he's dead."

"I can't believe it either," she agreed, "but I have to admit I'm not all that broken up about it."

"Bonnie! That's not like you."

"It's not? Anyway, if I remember correctly you were supposed to meet with that skunk last night, weren't you?"

"I was," he nodded, "but exhaustion hit me like a ton of bricks after dinner if you recall. I went to bed early and slept like a rock. What time did you come to bed?"

"Oh you know me and my insomnia," Bonnie said with the wave of a hand. "Elena and I stayed up puzzling until well after one AM. So, did you cancel the meeting?"

"Never had the chance," Roger lamented, "that must have been the reason he showed up at the zoo."

"And in Elena's elephant habitat to boot," Bonnie added.

"My God!" Roger exclaimed, "Am I responsible for my old friend's death?" Bonnie put her hand on top of her husband's.

"Don't be ridiculous darling. You can't blame yourself."

"I guess not," Roger said softly, "I guess not. Speaking of Elena where is she? I haven't seen her this morning."

"I haven't seen her either, but her Toyota is gone so I'm assuming she went with it."

At that very moment Elena James Ossidy sat in a chair inside Intelligentsia Coffee and Tea. She sipped on a cup of single origin Kangocho, savoring the subtle pomegranate notes.

"Everything okay here?" a waitress had swung by.

"Everything is a big word," Elena said and smiled, "but honestly things couldn't be better."

"Nice to see somebody had a good night," the woman said.

"Might have been the best night of my life," was Elena's   response.

"Well you go girl!" the waitress said and walked away. Elena sat and sipped for another few minutes then stood, walked over to the bin half full of dirty cups and placed hers inside. She found the waitress, surprised her with a kiss on the cheek, and slipped a slightly used 100-dollar bill inside her apron pocket.

"I think I'll go shopping," she said as she turned for the door.

"Who wouldn't want to be you!" the waitress called after her.

"At the present time can you determine the exact cause of death?" McCarron asked the diminutive doctor.

283

"And we were doing so well," Murphy whispered.

"That's redundant Scott," Yee said, "at present means at this time so 'at the present time' is not only redundant, it's verbose."

"Thank You," Murphy mouthed. Neither the doctor nor McCarron saw him.

"Duly noted," McCarron said, "but can you?"

"All signs point to one conclusion," Yee began.

"Which is?" McCarron butted in.

"This man failed to recognize the elephant in the room." For a second no one said a word then Brobdingnagian squealed in delight. A laugh so piercing Murphy thought about covering his ears.

"Good one Brob," McCarron had to admit.

"That's funny doctor," Murphy joined in.

"Of course technically there was no room," Yee was back to being all business. "It was the Los Angeles Zoo and more specifically the Elephants of Asia Exhibit."

"Thanks for clearing that up," McCarron tried to get in a dig.

"So he did die in the elephant exhibit?" Murphy ignored McCarron.

"As opposed to dying somewhere else and being dropped in the elephant exhibit at the zoo?" Yee asked.

"Yes," Murphy said. "As opposed to that."

"I can say with 100 per cent certainty that this man died in the dirt of an elephant exhibit at the L A zoo."

"Crushed," said Murphy.

"I'm sorry for your loss the young man who I recently started calling Murphy. I didn't know you knew the deceased." Murphy looked at him quizzically. "You just said you were crushed," Yee explained. "I was merely being polite by offering my condolences."

"Thank you but *I'm* not crushed. I simply deduced that Katterwomp here was and that's what killed him."

"Well, yes and no," Yee agreed and disagreed, "the man certainly was subject to thousands of pounds of pressure to his vital organs."

"So why the no? It sounds to me like he was crushed."

"His chest certainly was."

"But?" it was McCarron this time.

"But he may have had a heart attack before the pachyderm was finished using him as a step stool."

FROM PILLAR TO POST

Elena parked the Land Cruiser in her usual spot. The only difference today was instead of dogs she had shopping bags in the back. Well, not the *only* difference. There was the matter of a briefcase full of cash, the police crime scene tape encircling the exhibit, and the sign that read "Exhibit Closed Until Further Notice". The zoo, with the blessing of the LAPD, had called in several large animal veterinarians as well as a representative from the ASPCA to examine the elephants. They could find nothing out of the ordinary and determined all the animals were healthy, fit, and represented no further danger.

She left the keys in the car but grabbed Katterwomp's briefcase. After ducking under the yellow tape, she headed for the prearranged hiding place she had made for the money. She stuffed a couple handfuls of bills into her pockets and secured the rest. Her next stop was Beth Gable-Davis's office. She had called in sick but realized she needed to speak with her boss as soon as possible to lay the groundwork for keeping Bertha and the three other elephants in her care. She knew she'd be in for a fight.

Murphy Murphy and the Case of
the Commission on Cliches

McCarron left Murphy Murphy at the coroner's office claiming the need to get back to his desk and start what would be a stream of paperwork on the case. They divided up a few "next step" assignments and said goodbye for the time being. Left to his own devices Murphy dialed Do It Up Brown for a ride then got to work making his own list of where he wanted to go and with whom he would like to speak. Commissioner Katterwomp's office and Roger James topped each column. While he waited for Brown, he took another look at what he now considered the crime scene photos on his device. As hard as he tried he couldn't seem to find anything out of the ordinary in any of them. They all just appeared to be images depicting a tragic accident but something still gnawed at the detective.

"There has to be something more," he said quietly. "Why was Katterwomp even there?" That question made him think of the book. He called McCarron.

"Was there a book discovered near Katterwomp's dead body?" he asked after the detective had answered.

"What kind of book?" he asked.

"Not sure why that makes any difference," Murphy blurted, "but it's a book of cliches."

"Not that I'm aware of but I'll double check."

"Thanks," Murphy said and disconnected. The phone reverted to the photos and a couple of pictures caught his eye. They showed tire tracks taken around the perimeter of the exhibit. Tracks with very distinctive markings that Murphy felt deserved further investigation. He added that to his list. After hanging up with Murphy Murphy, McCarron called his partner to check in.

"Hey Scott," Karen Free answered. McCarron heard both a dog barking and a baby crying in the background.

"Howdy partner. Sounds busy there."

"Nonstop," she laughed, "but it's all good. What's up?"

"Just checking on you and I wanted to bring you up to speed on the case I caught while you're off lying on the beach."

"Very funny and thanks."

"We are still a team and I wanted to get your thoughts."

"I really appreciate that Scott," she said, and McCarron thought he heard a bit of emotion in her voice. "You're not as bad a guy as they say," she added but gave McCarron no time to respond. "So, give it to me."

"Who's they?" McCarron responded anyway.

"Nobody," she answered. "Well nobody expect Langer, Kelly, and Stricker."

"Jealous, all of them," the detective said and laughed.

Murphy Murphy and the Case of
the Commission on Cliches

Elena Ossidy knocked on her boss's door but opened it and walked in before receiving a reply. Beth Gable-Davis looked up from her computer.

"I thought you called in sick," the zoo director said.

"I did and I am. Sick that security in this place is so lax that any stumbling drunk can walk through the gates and end up dead in my elephant exhibit." Elena had decided to go on the offensive.

"Hang on a second Miss Ossidy," Gable-Davis said holding up a hand.

"Mrs." Elena corrected her.

"Before you go blaming me for zoo security," the boss plowed on, "you need to step back and think about the actions of those animals."

"I need to do no such thing, *MISS* Gable-Davis!," Elena shot back. "Those *animals* were doing what any creature would do under the circumstances. They were protecting their turf. So, what about that security? What did the cameras show? What did the security guard say?"

"Nothing," Gable-Davis said meekly, "and I don't know," she added.

"*EXCUSE ME?!?*" Elena poured it on knowing she had her boss on the ropes.

"Calm down, please," the director pleaded. "The cameras weren't functioning *again*," Elena thought she sounded sad, "and I haven't gotten in touch with the security guard who was on duty yet."

"Seems to me that would be priority number one."

"Priority number one is undertaking a full investigation into the actions of a rogue elephant that resulted in the death of an innocent man," Gable-Davis tried to go on offense herself.

"My elephant is not a rogue elephant," Elena said, her anger rising. "And the person who died was nowhere near innocent," she pointed a finger into her boss's face. "This zoo's unprofessional security operation is what's to blame here and that falls directly under your purview."

"First the elephant in question is not *your's*," Gable-Davis rose, "and how dare you make accusations against me!"

"If the shoe fits," Elena said as she turned to leave the office. Then she stopped and spun around. "If you go down the path of scapegoating those perfectly innocent elephants, I'll come for you with everything I have. That's not a threat, that's a promise."

"Get out of my office!" the zoo director screamed but Elena was already gone. Elena stopped just outside Davis's office door and took a deep breath. *That felt good* she thought before walking away.

"Where to boss?" Brown asked after Murphy buckled up.

"Back to the Commission on Cliches building."

"What's there?"

"I'm hoping a guard can let us in to find out," Murphy told him. Brown put the car in drive.

"A couple of things off the top of my head," Karen Free offered after McCarron had given her the low down.

"I'm all ears," her partner said.

"First, it sounds like this Murtry character can be a valuable asset."

"Murphy," McCarron corrected her but Free kept talking.

"Not as good as me, of course, but valuable. I'd use him."

"Understood and agreed. What's second?"

"Money," she said.

"Not following."

"You should be. Look, from what you told me and the way you told it, it seems to me that you think there is a crime here somewhere. This wasn't some random accident."

"Correct," Scott said.

"In my experience, which I admit isn't as extensive as yours, either money of jealousy is involved in most crimes. I don't know enough about the victim to assume the latter so if it was me, I'd zero in on the former. Find out if there's money floating around this crime."

"Smart," McCarron acknowledged. "And where pray tell might you start to look?"

"Bank records, silly, for both this Katterwomp dude *and* his questionable commission. I can help if you want."

"I'd appreciate that but you're not on the clock for at least another month."

"Scott, the city of Los Angeles is paying me to sit on my still fat from pregnancy ass and breast feed my baby. The least I can do is make a few phone calls and sniff around some bank records."

"You're a credit to the badge, Free," McCarron cajoled her. "I'll take Katterwomp and you dig into the Commission on Cliches."

"Consider it done," she said and hung up.

Do It Up Brown pulled up to the guard shack and Kip Henley and an attractive blonde came out. Murphy rolled down his window.

"Hello detective. Long time no see," Henley said to Murphy.

Murphy Murphy and the Case of
the Commission on Cliches

"Chris," was all Murphy said as a greeting.

"This is Lauren," Kip said with a head nod toward the blonde.

"Hey there," she said with a wave and a smile that showed perfect, white teeth. "The pleasure is mine. Chris has told me all about you."

"That, I doubt," Murphy replied. "In my experience I've found Mr. Henley here to be the type of person more likely to talk about himself than someone else."

"Touche," was her reply.

"Hello you two!" Kip spoke up, "I'm right here." Murphy Murphy ignored him and continued talking to Lauren.

"Can you get me inside?" he asked.

"I can get *us* inside," she replied, "and I will."

"This is exciting," Henley announced.

"Not you," Murphy poured cold water on Kip's enthusiasm. He looked at the guard. "Just you and me."

READING THE TEA LEAVES

Murphy found the office in much the same condition as he remembered it. While his recall was still pretty good part of him wished he had taken a few pictures the last time he was inside. A couple of questions immediately bubbled up. *Was the desk this clean before? Was that coffee cup here the last time? Wasn't there a briefcase in here and if there was where is it now?* But as far as the detective could detect there were no signs that A-OK hadn't planned on coming back. Murphy moved around the desk and started opening drawers.

"Hey, hey hey," Lauren piped up. "What do you think you're doing? Murphy ignored her and kept going.

"I'm looking for anything that might give me some idea of who might want Katterwomp dead," he looked up at her, "and why."

"Coolio," she said, "can I help?" Murphy reached into his pocket and pulled out a pair of latex gloves.

"Better put these on," he said tossing them her way.

"Why? You're not wearing any." She asked catching them.

"I've been in here before," he answered. "You haven't. My prints are already all over the place." He went back to testing drawers and doors. Most opened easily revealing files, shelves with books, trinkets, pens and pencils, and mementos. One concealed several decanters and half a dozen crystal glasses. Murphy pulled the top off one of the decanters filled with a deep red liquid.

"Wine?" Lauren asked.

"Port, more specifically," Murphy answered after a sniff, "and an expensive one at that."

"This one is locked," the guard announced after trying to open another cabinet.

"Interesting," Murphy said after trying it himself. "Do you see any keys?" he asked going back to the desk to look.

"No keys," Lauren said after a couple minute search.

"I guess I'll have to come back," Murphy said with a shrug.

"After getting a search warrant?"

"Yeah, after that. Of course," Murphy said wishing he'd brought his lock pick set.

"Hello Karen," McCarron answered his phone.

"Scott," she replied, "I think I may have something."

"Already?" the detective was impressed. "Something is a lot more than I've been able to get."

"Gotta take advantage when the baby naps."

"What did you find?"

"Money, money, money," she sang.

"I was hoping for some information not an ABBA song," McCarron ribbed his partner.

"Very good McCarron," she shot back.

"Hey, I saw *Mama Mia*!" They both laughed. "Tell me about the money."

"It looks like our victim transferred slightly more than $220,000 from an account belonging to the Commission on Cliches to a personal account under the Name of Adalindis Orval Katterwomp."

"Payment for services rendered or expense reimbursements?" Scott played devil's advocate.

"Neither would be my guess."

"Why is that?"

"Because there are other transactions earmarked for both of those things already. These transfers were in addition to those."

"Interesting."

"And it gets better," Free was on a roll.

"How so?"

The transfers are in dozens of increments. Never more than $9,500 at a time."

"Keep it under the radar," McCarron said more to himself than Free.

"Completely," she acknowledged, "if you ask me he's been planning to use this money for something specific."

"And planning it for a while," McCarron finished the sentence.

"Great minds think alike," she said.

"Nice work Karen," he complimented his partner. "Can't wait to get you back." He heard a baby cry.

"Somebody's hungry. Gotta go," she said. "I'll send over everything I have."

Murphy Murphy had Do It Up Brown wait in the driveway as he ran up to his room in Laurance's house to grab his pick set. He walked right past the giant nose sitting on the couch watching television.

"Hey Murph," Matthew called out as the detective passed, "what's the rush?"

"Holy hell!" Murphy screamed. "What in the world?!?" he stared at his actor friend. "You scared the crap out of me." He kept staring. "Is that? Are you? A *nose*?" he asked dumbfounded.

"As a matter of fact, I am."

"Why?"

"Because there are times when you can't *pick* your jobs. Get it? Besides I'm hard at work, you know, nose to the grindstone and all."

"Very funny," Murphy wasn't amused. "Seriously, why are you wearing a nose costume?"

"Doing a commercial for *Stop the Sniffles Sterile Saline Mist*," he said. "Available at a fine drug store near you."

"Impressive," Murphy lied, "but why are you still in *character*" he used air finger quotes, "at home?"

"Union lunch break. I'm back at it in ninety minutes and it takes two hours plus to get in and out of this booger." Laurance looked at his friend or at least Murphy thought he was being looked at. "What time you got?" Murphy started to look at his watch. "Never mind," the actor said, "studio driver should be here any minute to take me back."

"Sometimes I wonder if you ever wonder if being an actor is worth it," Murphy said shaking his head.

"The answer is plain as the nose on your face Murph," Laurance answered, "the money is nothing to sneeze at.

By the way how's the case going?" the actor asked
through his left nostril.

"Something about the whole thing stinks," Murphy
said.

"Good one," Laurance complimented his friend for
playing along. "Tell you what, why don't we have
dinner together tonight. I'll invite Mitchy over and you
can talk us through the case. You might think
something's important and we'll convince you that it
snot."

"You are not funny," Murphy said with a shake of his
head. "But that's not a terrible idea."

DON'T MINCE MATTERS

"Don't you worry about a thing Bertha," Elena stroked the massive elephant's trunk, "nobody is going to hurt you or take you away." The dogs sat near her feet and sniffed the air. Dundee growled causing Elena to turn. "Easy boy," she said to the Australian Shepherd.

"What do you want?" she asked the same fat security guard that, once upon a time, worked the shack at the Commission on Cliches entrance.

"I done what you asked," he scratched the ground with the toe of his work shoe.

"Let me guess," she stopped him, "the five thousand dollars I paid you just doesn't seem like enough anymore."

"Look," he said mustering up some courage, "you paid me *not* to patrol this particular area of the zoo the other night. I didn't know or care why but now I do. Somebody *died.*"

"Amazing," she said, "you *can* read."

"Saw it on the TV," he countered. "I was the one on duty that night and somebody is bound to ask me what I did or didn't see."

"Cut to the chase. What do you want?"

"The way I see it is another five grand seals my lips for good," he ran a stubby index finger across his mouth.

My God you're an idiot Elena thought. "You drive a hard bargain," she said, "but just in case you have third thoughts why don't we make it 10?"

"That sounds even better!"

"There's one condition," she added.

"What might that be?"

"I never see you again, this zoo never sees you again, and nobody you see or meet ever knows anything about this." The guard stared at her. "I'll know", she met his stare, "and these dogs bite." Dundee growled on cue.

"Deal," he said quickly.

"Good. Meet me at Foxy's in an hour. I'll have your money."

"Foxy's?"

"It's in Glendale. Google it."

Brown pulled the car next to the guard kiosk. Lauren stuck her arm out and waved, her head followed but didn't wave.

"Did you get the warrant?" she asked. As an answer Murphy waved a piece of paper from his side of the car and told Do It Up to drive.

"That's an old menu from the Ho Kee Café," the driver said.

"So it is," responded Murphy as he stuffed the sheet back in the glove box.

McCarron spent twenty minutes looking over the documents Karen Free had sent him. When he felt like he'd seen enough he grabbed his phone and called Murphy Murphy. It went to voicemail.

"Murphy," he started after the beep, "I think I found, well, actually my partner found, something interesting in regard to the Katterwomp case. Happy to share it with you so call me back."

Murphy listened to the message. "*With* regard to the Katterwomp case," he whispered. He set the phone down and went back to picking the lock on the commissioner's file cabinet. It was open less than thirty seconds later and Murphy sat staring at an old, metal lunch box with a cartoon Superman in full, one fist forward, flight. He flicked the box open.

"I think I found something interesting too," he said to the superhero.

"Any luck finding either your security guard or your elephant keeper Ms. Gable-Davis?" After hanging up with Murphy, McCarron immediately dialed the L.A. Zoo.

"Unfortunately the answer to both is no," the director lied and told the truth. "The man hasn't reported to work since the incident," she said skipping any updates on Elena. "We tried the number listed on his employment application but it seems to have been disconnected."

"That's a shame," McCarron said, hardly surprised. "Can you share his employment file with me? Maybe we can use our resources to track him down." He waited for a response. "Ms. Gable-Davis?" he asked after several seconds.

"Um… well," she finally stammered, "I hope you can appreciate that there isn't much of a file so to speak. It's so hard to find any kind of help these days. We were strapped and pretty much hired him on the spot based on his resume. He had been employed over the years as a guard for a number of reputable firms. I'm sure you understand," she said somewhat sheepishly.

"Of course," McCarron said not really understanding, "if the situation changes please give me a call. Thanks for your time."

"There is one more thing, detective."

"What's that?"

"I, uh, I mean we were wondering if it would be okay to reopen the Elephants of Asia exhibit. The animals have been examined and given a clean bill of health and It *is* our most popular attraction."

"It's still a little soon don't you think? Our investigation isn't over and I can't imagine you've wrapped up your internal inquiry."

"Actually, we are very close," she pushed back, "all of our signs point to it being a very unfortunate accident."

"I wouldn't rush to that conclusion, Ma'am but let me assess where we are and I'll get back to you. In the meantime please don't tamper with the crime scene."

Um, right, okay, we won't," she lied again.

"The world has gone crazy," McCarron said after hanging up. His phone rang and the detective recognized the detective's number. "Speak of the devil," he said answering Murphy Murphy's call. "Did you happen to find a large sum of money belonging to Katterwomp?" was his first question. Murphy answered in the negative then filled McCarron in on what he *found*.

STRIKE WHILE THE IRON IS HOT

"Wait just a doggone minute," Laurance said. He wiped his mouth with a paper napkin. The three men were enjoying pizza from Mozza2Go. Matthew had just swallowed a healthy bite of fennel sausage and pancetta pie. Mitch was scooping a spoonful of roasted cauliflower onto his plate positioning it between two slices of his Salame pizza which featured mozzarella cheese, Fresno chiles, and tomatoes. For his part Murphy had a slice of each pie and several meatballs. He passed on the cauliflower.

"Are you saying this Katterwomp character was robbing Peter to pay Paul?" Matthew asked. Murphy had filled the twins in on McCarron's news that the commissioner had withdrawn close to a quarter of a million dollars from the commission of cliches coffers which, of course, meant the American taxpayer.

"Believe it or not," Murphy said. "But it seems he withdrew the money but didn't deposit it anywhere. At least not in any accounts we could find so far."

"Why would he need the money?" Mitch asked.

"Embezzlement, paying for sex, blackmail," Matthew rubbed his hands together like a cartoon villain.

"God, you're dramatic," his brother scoffed.

"I guess any or all of that is possible," Murphy jumped in, "but it could also all be perfectly reasonable reasons."

"Don't bet on it," Matthew added. Where would one hide a quarter of a million dollars? He thought out loud.

"I could think of a dozen places," Mitch answered.

"Regardless, it seems like a whole new ball of wax as far as your case is concerned," Mitch kept the cliché train going.

"Remains to be seen," Murphy replied stabbing a meatball with his fork. "We'll keep looking for the money," Murphy replied as he stuffed the delicacy in his mouth.

"A lean toward a classic case of blackmail," Matthew said before folding a piece of pizza lengthwise and taking a bite.

"Or" Mitchy interjected, "maybe he's paying off a lover or a gambling debt. Remember that one Matlock episode in which I starred."

"*Starred*," Matthew mouthed rolling his eyes. "You mean the one that starred Andy Griffith and featured you as the attorney for a grieving widow who was actually in cahoots with her *not dead* husband to bilk the insurance company out of millions? That one?" Mitch just nodded and chewed.

"Or maybe, just maybe, he was using the money to buy back a book," Murphy said stoically. The three looked at each other.

"Nah!" Mitch broke the silence, "my scenario sounds way more plausible. Anybody else want another beer?" he asked getting up and heading for the fridge.

"Was he really on *Matlock*?" Murphy asked when Mitch was out of earshot.

"He was," Matthew conceded, "ten episodes but we might have mixed up that case with one from his time on *L.A. Law*."

"I found something else too," Murphy said changing the subject.

"Pray tell."

"Yeah, spill the beans," Mitch had rejoined the conversation.

"Love letters," Murphy responded, "an antique Superman lunchbox full of them," Murphy grabbed a beer from Mitch's hand and took a gulp.

"So, our quirky commissioner was a gay lothario?" Matthew asked.

"I hate to admit I don't even know what that means," Murphy admitted.

"It means a debonair fellow," Mitch answered for his brother. "A seducer of women."

"Ahh," Murphy nodded. "Well, in this case it was woman. Singular."

"Don't beat around the bush," Matthew said putting another log on the cliché fire, "is she anyone we know?"

"Bonnie Willows James," Murphy answered.

"Any relation to the guy who wrote the book?"

"His wife."

"Whose wife," Mitch asked confused, "what book? What are you guys talking about?"

"We're talking about how our good friend detective Murphy Murphy isn't about to look a gift horse in the mouth in his efforts to explore every avenue to solve the case of the commission on cliches," Matthew informed his brother.

"No rest for the weary," Murphy said raising his bottle, "I know where I'll be bright and early tomorrow."

Murphy finished his beer and bade the Laurance twins a good night. He went to his room, stomach still digesting, and got ready for bed. After fluffing the pillows, he leaned against them and thought about the case. Despite, or maybe because, of the newly learned information something nagged at him. He did what he always did when a case got to this point and made a list. Then he took a few minutes to make his goodnight call to Charlie hoping she was still awake. She was.

"Hey Doll," he said after she answered.

"Hello Sugar," was her sweet response. They caught each other up on the happenings of the day and then Charlie asked two questions. "Where does that leave the case," and "when are you coming home?" He had no real answer for the second and it took him a while to get through the first. When he had Charlie offered some advice.

"Go back to the basics," she said. "Talk to people, read their reactions and responses, you're great at that. And find that elephant girl!" Murphy thanked her, told her that he loved her, and they said goodnight. *Find that elephant girl* he added to his list then turned out the light and went to sleep.

Murphy Murphy met Scott McCarron at Dinosaur Coffee in Silver Lake at 8 AM. Unbeknownst to either policeman, Elena James Ossidy was only a few blocks up Sunset Boulevard making weekend plans with her new coffee shop friend.

"Interesting spot," Murphy said pulling out the chair next to his counterpart.

"I knew the original owners," the LAPD man said, "before they sold it and moved to the valley. They're gone but the joint still makes a great cup of joe."

"Tea?" Murphy asked.

"I'm sure they have it but for the life of me I couldn't tell you why." He blew on his beverage and took a sip. "You know what they say about tea don't you?"

"Actually I don't care," Murphy tried to stop him.

"If you replace your morning coffee with green tea you lose 87 per cent of what little joy you have left in your life."

"That's a good one," a third voice said and both men turned toward it. Johnny "Jack", Brian Katrek, Maginnes walked toward the table.

"Maginnes," McCarron said coldly.

"Boss," Murphy added without only slightly more warmth, "I didn't realize you were still in town."

"I'm not for much longer."

"Played every golf course you could weasel your way on?" Scott wondered. "Oops", he said with a smile, "was that my outside voice?"

"Couldn't manage to get on Bel Air Country Club," Maginnes answered unaffected, "but other than that, yes."

Murphy Murphy and the Case of
the Commission on Cliches

"Good for you," McCarron took another sip of coffee.

"I'm headed home," the captain said, "Chief Hill thinks I've spent enough of the department's money although I'm sure we'll get the LAPD to reimburse us for detective Murphy's time. I just wanted to say goodbye and good luck.

"Thanks," Murphy said.

"You two appear to have everything under control so my work here is done."

"Don't let the door hit you on the ass on the way out, Johnny," McCarron seemed to be getting more perturbed. Maginnes smiled and looked at Murphy Murphy.

"Don't overstay your welcome detective. People around here can tend to get a little rude." And with that he was gone.

YOU CAN LEAD A HORSE TO WATER BUT
YOU CAN'T MAKE HIM DRINK

McCarron and Murphy worked out a strategy after Maginnes hit the road, then fine-tuned it on the way to Roger James's home. McCarron filled Murphy in on the conversation he had with Bethany Gable-Davis about the security guard. Both agreed they needed to go back to the zoo and speak to the director again. Murphy showed McCarron his list with the last thing emphasized and the LA man agreed they had to find, and speak with, the "elephant girl" Ossidy. McCarron conceded the fact that they hadn't spoken to her yet was a huge gap in the investigation so far. The zoo didn't open until 10 so the first stop would be the James house in Los Feliz.

It was determined that Murphy would take the lead because he had the connection to Katterwomp and the commission on cliches. McCarron would serve as the authority in the room and for intimidation if it came to that. Neither cop knew if James had any connection to the death of Adalindis Katterwomp but he was their best chance at the moment. They didn't call ahead hoping to catch the man off guard. McCarron had gotten the address through DMV records after Murphy had identified this Roger James as the man who's photograph he had seen on the wall in Katterwomp's offices.

"Lives with his wife Bonnie," McCarron had said.

"That coincides with the woman's name on all of the love letters I found in the file cabinet."

"Tell me again how you found those letters detective?" Scott asked.

"Just lucky I guess," Murphy answered with a straight face. "The cabinet had been unlocked."

"I'm sure it had," McCarron said and left it there. He parked the Tahoe on the street and both detectives walked up the drive. At the sound of the closing SUV doors Cooper the Landseer started barking.

"What's up pal?" Roger asked the 150 pound animal.

"Roger," Bonnie called, "company. Looks like policemen, two of them."

"It took them long enough," James said under his breath as he and the big dog left his office.

Murphy rang the bell and seconds later Bonnie James opened the door.

"Good morning," she said. Murphy was impressed. She was on the shorter side but quite attractive, not nearly as pretty as Charlie, but well put together. No doubt a real looker in her day. He understood immediately how a guy like Katterwomp could be smitten.

"Mrs. James?" Murphy asked as both he and McCarron pulled their shields.

"I am," she stood her ground, "and who might you be?"

"I'm detective Murphy Murphy," he introduced himself and watched as Bonnie suppressed a giggle.

Well that's supernumerary," she said.

"I'm impressed," Murphy said with a nod.

"And I'm LAPD detective Scott McCarron," the other detective ruined the moment.

"May we come in?" Murphy asked.

"I don't see why not," Bonnie said, and the two men started forward. Bonnie didn't budge. "But at the same time, I don't see why," she added.

"We just have a few questions," McCarron stated.

"It shouldn't take up too much of you or your husband's time," Murphy added.

"It seems to me like you could ask them from right where you are," Bonnie replied.

"Oh for Pete's sake," a voice boomed from the hallway, "quit playing with your food dear and let them in. We have nothing to hide." Bonnie smiled what Murphy considered a fetching smile.

Murphy Murphy and the Case of
the Commission on Cliches

"Just having a little fun boys," she said backing away.
"Please, come in."

THICK AS THIEVES

Roger James was an imposing figure. Murphy figured him to be at least six foot four, probably 250 pounds and in great shape. He thought Roger and Bonnie James made a handsome couple. Since his brain was still somewhat stuck in Hollywood mode thanks to the Serious Crisis movie he couldn't help but think of Idris Elba.

"Welcome to our humble home," James said to the cops. He turned and walked down the hall clearly expecting Murphy and McCarron to follow. They did.

He led them to a large sunroom which included two comfortable looking chairs and a leather sofa. James took one of the chairs, the detectives shared the couch. Without prompting Murphy brought the man up to speed regarding his involvement in the case and his relationship with Katterwomp. Bonnie stuck her head in the room and asked if anyone wanted something to drink and all three declined.

"I'll leave you to it then," she said starting to close the door.

Murphy Murphy and the Case of
the Commission on Cliches

"Please stay," Murphy requested, "if you don't mind."

"Ooh, fun," she said entering the room and taking the remaining chair.

"What can we do to be helpful with your investigation?" James got the ball rolling.

Elena saw the black Chevy Tahoe parked in front of the house and knew immediately the police were inside. As noiselessly as possible, she pulled the Toyota into the driveway, got out, and headed to the side door that led to the rooms in her wing of the house.

"This could be entertaining," she said to herself.

"Are we suspects?" Bonnie leaned forward in the chair. Murphy could tell she was enjoying herself. "Do we need our attorney present? Is taking the fifth an option on the table?" The questions came rapid fire. Before either detective could respond her husband chimed in.

"Don't be impudent dear," he lovingly rebuked his wife, "you watch too many police procedurals. I said it before and I'll repeat it again, we have nothing to hide. Please continue detective Murphy."

Redundant thought Murphy. "None of that will be necessary, Mrs. James," Murphy said.

"Please call me Bonnie."

"And I'm Roger," the big man added.

"Right," Murphy regained control of the conversation. "Bonnie and Roger. Got it. Now, Detective McCarron and I are here purely on a fact finding mission. Neither of you are suspects," Murphy told a white lie. "In fact, we're not even sure a crime has been committed. From what we've been able to deduce so far in our investigation, this whole sad happenstance tragically appears to be an accident."

"If the shoe fits as they say," James piped in.

"That said," Murphy soldiered on, "sometimes where there's smoke there's fire."

"And you're the firefighter," Bonnie clapped her hands, "this *IS* fun."

"Can you tell us where you were and what you were doing the night Adalindis Katterwomp met his untimely end?" It was the bad cop McCarron.

"I can," Bonnie raised her hand while answering.

"You don't have to raise your hand Mrs. uh, Bonnie," McCarron smiled, "go ahead."

"He was here at home. In bed. Sound asleep." She put her hand back in her lap.

That sounds convenient thought Murphy.

"I know that sounds a little too convenient," Roger said as if he could read Murphy's mind, "but it's true."

"When was the last time you saw the victim?" McCarron asked.

"Oh gosh," James seemed to be thinking, "it has to have been several weeks if not months.," he said.

"Didn't you tell us," it was Bonnie, "you were scheduled to meet with him the night he died?" Both Murphy and McCarron leaned in.

"Yes, we had scheduled a meeting but I didn't hold up my end of the bargain."

"And you knew about this meeting?" Murphy turned his attention to Bonnie.

"I sure did," she answered. "Am I a suspect now?"

"Bonnie please!" her husband jumped in.

"No Ma'am," Murphy answered Bonnie who appeared disappointed. Murphy then looked back at Roger. "Why didn't you hold up your end of the bargain?" Murphy wondered.

"I trust you'll believe me when I say it wasn't because I didn't want to. It was simply because I was physically unable to."

"Please explain."

"Right after dinner an incredible exhaustion overcame me. I couldn't keep my eyes open and, in fact, didn't. I was in bed and out like a light by 8:30."

"And you can vouch for that?" McCarron asked Bonnie.

"Absolutely," she corroborated, "it's all true." McCarron nodded an "of course it is" nod.

"What about you?" Murphy asked Mrs. James.

"Moi?" she seemed surprised at the question. "I was home all night as well," she replied quickly.

"Can anyone attest to that?" Murphy pried.

"My daughter Elena," she said without missing a beat. "We watched TV for a bit," she paused to think, "an HGTV program called *Love It or List It*," she continued.

"Did Hilary or David win?" McCarron asked. Murphy looked at him as if he had suddenly grown a second head. McCarron just shrugged. "Hilary usually wins," he added sheepishly.

"We watched three episodes and I believe the tally was Hilary two and David one," Bonnie came to McCarron's defense.

"See," the LAPD detective said defensively.

"So, that's ninety minutes," Murphy continued.

"One hundred and eighty," Bonnie corrected the detective.

"Pardon?"

"It took one hundred and eighty minutes," she repeated, "each episode is an hour."

"Got it," Murphy did.

"But let me guess, that still leaves time for me to drive to the zoo and convince a four and a half ton elephant to squish Adalindis Kattrerwomp," Bonnie said. "Is that your theory detective?" Murphy had to admit to himself that it did sound unlikely.

"If the shoe fits," Murphy repeated Roger James's cliché. "So, what *did* you do after watching television?"

"We puzzled," Bonnie answered.

"I beg your pardon?" Murphy asked, puzzled.

"We worked on a jigsaw puzzle," she clarified. "This one right here to be more specific," she got up and walked to a round table. Murphy rose from the couch and joined her. He saw what looked more like a work of art than a puzzle. Intricately carved wooden pieces were arrayed in sections based on color. He saw one shaped like an eagle, wings spread in mid soar. Another depicted a hula dancer. The puzzle itself was a little more than halfway completed. The picture on the blue box showed a tropical sunset complete with palm trees and an outrigger canoe.

"This is exquisite," Murphy commented.

"I know," Bonnie nodded.

"Where did you get it?" he asked thinking it would make a great thank you gift for his friend Matthew.

"From a Boulder, Colorado company called Liberty Puzzles. They have hundreds and we've done dozens."

"I could see how this could keep you occupied," Murphy said picking up a pineapple shaped piece and sliding it into the correct spot in the puzzle.

"Well done detective," Bonnie praised him, "and yes, it can be addicting. This and a nice bottle of cabernet usually does the trick for Elena and me most nights." They both walked back to their respective seats.

"Roger," McCarron took up the questioning once Murphy Murphy and Bonnie sat. "I hope you don't mind my asking but were you aware that Mr. Katterwomp was in love with your wife?"

Good cop, bad cop again, thought Murphy, *well played McCarron.* His thought was interrupted by the deepest, most sincere sounding laugh he had ever heard. It came from Roger James.

"Only for as long as I have known him," James remarked once he'd finished laughing. "We both did," he nodded with a loving nod toward Bonnie. "I mean just look at her," he said with admiration, "can you blame him?" Murphy could not. Bonnie blushed. "She's meat and drink to me," Roger James said as he blew his wife a kiss.

"Your love is my balm in Gilead," Bonnie blew her own kiss right back. McCarron cleared his throat.

"Didn't Katterwomp's affection for Bonnie upset you?" Scott asked Roger.

"Not even a little bit," James responded immediately. "The man was his own worst enemy and my Bonnie would have no truck with a man like that."

"He was a strange, quirky man," Bonnie added, "from the get-go I kept him at arm's length."

"The fact that he fell in love with my wife was maybe the only normal thing about the man."

"Did he scare you?" Murphy asked Bonnie and he saw her smile again.

"If push came to shove," she said, "which it never did. I would have kicked his ass." Just then a clock, in another room, chimed three times followed by what sounded to Murphy like elephants trumpeting.

"Interesting cuckoo clock," Murphy said.

"Isn't it though," Bonnie jumped in apparently eager to change the subject away from Katterwomp's childish infatuation. "It was a gift from our son-in-law."

"I think we have everything we need," Scott McCarron said getting to his feet. Murphy rose too. The LAPD detective reached into his pocket and pulled out a card.

He handed it to Roger who had met them where they stood. "If anything else comes to mind please call."

"And don't leave town?" Bonnie added.

"Bonnie!" Roger semi scolded her, "I'm sure these detectives couldn't care less if we left town or not." *That's not exactly true* Murphy thought but didn't say. "Come gentleman," Roger said walking past the two cops, "I'll show you out."

This time through Murphy noticed the hallway was lined with pictures. He stopped at one that depicted a smiling family of four. Roger and Bonnie James and two young people.

"That's us," Bonnie had joined the procession. "Me and Roger obviously," she pointed, "and that's our son-in-law Grandi Ossidy and our daughter Elena." Murphy noticed a shadow of sadness wash across Bonnie's face. "Before the accident."

"Accident?" Murphy blurted.

"Grandi was killed by a falling coconut while he was working in Thailand. It was, and is, so sad." Murphy didn't know how to respond so he simply took one last look at the photograph and turned to follow James and McCarron to the door.

A SNARE AND A DELUSION

Once outside Murphy noticed the shiny red SUV in the driveway. He was sure it wasn't there before. Alarm bells figuratively went off in his head as he took a closer look at the vehicle, especially the tires. Murphy pulled out his phone and scrolled through several pictures until he found the ones of the tire tracks he had taken in the elephant exhibit at the zoo. The pattern was hard to miss and it matched. He took another picture, this one of the left rear tire, and upon closer inspection he saw it was a Yokohama Geolander Y-MT G005. The tread resembled a cluster of one inch sized maps of Australia.

"What are you doing?" McCarron asked but Murphy barely heard through the clanging bells still ringing in his head.

"Elena Ossidy!" he practically shouted.

"Who?" McCarron had walked up beside him.

"Didn't Bonnie James say her daughter's name was Elena?"

"I believe she did."

"And her dead husband's name was Grandi Ossidy?"

"Strange, I agree," McCarron wasn't getting it.

"And didn't Beth Gable-Davis say the elephant keeper at the zoo was named Elena Ossidy?!?" It finally clicked for McCarron.

"My god, you're right," he exclaimed. "It looks like we need to go back inside and speak to the daughter."

"We certainly do but let's get a warrant first," Murphy suggested.

"Good idea," McCarron agreed. "I'm sure we have enough but just in case I know a friendly judge."

Elena watched through a slit in the curtains as the two policemen examined her Land Cruiser then had a brief palaver. She could tell they were animated. The taller one turned as if to head back to the house but the shorter one, the one who had the instinct to get a closer look at her vehicle, put his hand on the other one's arm and said something that stopped him. The big one nodded and both climbed into the Tahoe and drove away.

Probably getting a search warrant she thought which, in her mind gave her at least an hour, maybe even two, before she'd see them again.

"Plenty of time," she said out loud backing away from the window.

COOL AS A CUCUMBER

McCarron ran the plates on the vehicle to validate that it belonged to Elena Ossidy. He went to work on the warrant including everything he and Murphy had discussed as well as everything else he could think of including the money trail and the fact that the zoo director claimed Miss Ossidy had yet to return to work since the night of Katterwomp's demise. It might not have been a slam dunk but McCarron figured it was enough to search Elena's office at the zoo and the James's home in Los Feliz. He was right.

Murphy Murphy and McCarron enlisted the help of a couple of uniforms and decided to start at the zoo. Gable-Davis met them and escorted the team to the Elephants of Asia exhibit and Elena Ossidy's office. The cops were disappointed to find that a thorough search produced nothing out of the ordinary, but it was abundantly clear that someone had been there to make sure the pachyderms had been fed, watered, and taken care of. The zoo director assured them it wasn't her so they all surmised it had to have been Elena. There were also two dog bowls and food. Gable-Davis mentioned the items were for Ossidy's two Australian Shepherds, dogs she used to help train the elephants. Murphy made a mental note that the only dog he had seen or heard at the James residence was the mammoth black and white Landseer. A beast that clearly belonged to Roger.

Unfulfilled but undaunted McCarron thanked the uniformed officers and Miss Gable-Davis for their help and he and Murphy headed back to Los Feliz. This time when they knocked on the door a young woman answered.

"Elena Ossidy?" McCarron asked showing his shield. Murphy showed his as well. "I'm detective McCarron and this is detective Murphy Murphy." Upon being introduced Elena wondered if this was the detective to which her friend Andy Rosenberg had referenced. *It wasn't Murray, it was Murphy* she thought.

"That appears to be a surplus of Murphy's," she said. Murphy shrugged.

"Is that your Jeep in the driveway?" McCarron asked ignoring the remark.

"No." was all Elena said.

"The red one?" McCarron kept on.

"Still no."

"Well it wasn't here when we came by earlier to speak with your parents," McCarron said, frustration rising in his voice.

"What wasn't?" Elena said clearly having fun.

"The *JEEP!*" McCarron insisted.

"Still isn't there," Elena was smiling now.

"This isn't funny Miss Ossidy," McCarron's anger was rising.

"Mrs." She corrected him.

"I don't know why you are insisting on being so combative," he practically spat.

"Me?" Elena said calmly.

"Ma'am," Murphy interrupted.

"You," she said turning her gaze to Murphy Murphy, "can call me Elena."

"Thank you Elena. Now, is that your vehicle in the driveway?" Elena looked.

"The red one?" she asked still yanking McCarron's chain.

"Yes."

"Yes."

"The Jeep!" McCarron chimed in.

"No," Elena shot back.

"Which is it," McCarron demanded, "yes or no?"

"It's both," she said and stared at the LAPD detective.

"Good grief," McCarron was exasperated. "What is your problem?"

"You."

"Elena," it was Murphy again. She turned to face him and smiled.

"Yes, detective Murphy Murphy. Such an unusual name," she added, "there has to be a story behind it."

"Oh, there is," he agreed. "A rather lengthy one."

"I've got plenty of time on my hands," she offered up the cliché.

"Maybe more than you think," McCarron said under his breath.

"You and detective McCarron seem to be at Loggerheads," Murphy went on. "Is there some confusion here?"

"Not as far as I'm concerned," she said confidently. "But you might want to ask your partner," she pointed at McCarron but her eyes never left Murphy. He thought they were beautiful brown eyes but he couldn't help detect a hint of sadness in them.

"You seem to be giving him two different answers to the vehicle question," Murphy offered.

"But I'm not."

"Is it yours" Murphy said as he turned and pointed to the SUV. Elena's eyes followed his finger.

"Yes."

"So, once again you're admitting the Jeep is yours," McCarron jumped in.

"No."

"Jesus!" McCarron cried and actually stomped his foot. Elena stared him down. "Sorry," he said sheepishly.

"Are you?" She asked.

"Can you please clear up the confusion," Murphy, the peacekeeper, piped up.

"There is zero confusion on my part," Elena said.

"Just help me out please," Murphy implored. She gave another withering look to McCarron then turned her attention back to Murphy.

"Sure," she said, "let me clear it up for you. I do not, would not, and have not ever in my life owned a *Jeep*," she looked once more at McCarron as she said the manufacturers name. "That red beauty, my vehicle," she pointed at her car, "is a 1973 Red FJ40 Toyota Land Cruiser expertly restored, at my great expense, by Geordy MacDougall and the team at Resurrection Land Cruisers in Orchard City, Colorado. It was first owned by my wonderful husband Grandiose Ossidy and is now owned by me."

"Seriously?" McCarron was nonplussed.

"Seriously," she said looking right at and through him.

"May we come in?" was all Murphy Murphy could think to ask.

"Of course," she said stepping away from the door and gesturing with her right hand down the hallway like a practiced butler. Murphy and McCarron looked at each other and went inside.

"We have a search warrant," McCarron said trying to regain his footing.

"This is all so mysterious and exhilarating," Elena said as she passed the detectives and led them down the hallway.

A little more than an hour later the two detectives found the young woman seated in the same chair her father had occupied earlier that day. There was a small table Murphy hadn't noticed next to the chair and on it rested a half-drunk glass of water. Elena had her legs crossed underneath her and she was reading a book as Murphy and McCarron approached. Two Australian Shepherds sat at the base of the chair, one looked up at the men and yawned while the other slept.

Murphy Murphy once again took in Elena James Ossidy. She was pretty in a rugged, outdoorsy, way. He could tell this was a woman of accomplishment and substance. One not to be trifled with. He perceived her as someone who had seen and experienced more than your average 30 going on 40 year old and he and McCarron should tread carefully. One of Katterwomp's cliches came to mind and he continued his examination, *still waters run deep* he thought. Elena looked up from her book.

"Find anything interesting? She asked.

"Quite a bit actually," McCarron fibbed hoping to get a reaction. He didn't. The search hadn't really uncovered much.

"Did you know Adalindis Katterwomp?" Murphy asked and he *did* notice a visceral reaction, almost a shudder. Murphy didn't know what to make of it and it was gone almost as quickly as it appeared.

"Of course," a composed Elena answered. "He was a colleague of my father's."

"Nothing more?" he prodded. Elena seemed to consider the question.

"I'm not exactly sure what you're getting at but no, nothing more." She took a sip of water from the glass.

"Did you know Katterwomp was in love with your mother?" Suddenly water sprayed from her mouth and doused the dogs who both started to bark.

"I'm so sorry Dundee and Timothy," she said in a soothing voice then she wiped her mouth with her sleeve. "Are you out of your mind?" she asked Murphy.

"Not that I'm aware of," Murphy answered with a straight face.

"I apologize but that's the craziest thing I've ever heard," she shook her head. "Katterwomp and *my mom*? No way. No how."

"How long have you worked at the zoo?" Murphy changed tack.

"Oh gosh," Elena paused to think, "coming up on half a dozen years now I guess."

"You guess?" McCarron asked.

"Well, time flies when you're having fun." She shrugged.

"Why elephants?" it was Murphy. He employed a tactic he had used over the years of asking rapid fire, sometimes unrelated, questions with the hope of tripping up the subject.

"Always loved them," she said without tripping, "ever since I was a little girl. You can ask my mom. Grandi and I both had a special affection for the beasts."

"I'm sorry for your loss," Murphy said because he was.

"Thanks. Me too."

"Why would an elephant attack a human?" McCarron wondered. Elena gave him another long look.

"Just for the record, I don't like you," she shot back, "and an elephant wouldn't. Not unprovoked."

"But one did," McCarron pressed on. Elena shook her head.

"Is that what happened?" she asked.

"You tell us," Murphy once again felt the need to jump in between them.

"All I know is I came home from work, had dinner with my folks, watched tv while enjoying a nice glass of wine and worked on a puzzle," she pointed to the table. "I found most of Diamond Head, that's a famous landmark on Oahu," she offered an unsolicited explanation. "And a humpback whale," she added proudly. "Then I went to bed. In the morning I found out about the unfortunate accident."

"Is that what you think it was? An accident?"

"I know Asian elephants detective, especially *my* Asian elephants. They are the smartest, gentlest, big animals on earth."

"That wasn't the question," McCarron jumped in.

"That's my answer," Elena said to Murphy.

"Are you a **Star Wars** fan?" Murphy asked after a couple of seconds.

"Well now, another question that I'm sure is intended to come out of the blue," Elena took a closer look at Murphy Murphy. "Is this your interrogation technique detective? Ask a random question and then gauge my reaction? Very clever."

"We found a voice altering Darth Vader mask under your bed," was all he said.

"That's weird," Elena tilted her head.

"Why is that?"

"Because I don't own a voice altering Darth Vader mask," she said.

"Not this again," McCarron huffed, stood up and left the room. Moments later he returned with the Star Wars trinket in an evidence bag and showed it to Elena.

"Oh that," she said with a nod and a wave of her hand. "That's a voice altering Kylo Ren mask *not* a voice altering *Darth Vader* mask."

"What's the difference?" McCarron asked.

"A generation," was her reply. "And anyway I'm more an Adam Driver fan than a **Star Wars** fan. I also have a **Logan Lucky** T-shirt. Did you find that too?" She could tell both detectives were lost. Murphy gathered himself.

"We also found tire tracks matching the ones on your vehicle inside the elephant exhibit."

"That's weird too," she said theatrically putting an index finger to her chin.

"Why is that weird," McCarron asked hoping they might have something.

"Well, it's weird that an elephant trainer would need a vehicle to patrol a bunch of acres inside an elephant exhibit. And that vehicle would leave tire tracks. Strange, don't you think?" She took another sip of water. Murphy conceded to himself that it wasn't strange at all.

"Elena darling," Roger James had walked into the room. The Landseer sniffed the Australian Shepherds and then plopped down at his master's feet, panting and drooling. "I see you've met detectives McCarron and Murphy."

"I have indeed."

"We're almost finished here, Mr. James," Murphy said. "Just one more question."

"For me?" both the father and daughter said in unison.

"For you sir," Murphy answered.

"Shoot," he said.

"Where's the book?"

"The book?" James asked, genuinely confused.

"The Book of Cliches. The tome you composed at the commission's bequest. The thing Adalindis Katterwomp claimed was at the crux of his disagreement with you and the entire reason I'm involved in this crazy case." Roger James laughed his deep, resonant laugh again.

"I wasn't aware A-OK and I *had* a disagreement. As for the book, it's right here," he said walking over to a shelf of books and pulling one out. "Always has been."

"I'll see you out," Elena said to the policemen.

McCarron turned to face the girl from the same step on which they had first met. He held up a couple of the evidence bags.

"We'll return this stuff to you when we're finished with it," he said.

"No rush," Elena replied and closed the door in his face.

Murphy climbed into the passenger side of the Tahoe and buckled his seat belt. McCarron started the engine.

"She's involved somehow," Murphy said more to himself than his temporary partner. He stared at the house. "I believe the mom and dad are in the clear but my gut tells me Elena has something to hide when it comes to Katterwomp's death."

"You might be right, and probably are but I have to say the reaction to the man and her mother being romantically involved question had to be sincere."

"I agree it appeared that way," Murphy responded.

"If she was acting she deserves a star on Hollywood Boulevard," McCarron conceded, "irregardless," he continued.

"That's not a word," Murphy said without hesitation.

"What's not a word?" McCarron asked.

"Irregardless," Murphy answered, "is not a word."

"Whatever," McCarron shook his head, "the point is I'll never be able to convince the DA to bring charges and even if, by some miracle I could, there's no way a jury would convict that girl on what we have."

"Sometimes I hate this job," Murphy lamented.

"I'll expend whatever resources I logically can to keep an eye on her for a while but I'm not going to get my hopes up and you shouldn't either."

"That's the way the cookie crumbles," Murphy said as McCarron drove away.

ALL'S WELL THAT ENDS...WELL

Murphy and detective McCarron stayed in relatively constant contact for several months but with no new revelations or suspicious activity from any of the James gang the phone calls became less and less frequent. They finally stopped altogether. Murphy did learn a few things including Beth Gable-Davis left the LA Zoo but McCarron was unclear if it was of her own accord. Murphy also found out Elena had taken a rather long vacation with a girlfriend, or friend who was a girl. McCarron either couldn't or wouldn't define it further. It was pretty much business as usual in Southern California. No new Bentleys or fifty-foot pleasure boats showed up in Los Feliz.

Neither detective subscribed to the Wall Street Journal so they didn't see the unbylined, three paragraph, report on the appointment of Roger James as the new head of the government's Commission on Cliches. In the same edition of the national paper Kimberley Strassel penned an opinion column calling for the dissolution of this unnecessary government waste. Something Roger James agreed with and did during his first day on the job. Murphy did see an uptick of sales on Amazon for

James's *The Dictionary of Cliches* and had even purchased a copy for himself.

Of course, the detective remained in close touch with his actor friend Matthew Laurance and from him got the news that **The Case of Serious Crisis** movie was soon to be released. Laurance promised to alert him about the premiere and he kept that promise. Murphy, Charlie, and Judith jumped on a plane and headed back to Hollywood.

Murphy was surprised to see Luca waiting at baggage claim with open arms which immediately closed around Judith.

"Will wonders never cease," Murphy said with a shake of his head. "I thought you said, she said, they were just friends," the detective addressed that comment to his girlfriend.

"Actions speak louder than words, I guess," Charlie said. "It would appear the relationship has gone from the ridiculous to the sublime."

"Enough," Murphy said.

"You started it," Charlie elbowed him lightly in the ribs.

"I guess I did."

As the two lovebirds sauntered off, they assured Murphy and Charlie they'd see them at the theatre. Then Murphy saw another familiar face.

"Mr. Snow?" he said to a rather large human waiting for bags.

"You found me," Snow said but it was clear to the detective that the man had failed to recognize him.

"Detective Murphy Murphy," he explained but Snow still looked uncertain. "We met on a flight some months back. You were headed out here for a job interview."

"The Rams job," Randy said remembering the flight.

"Did you get it?"

"As a matter of fact, I did not."

"Sorry to hear that," Murphy was. "So, what brings you back to Southern California?"

"A different job actually. A very good one."

"Do tell," Murphy encouraged the man.

"You may not believe it but there is a school out here that teaches people how to become sports announcers."

"Oh, I believe it," Murphy nodded. "Don't tell me you're going to be an instructor." The man laughed.

"Not my thing," he assured Murphy, "but in an effort to explore every avenue the guy in charge tapped me to recruit former athletes to join the program. He knew a guy who knew a guy who I played ball with back in the day."

"Who's the guy?" Murphy asked knowing it couldn't be Adalindis Katterwomp.

"The one who hired me or the one I played ball with?" Snow asked.

"Both, I guess."

"My boss is named Harold but they call him "the general".

"Slick back hair, fancy socks by any chance?" Murphy asked.

"That's him," Snow nodded. "It's an impressive set up over there and it sounded like his group and something called the Cloud Appreciation Society came into a lot of money thanks to the federal government."

"You don't say," Murphy said.

"I do."

"And just for grins who was the other guy? Your teammate?"

"Cat named Roger James. He could have gone pro but decided to take his life in a different direction, I guess."

"I guess," was all Murphy said. Then he realized Charlie had been standing there the whole time. "Man, how rude of me," he said touching her elbow, "this is Charlie Carlucci. Charlie this is Randy Snow."

"Hello," she said offering her hand. Snow took it.

"Pleasure to make your acquaintance," he said with one eye on the carousel. "Oh, there's my stuff."

"Good luck with the gig," Murphy said.

"It was nice to meet you," Charlie added.

"You too," Snow said striding away, "I guess we're about to see if you *can* teach an old dog new tricks."

"Something tells me he'll fit right in," Murphy said to Charlie.

With a few hours to kill Murphy had an idea and asked Charlie if she'd like to go to the zoo. She said she would. He took a flyer and called Do It Up Brown who just happened to be available to drive them. Along the way Charlie confessed to some misgivings about zoos in general.

"I just always feel a little melancholy at a zoo," she told Murphy, "have since I was a little girl."

"Why?" Murphy asked.

"I don't know," she answered honestly, "just a feeling that those poor animals are trapped in cages, behind fences."

"Like prisoners?"

"Kind of," she says, "but they really are all innocent."

"They also don't know any better and they're well cared for."

"I guess," she said with a smile, but Murphy could sense her sadness.

"How can you not enjoy the penguins?" he asked trying to cheer her up. Brown dropped them off at the entrance. He declined the invitation to join them but said he'd be there to pick them up when they were ready to leave.

"I got an idea," Murphy said. "Let's check out the elephants," he said.

"You're so subtle," Charlie said running her hand through his hair, "but first I need something sweet."

"A kiss?" he asked hopeful, and she kissed him.

"Nope," she shook her head, "sweeter." They bought an ice cream cone, mint chocolate chip, Charlie's favorite, from a kiosk.

"I can't believe you didn't get one," she said through a good-sized bite melting in her mouth.

"I'll just have a bite of yours," he said reaching for the waffle cone.

"No, you will not," she guided the cone just out of his reach.

"What? Why?"

"We've done that dance too many times," she replied. "I now know what 'I'll just have one bite' means in Murphy world."

"Fair enough," he had to admit. She handed him the cone.

If you didn't read the LA Times or watch the news you would have never known someone had recently died in the dirt of the Elephants of Asia exhibit at the Los Angeles Zoo. Dozens of people, mostly wide-eyed children appearing to be less than ten years old pointed at, giggled about, and called out to the pachyderms throwing dirt on themselves in the Southern California sun.

"They're getting all dirty!" One little girl yelled.

"Why do they do that?" A boy, no doubt the girl's little brother asked.

"That's a great question, honey, and there is a very good answer," the mother patted the boy on the head. "One reason is it helps protect them from the sun."

"Like sunscreen?" the girl asked.

"Exactly."

"What's another reason?" it was the boy.

"It helps keeps the bugs away," mom said.

"Bugs! Eeewww!" the kids cried out in unison.

"Yep. Bugs like flies and mosquitos just *love* elephants and the dirt helps keep them away."

"Can I throw dirt on me?" the little boy practically begged.

"Absolutely not!" was the reply.

A few feet away Murphy nodded knowing the mom was correct.

"It's known as 'dust bathing'," Murphy addressed the family. "It also keeps them cool." The mother gave Murphy a sideways glance and moved her family a few feet farther away.

"Weirdo," Charlie said jokingly, "stop bothering the children." He shrugged, grabbed Charlie's hand and looked through the fence. Three elephants were in view. The one taking a dirt bath, another lying in the shade of a tree, and a third, the largest, standing amid some hay. A woman who Murphy recognized as Elena James Ossidy, stood in front of the massive beast stroking its trunk. Two dogs lay panting at her feet.

"Is that her?" Charlie asked.

"It is."

"Do you still think she's guilty?"

"Of something," the detective stated simply. Just then Bertha the elephant wrapped its long grey trunk around Elena's waist in what looked very much like a hug. The trainer threw her head back and let out a joyful laugh.

"Mommy that efilint is hugging that lady!" The little boy squealed with delight. "I want a hug too," he added, happy face turned up to his mother. She squatted down and obliged.

Murphy took a moment to appreciate the scene then he smiled thinking the elephant in question would do anything for its trainer and friend. He'd bet dollars to donuts it had.

"Let's go see our movie," he said and they both smiled.

YOU CAN'T JUDGE A BOOK BY ITS COVER

All of this is because of Sarah. I said that after I wrote my first book and it's still true as I finished the sixth. She has always been there to support, encourage, and love me. None of this "reinvention" would have happened without her. I Love You Doll. Tons.

Thanks again go out to the two people who are the first ones to see what I write, Jake Hirshland and Susan Green. They are family, they are loved ones, they are friends, but most importantly they are editors and damn fine ones. Unflinching in their ability to tell me what works, what doesn't, and where the commas go.

This book is a work of fiction but that doesn't mean some of the character names aren't real. You know who you are, and you know this tale suffers without your blessing. Matthew, John, Brian, David, Judith, Charlie, Jeff, Joe, Lyndsay, Tim, Chris, Mitch, Bill, and Frank, you've been around the block with me before. Thanks for taking another lap. Scott, Courtney, Beth, Kip, Randy, K-Man, and Bonnie, I know this is your first rodeo and I appreciate you holding on for all eight seconds.

349

To Bobby Collins and the incredibly talented team at Beacon Publishing Group, I can only say thank you, from the bottom of my heart, for continuing to believe what I write is worth reading. Let's not stop here.

And to all of you, all the kind souls who have read this book and any of the others. Thanks for immersing yourself in this journey. I hope what I have written brings a smile, or a chuckle, or a laugh out loud. I feel like Murphy Murphy isn't just my character, he's our character and he'll be back.

Printed in the USA
CPSIA information can be obtained
at www.ICGtesting.com
LVHW040729061023
760252LV00024B/80

9 781961 504035